Praise for ...

"Grace has quickly become one of my favorite authors of Austen-inspired fiction. Her love of Austen's characters and the Regency era shine through in all of her novels." **Diary of an Eccentric**

"Maria Grace is stunning and emotional, and readers will be blown away by the uniqueness of her plot and characterization" **Savvy Verse and Wit**

"Maria Grace has once again brought to her readers a delightful, entertaining and sweetly romantic story while using Austen's characters as a launching point for the tale." **Calico Critic**

"I believe that this is what Maria Grace does best, blend old and new together to create a story that has the framework of Austen and her characters, but contains enough new and exciting content to keep me turning the pages. ... Grace's style is not to be missed." **From the desk of Kimberly Denny-Ryder**

A Less Agreeable Man

Maria Grace

White Soup Press

Published by: White Soup Press

A Less Agreeable Man
Copyright © 2017 Maria Grace

For information, address
author.MariaGrace@gmail.com

ISBN-10: 0-9980937-4-2
ISBN-13: 978-0-9980937-4-1 (White Soup Press)

Author's Website: RandomBitsofFaascination.com
Email address: Author.MariaGrace@gmail.com

Dedication

For my husband and sons.
You have always believed in me.

Chapter 1

There are as many forms of love as there are moments in time.— *Jane Austen, Personal correspondence*

THE LITTLE CHAPEL hummed as it filled with Sunday morning congregants. Mary plucked at the braided trim of the periwinkle blue calico gown that she wore every Sunday.

Charlotte slapped her hand lightly. "You will spoil your dress. He will be here. Stop fretting."

Mary laced her hands tightly in her lap and glanced over her shoulder. The Hunsford parish church appeared exactly as it always did: stark slate floor and grey stone walls. Sturdy dark wooden pews scarred with use, just a few more than absolutely necessary to accommodate the church-goers. Several cobwebs dangled in the corners, and the windowsills needed dusting.

But this Sunday was like no other.

Mr. Collins minced his way to the pulpit. Did he enjoy the way all eyes were on him as he paraded past? Although he professed his humility to any who would listen, it seemed that a man so assured of his modesty would necessarily be prideful of it.

One more topic to avoid at the Collins' dinner table. It might have made for interesting conversation, though.

He climbed the three steps up into the dark-stained walnut pulpit. A hush fell over the chapel. "I publish the Banns of marriage between Graham Allen Michaels of Hunsford parish and Mary Susanna Bennet of Hunsford parish. If any of you know cause or just impediment why these two persons should not be joined together in Holy matrimony, ye are to declare it. This is the first time of asking."

Lady Catherine slowly stood, her purple silk ball gown rustling against the front row pew. "Where is he?"

Whispers and cloth-muffled shuffles mounted, gathering with the force of storm clouds. Mary glanced over her shoulder. Too many people were looking at her, although just as many were scanning the chapel for Mr. Michaels.

Lady Catherine turned to face the congregation. "Where is he? How can I know if I approve if I cannot see him? Present him to me now."

"He is not here, your ladyship," Mr. Collins stammered, heavy beads of sweat dotting his forehead.

"I do not recall giving permission for him to be elsewhere. I am quite certain of that. I insist—"

The church door groaned and swung open. Two men paused in the doorway, silhouetted in bright sun.

"Richard Brandon Fitzwilliam! Young man, why are late for—"

"Your ladyship." Mary stood, her knees having all the substance of calves' foot jelly. "May I present Mr. Michaels?"

"Michaels? Why do I care to receive him into my acquaintance? Come and sit down this moment, Richard." She pointed to the empty spot beside her and sat as if on a throne.

Colonel Fitzwilliam scowled—an expression that would likely bring an entire regiment to order— and stalked to the family pew. Mrs. Jenkinson whispered something—probably very serious given the tight lines around her mouth— to Lady Catherine.

She threw her head back and cackled.

Mr. Michaels slipped in beside Mary, offering a supportive glance to Colonel Fitzwilliam.

Mr. Collins cleared his throat, waited for silence, and returned to the order of service. Once he exhausted all the words of his sermon and a few thousand more, he dismissed them and the congregation dissolved into a throng milling in the cheerful morning sun just outside the church.

Mr. Michaels beckoned Mary aside to a stand of shade trees, just far enough away from the crowd for a little private conversation but not so far as to raise the attention of the gossips, but Mr. Collins trailed after them like a terrier on a rat.

"Late to services, sir?" His tone had an edge which suggested this dialogue might well last all day. "I cannot condone it. Think of the precedent it will set among the parish. You see how it distressed her ladyship."

"I assure you it was not by intention or neglect. I was called away for a bit of an emergency—"

"What happened?" Mary and Mr. Collins asked simultaneously.

"Not to worry; the issue is quite resolved. There was just a small misunderstanding on the road." Michaels glanced over his shoulder toward a sandy patch near the church door where Lady Catherine, flanked by Mrs. Jenkinson, held court. Her fondness for that particular spot was not accidental. Her proximity to the stone building caused her voice to broadcast farther than it would if she stood anywhere else.

Mr. Collins' face changed entirely, his critical tone fading. "Was her ladyship involved?"

"The matter is resolved, and no further discussion need be had." He offered Mary his arm.

"I am most gratified to hear that, sir. Most gratified." Mr. Collins trundled off toward the church door with his peculiar step-hop gait.

Lady Catherine took Colonel Fitzwilliam's arm and slowly made her way past the crowd toward her waiting carriage.

"I do hope Collins can keep his mouth shut." Michaels muttered under his breath.

"He does seem to upset her as often as not." Mary winced as Mr. Collins reached Lady Catherine and started talking.

Michaels leaned close. "She pitched Colonel Fitzwilliam from the carriage halfway to the church. She did not recognize him and refused to permit a strange man to ride in her carriage."

"This is the first time she has failed to identify him," Mary whispered behind her hand.

"I came on them in the road as it was happening. It took some time to calm him down."

"An excellent reason to be late."

"On the first Sunday our banns are read. I know, and I am sorry." He frowned a little. He always did when they disagreed over timeliness.

"What are you discussing, so low and private?" Charlotte waddled up to them, her drab, high-necked gown showed the outline of her belly. It would not fit for much longer.

"Certainly not what you would expect." Mary glanced toward Lady Catherine.

Charlotte's smiled faded. "Would you have dinner with us this afternoon, Mr. Michaels? It has been so long since we have enjoyed your company."

"I should like that very much, thank you."

Charlotte nodded and shuffled off toward Mr. Collins and Lady Catherine.

"I think I shall follow the carriage back to Rosings in the event Lady Catherine suffers any more confusion. In any case, I should speak to the Colonel about a few matters—"

She squeezed his arm, a bit harder than might be decorous. "It is Sunday. You should rest. You work late into the night, and you start far too early in the morning. Once you begin, it is difficult for you to stop."

"Why do you not come out directly and say it? You fear that I might miss dinner altogether and thus offend the Collinses."

Mary stared at her feet.

"And offend you as well?" He laid his hand over hers and pressed firmly. "You are right. The situation at Rosings has been so overwhelming it has brought out a level of single-mindedness in me that I know is both a blessing and a curse."

"It is pleasing that you work so diligently, and that you are so good at what you do." He always intended to keep his promises. Nonetheless, there was a better than average chance he would fail at the endeavor.

Still, it was good that he should be so hardworking and committed to those he served. Or at least Mr. Collins said so. If only he were so dedicated to her.

Mr. Darcy's devotion to Lizzy was the stuff of novels, running after her to rescue her from the clutches of Lady Catherine. And Lydia—who would have thought? She inspired her Mr. Amberson to walk all the way to Pemberley and demand an audience with a man so far above him that they should never have otherwise met. Apparently passionate tempers like Lizzy's and Lydia's inspired grand shows of affection.

Mary's did not.

But comparing herself to her sisters never brought pleasure. There was nothing good to be had from it. Michaels had chosen her from among all her sisters. That was the thing she had to focus on. He could have courted any of them. Not that Lydia would have paid him any mind or that Lady Catherine would have permitted Jane a suitor she did not select. Still, Michaels chose her, purposefully, intentionally because her disposition—serious and practical—matched his. He cared for her exactly the way all conduct books declared he should—faithful and steady, pleasant and companionable. Complaining about such a man was the height of ingratitude.

"Shall I walk you to the Collins' then?" He gestured across the rutted, uneven lane toward a little used footpath that led into the Rosings' woods.

Tall hardwoods lined the path, their branches arching out and tangling with one another to form a covering that kept out the sunlight. Some found it ominous—even called it haunted at times—but that only ensured they would have a modicum of privacy to converse.

Honeysuckle vines twined around the trees, winding into the canopy and filling the air with sweet perfume. Too bad there were no flowers in reach. Each flower had only a drop of nectar, but she relished the secret indulgence. If Michaels knew, would he find it endearing or ridiculous?

"You were concerned because I was away a fortnight longer than I had predicted?"

She clasped her hands behind her back with a shrug. "I know you had a great deal to accomplish."

How could she tell him the local matrons were quick to believe that he would abandon her if he left Kent for any time at all. No doubt they did not think her sufficient enticement to keep his attention once he was exposed to the wider society of London. Surely there, prettier, richer girls would vie for his consideration, and she would necessarily be the loser.

It was decidedly unpleasant to know that people thought her likely to be jilted.

Why was it the woman always suffered more being jilted than the man? He might walk away with barely any damage, but her reputation would bear the stain forever.

"Was your trip to London unsuccessful?"

"It was more complicated than I anticipated. I have finally untangled Rosings' records, but it is just the beginning."

"You look so weary."

"I am certain the colonel expects the debts to be paid off quickly, with little privation on his part. The expenses of the manor are extreme, and I suppose the colonel would prefer to maintain a lavish lifestyle. I cannot imagine he will be amenable to plans of economy. It is hard to see how, under those circumstances, the estate might be unencumbered in even ten years." He rubbed his eyes with thumb and forefinger.

"I know you will find a way." She touched his arm.

He turned to her, smiling. "I am glad to be home and privy to your good sense and encouragement. Now you must tell me how things have been in my absence."

"Mrs. Collins is faring well as she increases, though it seems to be progressing far more rapidly than anyone has expected. The midwife has expressed some concerns."

Michaels shook his head, the corners of his lips turning up. "It is difficult to picture a household of tiny Collinses running about. Perhaps it is a good thing he is the kind of man who will have little to do with his children."

Was it wrong to agree? "He received word that he has inherited the estate that had been entailed upon him. I expect the topic will be discussed … extensively … at dinner tonight."

The edges of Michaels' eyes creased as his brow furrowed. "He will wish to seek advice in hiring a curate, no doubt. Something that is unlikely to please his patroness."

"I expect not. As it is, she no longer comes to

call."

"Collins cannot like that."

"Not at all. There are some days she is driven past in the phaeton. He waits near the windows watching for them. She usually waves as they pass, and he appreciates that. Mrs. Jenkinson believes that the fresh air is beneficial for her spirits. According to her, Lady Catherine has some good days in which she is quite aware of what is going on around her and demonstrates strong understanding. She will direct menus and even engage in conversation with Colonel Fitzwilliam."

"You mean try to tell him what to do?"

Mary snickered. "The darker days are growing more common though, and very unpredictable. I saw bruises along Mrs. Jenkinson's face last week. She claimed that she was distracted and ran into the door frame. I am not inclined to believe that."

"If Lady Catherine is indeed becoming dangerous, then we must have some way to manage her." Did he really need to call out the obvious?

"I plan to call upon Mrs. Jenkinson and the housekeeper tomorrow to discuss what might be done to make Lady Catherine more … comfortable."

"Perhaps you might have a few words with Colonel Fitzwilliam? I think he could benefit from your advice."

"If you wish. Just pray, let not Mr. Collins be informed. He is uncomfortable with me meddling in the affairs of my betters. The notion that Lady Catherine must be managed agitates him. Whilst I can bear his anger, Charlotte cannot. Her condition is fragile. She should not be taxed."

He took her hands and pressed them to his chest.

"How do you always seem to know what everyone around you needs? I may be steward of the land here, but I am quite certain you are steward to all the people."

"Do you disapprove?" She bit her lower lip.

"I approve." He leaned down and kissed her, gentle, chaste, controlled. His lips were dry and warm, a little rough from traveling.

Her heart fluttered, just a mite, restrained as much as he. Was it wrong to wish she could give it free rein to soar? Soon, very soon, they would be wed. Perhaps it would be different then.

Early the next morning, Colonel Richard Fitzwilliam, formerly of His Majesty's Army, navigated the treacherously steep servants' stairway that smelt of old stone and damp. Half the steps were too narrow to accommodate his foot. They creaked with each step, threatening to reveal him to the enemy. Cobwebs dangled from the walls, reaching for him and clinging to his navy blue wool coat as he passed.

Did the servants not clean these passages? Probably not—who would have noticed or cared until now?

The mysterious dark passage had been fun to explore as a child. How often had he and Darcy startled servants as they scurried on their errands, thinking themselves sequestered from the family? Their surprised looks had been mightily entertaining, then.

Now they were irritating.

Irritating and embarrassing.

The master of a house should not be hiding like a rat in the walls, avoiding a cat—or in his case, a mad dowager. Yet that was exactly what he was doing.

He had faced cannon fire and sabers, taken a musket ball to the shoulder and another to the thigh, stood against Napoleon and lived to tell of it. Never once had he hidden nor run. But Aunt Catherine—she had him scurrying into dark corners like despicable vermin.

Had she been on Napoleon's side, he would have won.

Which was why they had run out of port last month. Now the stores of brandy were growing low as well. If things did not change soon, he would have to turn to gin.

He shouldered open the door to his office, but it resisted. Another shove and it gave way just enough to slip through. He stumbled and tripped, catching himself on the hall chair stacked with ledgers that he had left in front of it yesterday. Too damn drunk to remember to leave his own escape route clear.

Bloody hell, how had it come to this? He dragged his fist across his prickly chin. Drink had always been a pleasure, never a necessity. When had that changed?

Yes, the unexpected inheritance was astonishing, and he was grateful. Finally he was a proper gentleman in the eyes of society with an estate and connections that would make him welcome in nearly any company.

But it was also ruining him.

He fell into the generous armchair behind his desk. Bright sunlight streaming through two tall windows revealed every book and paper out of place, every piece of furniture than had been uprooted as he searched for papers he had mislaid. He scrubbed his face with his palms.

The new butler—blast it all, what was his name?

He was of average height, average looks, average everything. There was not a single distinguishing thing about him, right down to the average color of his suit. How dare he be so unexceptional. Dash it all, he would be Tom from here on out—Small Tom, though, as he bore little resemblance to Long Tom whom he replaced—entered and waited until Fitzwilliam cast an irritated nod his direction. "Sir, Mr. Michaels has arrived. Are you at home to him?"

"Am I at home? What does it look like? I am drowning in a sea of documents and in need of a man who can swim. Damn it, yes! I am at home."

Small Tom bowed a very average bow and shuffled off.

A moment later, Michaels strode in, a portfolio under one arm and a bag in the other. He navigated around the piles of books and other debris on the floor and sat on the leather wingback near the desk—the only seat in the room not covered in detritus.

"What news have you for me? It had best not be all bad, or I shall surely run mad with my aunt. Wait, wait, shall I retrieve the brandy before or after you open that portfolio of disaster you keep always by your side?" He laughed, mostly to control his nerves. It sounded hollow even in his own ears.

Michaels rifled through his case. "The news is mixed, sir. Regardless, these are matters best approached with a clear head."

"You mean a clear headache." Fitzwilliam rubbed his temples. "If you are going to deny me liquid comfort, give me good news to console me."

Michaels pulled papers and journals from his bag. Dear God, how much could such a small bag hold?

"To sum it up, I have negotiated with all the

known creditors. Needless to say they are unhappy, but they understand they are more likely to be paid back if no one ends up in debtors' prison."

Aunt Catherine would probably prefer Bedlam to debtors' prison in any case.

"To that end, I have drafted a plan of economy. An extensive plan." He tapped a folio and laid it on the desk. "I suggest we review in detail. My proposal is comprehensive and will require a vast array of changes to all aspects of life at Rosings."

Fitzwilliam muttered under his breath. While change was not anathema to him, the same could not be said of Aunt Catherine.

"Though it may be—challenging—for some time, I am confident that the strategy will allow the debts to be repaid in the foreseeable future."

"Foreseeable? Just how long is a 'foreseeable'? It is not on a unit of time with which I am familiar."

Michaels chuckled.

Thank God he had a sense of humor.

"The debts should be cleared in ten years, or less depending on what you are willing to tolerate. The heaviest burden, though, is in the first three. Then there is another break after five, and then after seven." Michaels shoved a sheet of paper at him.

"So, you say we will live like paupers on the streets begging for three years, then rent an attic room in a fourth rate town house after that?"

"If you wish, sir. That would pay off your debts several years earlier. I can add that as an option if you so choose. I simply began with the belief that you would prefer to have a roof overhead for the entire period."

Fitzwilliam threw his head back and laughed. "Yes,

indeed that is probably a better plan. Or I could simply marry an heiress and avoid all this unpleasantness altogether."

"I draw the line at arranging marriages. For that you will have to consult your mother, the countess."

He was right. Mother would only be too happy to be given such a charge. Far too happy.

"If you are amenable, there are a number of articles in the latest *Agricultural Review* that would help explain my recommendations for the eastern fields, the ones prone to flooding." Michaels skirted around the desk to the bookcase behind him, every movement brisk and efficient. Did the man ever relax or enjoy himself?

Even his choice of bride was efficient. The plainest, hardest working of the Bennet sisters, she had little remarkable about her, save how unremarkable she was. Just the kind of wife for a man who specialized in retrenching estates and repaying debts.

What else would a man like him do? He would not want a woman of great passion and fire. One who could enflame him like a courtesan, and comfort him among sheets of silk. No, a quiet woman who would be a mother to his brood of well-mannered children and mistress of his efficient house would be his preference.

If only one could find passionate fire in a practical woman, now that would be a treasure indeed. Would there be such a woman who would also tolerate the domestic situation at Rosings?

Fitzwilliam frowned, chewing his lower lip. "There is one other matter I would bring up with you, though. Mrs. Jenkinson is simply not up to the task of serving as my aunt's companion. I was wondering if

Miss Bennet and perhaps Mrs. Collins might be willing to help me find an appropriate companion for her."

"Not up to the task, or has Mrs. Jenkinson given you notice she wishes to leave Rosings at the end of the quarter?"

Fitzwilliam grumbled under his breath. He should never play cards with Michaels. "Assuming Mrs. Jenkinson does not change her mind—and I see little possibility of that happening—then yes, Aunt Catherine will be without a companion at the end of the quarter. Perhaps sooner if she displays another bad spell of temper. I shudder to think what will become of the household if this continues. We are losing staff at an alarming rate. Even Parkes, the housekeeper, is at sixes and sevens. She may be making plans to leave as well."

"Perhaps in addition to helping you find a companion for Lady Catherine, Miss Bennet might be able to offer you some suggestions on living with her more peaceably, too. She does have a remarkable way with her ladyship. Dealing with ones in your aunt's condition is not, after all, a skill expected from His Majesty's officers."

True enough, but take advice from the unremarkable Miss Bennet? "I suppose it cannot hurt. Tomorrow, after we have dealt with the real work at hand." Fitzwilliam picked up the nearest sheet of paper. "So tell me about this campaign of economy."

Chapter 2

MARY STORMED BACK to Rosings manor from the remains of the newly planted section of the kitchen garden. Her half-boots crunched along on the gravel while her skirts swished in an irate whisper. A trickle of sweat fell on her lips; she licked away the salt. Yes, she would arrive in an absolute state of inelegance, but few women could affect angry sophistication under the best of circumstances.

Not long ago, she had sat with Mr. Michaels and Colonel Fitzwilliam offering insight on how to manage Lady Catherine and even how to bring up the subject of hiring a curate for the parsonage. It seemed like he had listened to her, taken note of what she had said. But now it was a se'nnight later, and he had apparently ignored it all.

First he chided Lady Catherine for wearing a dinner dress whilst receiving Mary for a morning call. It took mere moments for the scene to devolve into shouting and stomping and shrieking and required the whole afternoon to restore Lady Catherine's equanimity. Now today he permitted her to walk the gardens alone. Why could he not understand that she must never be allowed outside without a companion?

Lady Catherine had become confused and wandered into the kitchen garden instead of her flower garden. The confusion turned to fear and then anger against the plants themselves, tearing out most of the seedlings and hothouse transplants. It was only by Providence alone that Mary had been walking one of the footpaths near enough to hear the commotion and intervene.

It took an hour complete, but she was finally able to calm Lady Catherine and place her back in Mrs. Jenkinson's care, with firm orders that she not be left alone again. The damage to the garden, though, was extensive, a loss Rosings could not afford.

It could all have been avoided had Colonel Fitzwilliam merely heeded her advice. Mary clenched her fists until they ached. If he was too stubborn to listen, then he deserved whatever happened.

But the rest of them did not—not the staff, not Rosings' tenants, not the inhabitants of the parsonage. For their sakes she would get involved.

Barkley—whom the colonel called Small Tom now—opened the great carved mahogany door and dodged out of her way. Wise servant that he was, he seemed to realize she was not to be gainsaid and did not even make a show of attempting it.

She paused on the marble tile of the front hall, allowing the cool air to soothe the edges of her temper.

Her eyes slowly adjusted to the dimmer inside light and she made out Small Tom as he watched from a safe distance, impeccable in his dark suit and white gloves.

"The colonel?"

Small Tom pointed down the hall.

She gathered her skirts in one hand and stalked toward the study.

She flung open the imposing paneled wood door and marched inside into nearly blinding sunlight pouring in through the tall windows.

When the room had been used by Lady Catherine, it had been immaculate—granted that almost certainly meant that no real work was ever accomplished within its walls, but at least it was respectable. Now it looked—and smelt—like a public house near closing hour. The scents of alcohol, stale food and sweaty men hung like cobwebs in every corner. Books, dirty dishes, even furniture were strewn about as though the room were inhabited by Eton students with no housekeeper.

Mr. Michaels and Colonel Fitzwilliam sat on opposite sides of the desk, hunching over several ledgers. They sprang to their feet, jaws dropping as the door slammed against the wall behind her.

"What did you think you were doing?" She stormed toward them, stopping at short edge of the desk.

"Excuse me?" Colonel Fitzwilliam scowled—probably an expression that cowed lesser officers.

"You sought my advice yet you have summarily ignored it. Now see what your wisdom has wrought. The kitchen garden has been ruined." She slapped a small space on the desktop not occupied with masculine detritus.

"Mary?" Why did Michaels look so surprised?

"How dare you march in here—" Colonel Fitzwilliam slowly leaned forward on the desk, most likely hoping to tower over her and intimidate.

She matched his posture. "And how dare you go on expecting that I will placate Lady Catherine when you will not do me the courtesy of doing as I have suggested."

"You have no place to be instructing me as to what I should be doing."

"Perhaps not. Since you are an all-wise and knowing officer of His Majesty's service, you are free to apply your understanding to the management of your relations. I shall be happy to keep away from Rosings, and mind my own business. It is not as though I need your assistance to keep myself occupied."

Colonel Fitzwilliam's jaw dropped.

Michaels flinched. He had not seen her fury before. Doubtless best that he know now, before their wedding.

"Good Lord, talk some sense into your woman, Michaels!"

"I am hardly without sense—or have you forgotten you sought my advice? I might remind you, I have no duty to look after Lady Catherine, particularly after all the harm she has wrought on my family."

"Mary, please!" Michaels' face turned puce. "What has come over you?"

She whirled on him, shaking. "I am not a servant of Rosings! I will be treated with the respect due a gentlewoman! If you will not heed my counsel, then do not expect me to deal with the aftermath."

"I will not be spoken to in this manner." Fitzwilliam clasped his hands behind his back and pulled his shoulders erect.

"And I will not, either. Good day." She spun on her heel and stormed out.

Small Tom was waiting in the hall to escort her out. Was that the hint of a smile playing about his eyes?

She half-ran all the way to the outskirts of the parsonage's fields. No rush to get back to the Collins' house. As fast as word traveled at Rosings, Collins would already know about her outburst by the time she arrived. There would be a price to be paid for that, a dear one no doubt.

Usually she controlled her temper so well no one knew it was even there. Charlotte had seen hints of it—living with Mr. Collins' ridiculousness had pushed Mary to her limits. Lizzy had observed it once or twice, but no one else. It had been her secret.

Would Mr. Michaels despise her for it now and jilt her like the matrons believed he would?

No, he was a patient man, a practical man. A broken engagement would be far too much trouble for a mere outburst of temper. But in all likelihood she had lost some of his esteem. There would be a touch of disappointment in his eyes next time they met.

She gulped back the lump in her throat. It was not as though she had never seen that expression before. She would survive. It would motivate her to try harder and be successful at reining in her temper and her tongue once again. Perhaps this was a good reminder of what would be required of her as a married woman.

Fitzwilliam stood rooted in place. The fire and the fury that had just stormed from his office, had that truly been the mousy Miss Bennet?

"I pray you will forgive her. With the wedding so close, she has a great deal on her mind." Michaels shrugged a bit, clearly baffled by his woman's reaction.

Had he never seen this side of her? Oh, that was rich!

"I am sure living with Collins is enough to drive anyone to distraction." What a struggle it was to keep a straight face.

"I am grateful for your understanding. Shall we get back to the business at hand?" Michaels tapped the ledger between them.

"Let us return to this tomorrow. Perhaps you might take the afternoon to survey the fences along those eastern fields."

"Very good." Michaels gathered the papers into a neat stack on the corner of the desk, bowed, and strode out.

Fitzwilliam picked his way to the cabinet between the windows. Blast and botheration. The bloody decanter was empty.

Of course it was.

He fell into a worn leather wingback by the fireplace, mate to the one Michaels used near his desk, and dug his fingertips into the back of his neck.

Gah! Drilling fresh recruits never left him as tense as trying to make sense out of Rosings' accounts. He needed a drink.

A glass, a large glass, a very large glass, of some very good brandy. Or port. That would set him up very well indeed. Even gin was sounding tolerable at this point.

Great Jove above! His stomach knotted in on itself. Andrew said nearly the same thing when he began his descent into opium eating.

What kind of barbarian was he becoming? His behavior had already turned shocking. He might have been well within his rights to have spoken harshly to Miss Bennet, but it was hardly gentlemanly. She had been right in that, it was not the way one treated a gentlewoman. Usually he had better mastery over his irritation. It was not Michaels'—or Miss Bennet's—fault that Aunt Catherine belonged in Bedlam.

If only he could make those arrangements and be done with the old woman. But nothing was so simple. As much as he hated to admit it, his parents were right. The family's reputation would suffer if her condition were made more widely known. Mad relations were not exactly a fashionable accessory this season. So he was effectively saddled with her until she died—which with his luck, would be a sore long time.

Her presence would also make the prospect of finding an heiress to marry and save Rosings particularly difficult. Who would want to marry into these circumstances? But if Aunt Catherine might be managed more effectively …

How many times had Miss Bennet had warned him to tread lightly and not antagonize his aunt? A colonel in His Majesty's army was used to issuing orders and seeing them obeyed, not being patient with someone who did as she pleased. What Miss Bennet asked—nay, demanded— was entirely impossible.

But she was the only one who seemed able to adequately manage Aunt Catherine. For that, she deserved better than his disrespect.

He needed to apologize. Quickly.

Unlike his father, he was not too proud for that.

He straightened his cravat and patted his hair, turning this way and that before his long mirror. It had been months since he had dressed so carefully. His dark blue wool hammer-tail coat nipped in nicely at the waist, held securely by shining brass buttons. A hint of burgundy silk from his embroidered waistcoat peeked just about the lapels, over a fine starched white shirt. Buckskin breeches and polished boots completed the ensemble.

He was not a bad looking man, certainly not the dashing dandy some of his fellow officers had been, nor as handsome as Darcy. In truth he was actually ordinary and even a little plain. Something his sister never hesitated to remind him of. But he cleaned up rather well, and his manners could make up for what his face might lack. At least when he made the effort at it.

Undoubtedly, Miss Bennet would see his good intentions. She was like Elizabeth, annoyingly perceptive that way.

Bright sunlight and cool air slapped his cheeks as he left the shadow of Rosings Park, his boots crunching crisply on the wide gravel path. It was a satisfying, purposeful, official sound, invigorating, even powerful. Perhaps he should get out of the house more regularly. He had not felt this alive in days—maybe weeks.

He caught the scent of sheep on the breeze. In the distance the shepherds were moving a flock from one pasture to another. Sheep were soothing to watch. They were usually so obedient to their shepherds, like good soldiers to their officers.

It might behoove him to plan a speech for his arrival at the parsonage. He laughed under his breath. It was the sort of thing Darcy was apt to do, and he was apt to laugh at him for. Words, after all, had always been friendly to him, easy enough to deliver on cue—why should he bother himself about what he was going to say?

Recently though, they had become far more stubborn, quite in line with the shortness of his temper.

So then, what to say? Pretty words alone would be more likely to condemn him than raise his fortunes. Sincerity would be the thing …

What was that?

A dark blur raced along the corner of the fence marking the parsonage's land. It paused at the stile, climbing across it with measured, dainty steps. On the other side, it picked up speed again, toward the woods—decidedly feminine in all its motions.

Fitzwilliam chased after in a long easy lope, following at a discreet distance. The form was familiar, but the urgency of its movements was not. Who was it?

His heart pounded and his breath came in measured pants as she turned down a little used path. Estate legend held the path was haunted by the ghosts of long-forgotten squatters who lived in a shack, now gone to ruin. Few even knew about the place anymore, and fewer still visited there. Whoever it was knew her way around Rosings very well.

She stopped at the end of the footpath, between the tiny tumble-down wood hovel and the lopsided stone well that contained a bubbling spring, in a patch of sunshine that broke through the dense hardwood canopy. Her swishing skirts wrapped around her and clung to well-shaped legs.

Fitzwilliam ducked behind a conveniently large oak—it had grown since the days he and Darcy had played hide-and-seek here—and peeked around. To whom did those delightful limbs belong?

Head thrown back, the figure untied her bonnet and cast it aside with one hand, attacking the buttons of her spencer with the other.

Fitzwilliam gulped as the spencer followed. Miss Bennet leaned against the stone well, shapely bosom heaving, gasping for breath.

Great Lord!

She liberated her fichu from her bodice and yanked it free, exposing the pale swell of her chest to the sun and wind—and him. Sunbeams glistened off a fine sheen of sweat.

His mouth went dry, and every fiber of his being tightened, aching to respond. Tree bark ripped from the trunk and crumbled in his hand. How long had it been? Far longer than ever before. Maddeningly, painfully long.

She dipped her hand into the well, reaching deep. Just a little farther and her bodice might cease to contain her. He licked his lips.

What had he become? She was betrothed to another! He slipped back behind the tree.

Was he a peeping Tom now, lusting after gentlewomen? Willing partners had never been difficult to find back when every spare penny was not tied up in the cursed estate.

He peered around again.

She drank from cupped hands, water trickling down her cheek and neck, staining the edge of her grey bodice dark. Her breathing slowed as she half-sat at the edge of the well, feet dangling just above the ground. Tendrils of hair escaped their pins and framed her face, backlit against the sun.

Her figure was better than he had given her credit for. Far better. Her curves were generous but her frame slender, and she moved with fluid ease. How many women would have envied her grace?

Her face caught the sun and became nymph-like, no longer so plain, but intriguingly different.

Did Michaels know she came here like this? Would he approve, seeing her this way—wild and impractical, running free in the sun like a colt before it was broken to the saddle? Not likely. What would he do when he found out she was not what he expected?

Fitzwilliam licked his lips again and swallowed hard.

Mary—Miss Bennet—pushed the dripping water from her neck with her hands, then dragged her palms over her cheeks.

Good Lord, the woman was crying. A red mark traced the crest of her cheek, tinges of purple showing through.

His ardor shifted into something less troubling but no less potent.

She slowly reassembled her walking ensemble, tied her bonnet and wandered to a rough-hewn stone bench in front of the shack. Slowly, very slowly she lowered herself onto it. What other pain was she concealing?

Fitzwilliam counted to one hundred. That should be long enough. He sauntered out from behind the oak and dipped out a cold drink from the well before pretending to notice Mary for the first time.

"Good day, Miss Bennet."

The poor girl jumped so violently she nearly fell from her perch. "Colonel Fitzwilliam! Forgive me, I did not mean to trespass ..."

"By no means, you are most welcome. Darcy and I used to play here as children. The shack was in little better condition in those days, but the well was as sweet." He shook water droplets from his hands.

"Thank you. I should go." She rose and straightened her simple grey skirts.

It was a damn shame to lose sight of her lovely legs.

"Pray, do not." He stepped closer.

She averted her face, turning the reddened cheek away from him.

He ducked to that side and peered close.

She covered her cheek with her hand.

"What happened?"

"It does not signify."

"Does Michaels know?"

"Know what?"

He caught her chin carefully and pushed her bonnet back. "This." He traced her cheekbone with a fingertip. No, it was not proper. Yes, it was far too intrusive, but ...

She winced and pulled from his grasp. "It is not your concern." That was a good sign, a bit of fire returning to her voice.

"I beg to differ. It is not the example I wish my clergyman to set for the parish."

She stepped back and replaced her straw bonnet, plain as her gown, tying it a little more firmly this time. "He is my cousin, and I, a member of his household. It is his right to maintain order."

"I knew there was reason I did not like him." His lip curled back.

"It was my fault. I should not have lost my temper."

"How would he know about that?"

"Nothing moves faster at Rosings than gossip." She wrapped her arms over her chest. "I should return to the parsonage. Mrs. Collins will need me."

"I was on an errand there myself. Might I walk with you?"

"Mr. Collins might not…"

"Might not approve? I scarcely see how he is in a position to judge my behavior."

"But he does examine mine."

"I shall make it clear that I sought you out."

Her eyes narrowed in an expression uncomfortably like her sister's. Elizabeth always knew too much when she looked at him that way. "Why, sir?"

"Because you are my errand, Miss Bennet." They walked several dozen steps in silence. Why did the words come so slow now? "My behavior has not been gentlemanly toward you."

"Lady Catherine has left you rather frayed." She shrugged as though to dismiss him altogether.

"That is no excuse for my boorish conduct."

"You may not find it a compliment, but I hardly noticed."

He threw his head back and laughed. "I do not know how to take that. Is my behavior so bad, or are you so accustomed …"

She looked aside, silhouetting her face in the sunlight.

Still nymph-like. He would always see her that way now.

"I am sorry that you have such low expectations of the men around you."

She shrugged again, fire fading away, her mild-seeming façade—that is what it was, was it not?—replacing it.

Bloody shame, but probably safer that way.

She kicked a clump of dry leaves aside. "I believe I owe you an apology. I must remember my place and the great condescension I am offered by Rosings Park."

Damn that bloody old finger-post. "Collins is wrong on many counts. I believe you are due an apology."

"That is thoughtful of you. But forgive me for being plain: it is rather a dangerous sentiment, one that I would beseech you not to utter in Mr. Collins' hearing."

They walked the next mile through the haunted path in silence. But the ghosts whispered on the breezes.

Chapter 3

SOME MIGHT CONSTRUE she deserved Collins' correction, but some might equally construe it was Fitzwilliam's fault that she was put in such a position in the first place. He lifted his hat and raked his fingers through his hair, ruining his valet's careful work. Had he behaved in a more civilized fashion, she would never have had reason to address him in the manner she had. A colonel of His Majesty's army should be in better control of himself.

He glanced at her, bathed in the deep shadows, touched by hints of some flowery scent descending from the dense tree canopy. She said nothing, but something in her posture spoke her awareness of his presence. It was a companionable, comfortable sort of silence.

What would Michaels do when, not if, but when, he found out about Collins' temper?

Great heavens! That might be the final straw for him. That was not to be borne …

He scrubbed his lips against his palm.

Miss Bennet cast a quizzical look his way, but he shook his head, and she returned to her private reverie. Funny, their steps were synchronized now.

Why had Darcy never told him how many personalities were involved in managing an estate? Father had never dealt with such things. No, he was above handling mundane matters himself. That is what the steward was for, that and supervising the place whilst he was away—and he was away a great deal.

How often Father criticized Darcy for spending so much time at Pemberley, sullying his hands with the running of the estate. Was that why Pemberley ran so well? Father had always said it was because Darcy had a particular knack for finding good stewards.

The parsonage rose up on the horizon, quaint and covered with roses and ivy. A pretty looking little abode for so odious a man. Miss Bennet hesitated and nearly stumbled. He steadied her by the elbow.

They left the haunted path and crossed the lane in front of the parsonage. Was Miss Bennet dragging her feet? Certainly she would not admit to it, but yes, indeed she was.

Collins himself—lovely chap and gracious host that he was—met them at the door and let them into the tight vestibule.

Really, the space was hardly large enough to be called that. It was an odd sort of empty spot between halls and rooms and stairs that caught visitors as they walked into it. Painted a sort of dirty off-white color, the walls held two portraits of no-one-knew-who and a half-table pushed up against the wall bearing a green earthenware vase with a scraggly bunch of garden flowers that smelled a day too old. With all the elbows and arms and shoulders, it was a wonder that the vase had not been knocked off yet.

"Colonel Fitzwilliam? How good of you to call upon us this morning." Collins took Fitzwilliam's hat and coat, nearly elbowing the flustered housekeeper in the face, all the while glowering at Miss Bennet. "I pray my cousin has not been a trial to you."

"Her company has been most pleasant, I assure you. I fear I am the one who disturbed her when she would rather have been left alone." Fitzwilliam assisted her with her sweat-marked spencer and bonnet despite her protests, passing them to the housekeeper as Collins looked on, feathers bristling.

"Shall we adjourn to my study, sir?" Collins turned his shoulder to Miss Bennet who retreated half a step toward the stairs. One more word and she would probably disappear to her chambers, happy for the dismissal.

"I do have several matters I would discuss with you, but I would include Mrs. Collins and Miss Bennet, too. I value their insights."

"Certainly, certainly, sir. Pray, follow me. " Was Collins speaking through gritted teeth?

He trundled them through a dimly lit corridor too narrow for two men to pass comfortably side-by-side. The back room was furnished as a woman's sitting room—a rather ugly one—but what an odd arrangement to locate Mrs. Collins' room with such an unattractive view? Why would the man's study face the road and the more favorable prospect?

Mrs. Collins reclined on the faded red floral fainting couch, the room's dominant piece of furniture, placed so it might benefit from the light from two narrow windows on the longer wall. A small writing desk and chair, cast-offs from Rosings that Collins must have received with obnoxious gratitude, sat near the window on the short wall. An odd pair of wood and wicker arm chairs with tables to match, and a curio cabinet, also all cast-offs from the manor, completed the room. He stared at the couch again. Damn! It was from Rosings, too. The entire room reeked of Rosings Manor!

Had Aunt Catherine insisted that Mrs. Collins leave behind any evidence of her more humble upbringing, or had she already filled every room before the happy couple took residence?

Mrs. Collins pushed up awkwardly from the fainting couch, like some sort of large sea creature washed up on the shore.

"Pray, madam, do not rise on my account." Fitzwilliam waved her down.

"Mrs. Collins!" Collins glowered as she lowered herself.

"Are you contradicting me?" Fitzwilliam pulled himself up a little taller and adjusted his tone to one more appropriate to drilling men.

"By no means, sir." Collins hopped several steps back.

His reaction should not be so satisfying.

"I shall ask the housekeeper for refreshments." Miss Bennet ducked around him and left, calm dignity in every movement.

Collins bowed deeply. "Pray, sit down, sir. We are at your disposal for whatever you may need. I am honored that you would consider my assistance useful in any manner."

Fitzwilliam turned the largest chair in the room to face Mrs. Collins and settled into it with far more ceremony than necessary. But it seemed to make an impression on Collins, and that was his purpose.

Miss Bennet returned and perched beside Mrs. Collins. Collins stood behind them, hand lightly on the couch, clearly waiting with bated breath.

Fitzwilliam leaned back and crossed his ankles. "I have a number of issues on my mind this morning. I think perhaps you and your wife are particularly suited to assist me with them. To start, I want your advice in dealing with on a ... sensitive matter on the estate."

"Certainly sir, I am most obliged to offer what wisdom I may."

One must not roll one's eyes. It did nothing to maintain a look of authority in any situation.

"It has recently come to my attention, quite accidently, that one of the tenants has been behaving in a way I most heartily disapprove. I suppose by strictest definitions, he has done nothing wrong, but I find his behavior abhorrent, so much so that I should wish him off Rosings immediately, should I have my way. But, there are, of course, those who depend upon him who might be injured if they were suddenly uprooted."

"Might I ask, sir, the nature of the man's transgressions? I am certain that your judgment of what is acceptable at Rosings Park is by everything good and correct. I only ask as a means of helping me to determine how the situation may be approached, you see." Collins thumbed his lapels.

It would be a delight to see that ghastly self-satisfied expression fade away.

"Of course." Fitzwilliam rose and paced along the length of the room, feeling Collins' eyes following his every step. "You must understand. I am not opposed to a show of force when that is the only way by which a wrong may be righted. My service in France should make that point clear. There are some situations which might only be met with a show of might to stop a great injustice."

"Absolutely, sir. I do not believe anyone would question the rightness of that action."

"However," Fitzwilliam turned very slowly until he faced Collins, looking him in the eye. "I find it repulsive and cowardly when force is used against a weaker party. There is never an excuse for a proper gentleman to use strength against one whose position is weaker than his own. That is not only ungentlemanly, it is unmanly and not to be tolerated."

Collins ran a finger around the inside of his collar and tugged it away from his throat.

Excellent! No more self-satisfaction. What would one call that expression replacing it? Mounting anxiety, perhaps?

Fitzwilliam resumed pacing. "Quite by accident, I came across a scene I thoroughly disliked. A tenant enacted violence against one of his family. No doubt the whole affair would have been hidden from me if possible, but as it was, I witnessed the evidence with my own eyes."

"It is necessary for a man to keep his household in order. Sometimes force is required." Collins' eyebrows rose as he cocked his head.

"I thought that might be the case, but upon investigation, I can only conclude it was a brutish show of temper, designed to bring ease to the man."

Miss Bennet's face colored, and she stared at the floor. Mrs. Collins looked back and forth from her to Collins.

"I should like to remove the brute from my property and never see him return."

Mrs. Collins' eyes bulged, and she pressed a hand to her chest. Poor woman had far greater sense than her shallow-pated husband.

"Perhaps, sir, that is too harsh, considering the conditions. You have not said there was great injury involved," Miss Bennet whispered, a little look of pleading in her eyes.

Did she not realize this was for her benefit? Difficult woman!

"In truth, I am not entirely certain of the extent of the injuries, nor do I know for how long this has been going on." He clasped his hands behind his back and clucked his tongue.

Dr. Grant from Cambridge would be proud to be aped so well.

"Perhaps one should assume the best?" Miss Bennet's voice trailed off as Collins turned a glower on her.

Fitzwilliam cleared his throat hard. "And simply forget it all? No, I can hardly abide such a suggestion. That would leave me to do nothing, and I am a man of action."

"Then perhaps the minimum action possible: a word of warning, a gentle word of warning."

"Cousin, I am quite certain the colonel is in no way interested in your opinions—"

Fitzwilliam leaned toward her. "Are you suggesting that he might be apt to behave better were I simply to warn him it was necessary?"

"I have known that approach to work."

"Then you have dealt with a far different sort of person than I. Most only respond to threats and consequences."

Collins cleared his throat. "As I was saying, Colonel, it is my opinion—"

He caught Collins' gaze and held it in a crushing grip. One, two, three ... ten measured breaths, until Collins' face turned ashen, and he withered.

Better, much better.

"Perhaps, Miss Bennet, if you are so certain, I shall give your approach a try first. Then, if it proves unsuccessful, I can resort to measures more comfortable to a soldier. After all, I have great admiration for your advice and your wisdom. You are a font of good sense, and it behooves one to pay attention to..."

Miss Bennet sprang to her feet and met the housekeeper at the doorway. Those were not the steps of a woman who was pleased with him.

He might be laying it on a bit thick, but Collins was not a smart man, and subtlety would surely be lost on him.

Miss Bennet took the tray from the housekeeper and placed it on the table nearest Mrs. Collins. "Tea, Colonel?"

"Thank you." Fitzwilliam returned to his seat. Maybe for the ladies' sake he should change the subject. He took a plate of dainties from Mrs. Collins. Nothing fancy, some cucumber sandwiches, shortbread biscuits, some toast with jam and clotted cream. Clearly thrown together at the last moment, probably under Miss Bennet's direction. A possible enough show of hospitality all things considered.

Damned efficient woman.

Tea in hand, Collins managed to find a chair for himself. Sweat trickled down the side of his face, and he avoided looking at Miss Bennet. As dense as he was, perchance the message had got across.

"Was there another matter on your mind, Colonel?" Mrs. Collins' teacup rattled subtly in her hand.

"Indeed, I have a favor to ask of you and Miss Bennet."

Collins jumped, knocking a biscuit off his plate. "A favor? Whatever it is, they will be happy to accommodate."

"Whilst I appreciate your enthusiasm, sir, I would much prefer to hear from the ladies themselves after I have explained my request." Fitzwilliam drummed his fingers along the side of his tea cup as he balanced it on his knee. The china had not come from Rosings. At least there was something in the house that Aunt Catherine had not orchestrated. " You are aware Lady Catherine's condition does not improve. Mrs. Jenkinson has made it clear that she is not equal to the task of managing her care any longer. Aunt Catherine will be in need of another companion or, perhaps more properly a nurse, very soon. Both of you ladies seem much more adept at accommodating my aunt's needs than I, particularly you, Miss Bennet."

Collins' hand flew up, much the same way he emphasized a point during his sermons. Far too dramatic for Fitzwilliam's liking. "Cousin Mary is indeed the embodiment of compassion and understanding for her ladyship. I am quite certain she would be happy to fulfill the commission—"

Miss Bennet gasped.

"Excuse me, Mr. Collins. Have you forgotten Michaels is to take her as his bride soon?"

"But what is marriage to the opportunity to serve—"

Fitzwilliam slammed his fist on the arm of the chair, nearly dislodging his teacup. "Enough, man! Are you daft? I am not asking for her to be Lady Catherine's companion, but for her and Mrs. Collins' assistance in finding one! Would you make inquiries on my behalf and recommendations on how to fill the position?"

Mrs. Collins glanced at Miss Bennet. "I ... we ... would be honored to assist in any way we can, sir."

"Certainly they will." Collins bowed from his shoulders. "And if there is any way in which I might offer up my own wisdom—"

"They are entirely up to the task without your interference, Mr. Collins. Keep yourself to the concerns of the parish and allow the ladies to manage this undertaking on their own. I shall be very displeased if I hear you have been meddling in their affairs."

Great lord above! He sounded just like Aunt Catherine!

"Of course, sir, of course. I would never meddle. I only want to ensure—"

"Then follow my instructions, and let them be about their business." Fitzwilliam slapped the chair's arms again.

"As you say, sir, as you say." More obsequious bowing.

"We are honored that you would trust us with such an important task." Mrs. Collins wrung her hands in her lap.

"With your permission, sir, I shall enquire of my sister Mrs. Darcy as well—"

Collins whirled on her, and she flinched, not subtly

either. Fitzwilliam nearly jumped to restrain Collins. That was the final straw. A curate would have to be found straightaway.

"You will do no such thing. What has she to do with Rosings? You know how Lady Catherine feels about that … that—"

"Hush, Collins! Pray continue, Miss Bennet." Fitzwilliam clenched his fists until he lost feeling in his fingertips. Better that than lay hands on Collins.

Miss Bennet stared at her lap. "I only thought Mrs. Darcy, with her connections in society, might know of appropriate candidates for the position: widows of good character, spinsters whose brothers may no longer need their assistance."

"Excellent notion. I know of no one with so much good sense. Ideas like that are exactly why I have asked for your aid. In fact, you have given me an outstanding thought of my own. I should like to invite you to Rosings as Lady Catherine's guest, whilst you engage in this favor. It is only fitting that you should enjoy Rosings' hospitality whilst you exert such efforts on our behalf."

Miss Bennet did not look entirely pleased with the suggestion—no, she looked entirely annoyed and ready to argue. Contrary creature, what was there not to appreciate?

"Sir, I … I do not know what to say. I am quite able to accomplish the charge here, with Mrs. Collins."

"Nonsense, it is the least I can do to express my gratitude. Mrs. Collins is most welcome to come to Rosings to work with you. I shall see one of the small sitting rooms upstairs made into an office for your use. I would not wish Mr. Collins to be disturbed. I know that you have parish business to attend. Nothing should distract you from your sacred tasks."

"You are most generous, Colonel Fitzwilliam. I thank you for the hospitality and condescension you extend to my … cousin." Collins' voice was strained and tight—no doubt he meant to say "undeserving cousin,", but it was good that he restrained himself.

"Then it is settled. A servant will be sent for your trunk. Shall I tell Mrs. Jenkinson and Lady Catherine to expect you for nuncheon this afternoon?"

Miss Bennet glared at him.

So blasted difficult.

"Excellent. This afternoon then." He bowed, and departed.

One advantage to a house this small, it took little time and effort to get to where one wanted to go.

The housekeeper chased behind him, trying to hand him his coat and hat. He snatched them out of her hands, but he did not pause to put them on. Better to be out of the vicarage as quickly as possible. A moment longer in Collins' proximity and he might say or do something regrettable. How had Aunt Catherine selected him for the living? More importantly, how soon might Collins sent packing to his new estate in Hertfordshire?

Icy, prickly cold descended in Charlotte's parlor. The kind of cold that frequented the house when Papa had a bad day. The kind of cold that sent Lydia and Kitty running for cover and Mama to making him tea with a liberal dose of brandy. The kind of cold that Lizzy had no choice but to put on a brave face for and withstand.

She would follow Lizzy's example.

Mr. Collins stared dumbly at the doorway and empty hall. Mary clenched her fists in her lap, the pain of Charlotte's gaze rasping her skin nearly too much to bear.

The front door squealed and thudded shut. Mary held her breath.

He rose slowly, turning his back to them, and stalked away, muttering about the need to write a sermon.

Mary counted silently. At thirty-five, the door to Mr. Collins' study slammed shut. She closed the sitting room door and leaned back against it.

"What happened after you ran from the house?" Charlotte probably did not intend to sound so accusing.

Mary covered her eyes with her hand. "I did not go seeking the colonel if that is what concerns you. I went to the spring well by the old shack, at the end of the footpath no one uses. I thought no one would be there. With good reason, I might add. But in some perverse mischance, the colonel appeared. He said he was on his way here."

"I do not know why he should be there. It is hardly on the way to the parsonage." Charlotte pushed up from the couch and pressed her hands to the small of her back. How much her belly had grown even these last few weeks. "What did you tell the colonel?"

"Nothing, absolutely nothing. Do you really think so little of me?" She turned her bruised cheek toward Charlotte. "But he is no fool. He knew where this had come from without a word on my part. And yes, I begged him to leave the matter lie."

Charlotte inched closer and inspected Mary's face.

"I know Mr. Collins has a bad temper. I suppose it is a trait shared by the men of your family. He has not been apt to behave that way with me, though. I do not know why—"

Was that indictment or commiseration? Apparently, she had no idea that bowing to every whim and agreeing with his every declaration would render him more docile? What a coincidence, then, that she managed to do all those things correctly.

Mary balanced her forehead on her fist. "What difference does it may why he should find me so disagreeable? What is done is done."

"I do not see why you are so disturbed. I know your father—"

"Charlotte! Are you actually defending them?"

"I am merely being realistic." Charlotte waddled to the farthest window and leaned against the writing desk. She traced the chipped paint on the window mullion with her fingertip. "What else is there to be done? The law does not agree with you. It is ours to endure and to be gentle and mild."

Mama often espoused the same sentiments. "So I have read, but I do not know that I believe it anymore. I am not certain it has served any of us well. At the least, it was gallant of the colonel to stand up on my behalf."

"I would caution you. Be careful of him." Charlotte looked over her shoulder at Mary.

"What are you talking about?"

"Are you not suspicious of his expectations for your company?"

"Do not be ridiculous!"

"He is not the kind of man you are accustomed to."

"I am betrothed to his steward and sister to his cousin. Not to mention I am hardly a beauty, nor have I any fortune. There is no reason for him to pay attention to me." Mary wrapped her arms around her waist.

"A man does not reason beyond lust."

"Charlotte! I cannot accept what you are suggesting." How annoying that the carpet should muffle her foot stomp.

"As you will." Charlotte turned back to face the window. "I am only concerned for you. You are my friend."

Why did silence always have to be so awkward?

"Will you still be with me for my lying-in and confinement?"

"Of course I will. You need only send word, and I will be here. I have promised you that."

"Do you want help packing your trunk?"

And be instructed on Lady Catherine's way of folding gowns? No. "You should rest. I think your ankles are swelling again. You need to put your feet up." She guided Charlotte back to the couch and helped her to arrange her feet.

"I will miss your company. Who will tell me to rest if you are not here?"

"With all my regular calls, you will hardly know I have gone. I am sure Mr. Collins will be in a better humor without me. Take a fresh cup of tea and a few sandwiches to keep up your strength. Eat, then close your eyes and rest for a bit. I shall not go without taking leave of you."

"You are a good friend." Charlotte patted her hand and sipped her tea.

Mary slipped out and tiptoed past Mr. Collins' study.

Her heart hammered in her throat. Who did Colonel Fitzwilliam think he was, highhandedly managing her life that way? It seemed he was more like Darcy than Elizabeth knew. Perhaps it was a family trait among the Fitzwilliams. Lady Catherine certainly demonstrated her share of it.

She dragged her trunk to the middle of the room—it had not been properly aired and stored in the attic—and flung it open. Botheration, it smelt musty. Would that scent never come out of it? Maybe Parkes could assist her with that whilst she stayed at Rosings. She minced around the trunk, fighting to get around it and back to the closet for her things.

Getting out of the Collinses' house was a blessing, full stop. The man was obsequious and shared all of Papa's worst traits, filtered through his vicar's robes. He was only tolerable with the knowledge that she would soon be moving to her own establishment with Michaels. Maybe she should be gladder to be getting away from him.

But the price was far too dear to appreciate easily.

Now she was stuck with Lady Catherine and the denizens of the manor. The servants would be turning to her as they had to Lizzy, the only practical head in the house. Effectively being mistress of a grand manor might be an amusing mental exercise, but it was a great deal more work than she cared to take on, particularly when she could look forward to being questioned and meddled with at every turn.

She yanked open a sticky drawer and nearly tumbled backward into the open trunk. With one hand she scooped out her body linens and with the other flung them into her luggage. Who would know they had not been folded properly?

Had the kind and generous colonel realized the breadth of what he was asking of her? Honestly, probably not.

Why did these interfering men never bother to ask her opinion? They simply decided for her as if she were some simpleton!

In some part, though, she should be grateful. He had swept in, rather like a knight in armor, to protect her from a very real ogre. That was sympathetic of him. And the way he looked at her at the well ... how long had he been there, and what had he seen?

Oh! Gracious!

Her cheeks heated, and she pressed her palms to her face. Had he seen her indecorous display, water dripping down her décolletage? She winced. No doubt he had.

Could that explain the look in his eyes, the way he licked his lips as he stared at her?

Heat crept up her jaw and neck. No man had ever looked at her that way. Michaels certainly had not. Should it please her, or disappoint her that he did not?

She should not like that Fitzwilliam did, but the memory of his eyes, his voice, sent a chill down her spine and a frisson to her belly.

No, no, no! This was not how she should feel and not how she would feel!

She huffed out a jagged breath and then another. There, that was better. She would be in control; her sensibilities would not overwhelm her good sense.

For the first time, Lydia's impulsiveness and the liberties she allowed to her person made a modicum of sense. Was that a good thing?

Great heavens—did Charlotte suspect? Was that why she had offered her warning? If she thought she saw something, did Collins suppose something as well? What about the colonel?

Oh, goodness!

She dropped to the edge of her bed, feet balanced on the edge of the trunk and face in her hands, gasping for breath.

No, no. She was letting her imagination run away from her. Collins was too self-absorbed to pay attention to anything so subtle, and Charlotte? Surely, it was mere coincidence. No doubt she found her husband's attentions disagreeable and assumed all men were as he.

She shuddered. Those were thoughts she did not need in her mind.

Not at all.

Breathe, just breathe.

Enough of this foolish speculation! She threw gloves, shoes, and pelisse into the trunk. Lady Catherine would be appalled, but it would do to travel from the vicarage to the manor. She flung the lid shut and donned her bonnet and spencer.

Best not leave anything behind. No telling what Collins might arrange to have happen to anything of hers left here in her absence. She added a smaller trunk she had never unpacked and a large carpet bag that contained her sewing and letter writing supplies to the pile.

What an entirely untoward thought. She needed time for repose, to gather herself before facing Rosings.

After taking her leave of Charlotte, she would take the long way to the manor. The very long way.

✣ Chapter 4

SEVERAL HOURS LATER, Small Tom—she had started thinking of him as that—ushered her into the great expanse of the front hall that contained more furnishings—half tables, chairs, a cabinet, and many vases of flowers—than some of the rooms in the parsonage. Sadly, the man looked more like a Small Tom than a Barkley; he was barely as tall as Parkes and not nearly so stout. At least he did not seem to mind the appellation.

"A room has been prepared for you, Miss Bennet. Parkes has already assigned a maid to your service. Your belongings arrived earlier and have been arranged for you." His eyebrow rose slightly, but not enough to be impertinent.

No, she was not going to answer that question.

He led her up the broad marble grand stairs. How much easier it would be to help Charlotte down these than the ones at the vicarage. Three, maybe four people could traverse these steps abreast and never crowd one another.

"Parkes and Cook have asked to be notified at your arrival. I believe they are in great hope of garnering your input into household matters. Shall I send them up, or would you prefer to rest first?"

Mary paused and gripped the smooth mahogany banister a little more tightly. "Colonel Fitzwilliam said something about a sitting room that I might use as an office."

"Indeed, Miss. Your chambers are across from a sitting room. A writing desk, fully supplied, has already been moved into that room for your use." He gestured toward an open door, halfway down the corridor.

"I shall see them there in a quarter hour." Mary chewed her lip.

Oh, the words she had for the colonel right now. How smug he would be, thinking he had done her such a favor. How could she hold her tongue if he gloated over his good deed? She forced a smile, just to practice. It was not as if she had never held her tongue. In fact, she was a great proficient at it.

At least he was truly trying to do her a good turn.

She held her breath as she peeked into the sitting room. Peach striped paper-hangings covered the walls, a pleasing contrast to the navy brocade drapes and upholstery on the sofa and matching pair of bergère chairs. Surprisingly little ormolu appointed the room—only on the candle sticks, accenting the lancet-shaped mantel clock, and on the mirror's frame that reflected the landscape from the windows near the dainty, feminine writing desk. Small, elegant oak tables dotted the room, exactly where they might be most useful, including one near the fireplace, between the sofa and chairs, bearing a large vase of fresh white peonies.

The relatively plain furnishings no doubt represented some of the oldest pieces at Rosings, but they were very much to her taste. How astonishing.

The light was good for letter writing, so that was an added blessing. Moreover, the room was away from the main stairs and Lady Catherine's usual paths. Surely that was no accident, either.

Perhaps she would be able to endure Colonel Fitzwilliam's hospitality after all.

Parkes and Cook found her at the quarter hour. Parkes was an excellent housekeeper, but she had been cowed by Lady Catherine and needed confirmation on all her plans. Colonel Fitzwilliam might have served the same purpose, but Parkes had little confidence in his ability to run the manor.

Cook expressed concerns about the budget. That issue would take some time to sort out, but it would be straightforward enough. Numbers generally were. They told a true story without wheedling one into another opinion. All in all, numbers were often far easier to deal with than people. Tomorrow morning, after she wrote a few letters, she would begin balancing the household accounts. Michaels would be pleased to know she was handling the task.

Parkes and Cook left, only to be replaced by Colonel Fitzwilliam's valet and Small Tom in turn—every upper servant in the manor except Lady Catherine's lady's maid.

Over an hour later, Lady Catherine's lady's maid appeared at the door. "Her ladyship heard you were here and has decided it is time for tea. She … ah … requires your company, Miss. But first, may I ask your opinion on a small matter?"

"Are you enjoying your tea, Miss Bennet?" Mrs. Jenkinson leaned close and whispered. She was a mousy woman with a nose barely wide enough to hold up her glasses which twitched when she spoke. Slightly taller than Mary, her skin stretched tight over her skull, emphasizing high cheekbones and watery blue eyes.

The hushed voices were hardly necessary. Lady Catherine's head lolled back on her throne—as Lizzy called it—in the small downstairs parlor. Just prior, Lady Catherine had kept up a rather animated, if difficult to follow, conversation for a full half hour. Apparently, shoving that many words into such a short span of time had been exhausting.

She snored loud enough to set the beaded valance beneath her chair rattling between the gilded sphinxes. What a ridiculous piece of furniture.

The rest of the room matched, with ostentatious red upholstery on too many sofas and chairs for a room of its size, three and eight respectively. Too many ornaments on too many tables, all of them seemingly covered in ormolu. The eye could not rest and take in any one; it just jumped from one piece of ostentation to another piece of hideousness. No, that was not fair; just because tastes differed did not mean they were wrong.

Except in this case where it was all ugly and showy and unpleasant, crowding in on one and making her long for escape before she suffocated in pretense.

"The tea is excellent. Thank you." Mary placed her teacup bearing the de Bourgh family crest almost soundlessly on its saucer and peered over Mrs. Jenkinson's shoulder.

Colonel Fitzwilliam stood just outside the doorway, and beckoned her with a nod.

"Pray excuse me." Mary pointed toward Colonel Fitzwilliam with her chin and slipped past Mrs. Jenkinson who looked as though she might protest, but then seemed to think better of it.

Fitzwilliam bowed his head in a gesture of thanks and tiptoed down the wide hall toward his study. He urged her inside and shut the door with exaggerated care.

His confidence seemed to return, and he leaned against his desk. "How do you find your quarters, Miss Bennet?"

She leaned back slightly and studied him. His previously impeccable dress had devolved into something far less tidy. His loosely tied cravat nearly masked the open top button of his waistcoat. Ink smudged the cuff of his shirtsleeve, and his hair must have been raked through multiple times. The study matched his manner of dress, with piles of papers on every flat surface ... and on a few not-so-flat ones. Empty glasses kept them company.

How much had he been drinking?

"Your quarters, are they suitable?"

"I have not actually been able to see them yet, so I do not know. But the sitting room is quite lovely, and the desk installed there will do nicely for my needs. Your staff has been most attentive."

"Good." He strode to the fireplace, managing to look graceful as he dodged the books, small tables, and chairs in his path. "I am pleased to hear it."

"Forgive me, sir, if I observe you appear to be rather unsettled right now. Is there something I might do for your distress?"

He leaned against the mantel, his back to her, and raked his hair. "Are all your sisters apt to be so observant?"

"I do not find Jane and Kitty to be so, but Lydia has demonstrated herself to be a far better study of her surroundings than I previously gave her credit for."

Fitzwilliam chuckled under his breath. "I am grateful that you still retain a sense of humor about you."

"Why would you be concerned about that?"

"I have been expecting a proper tongue lashing." He glanced at her over his shoulder.

"Indeed, sir? And why would that be?" She crossed her arms over her chest.

"Is it not bad enough to waiting for one's executioner? You might have the mercy not to force me to pronounce my own sentence as well."

"I am by no means requiring anything of you. Perhaps your conscience is troubling you?"

"There are many who would argue I am without a conscience."

"Yet you have proven them quite wrong, have you not? Clearly you are troubled, although you refuse to tell me the nature of it."

He cleared a chair by shoving the journals it contained to the floor and fell into it. "You asked me not to become involved, and I ignored your request. I interfered, dramatically one might say. Not only did I make it clear to that dolt that I knew what he was about, but I also interjected my own solution and forced you to go along with it. There, is that confession enough?"

The corners of her lips rose in spite of herself. "It is a rather thorough one, I have to say. I cannot disagree with any of the facts as you have stated them."

"So then, state your case. Express yourself, and leave me in no question as to the depth of my transgressions." He waved his hand in the air.

So he enjoyed a touch of the dramatic. Somehow it was fitting.

"Why? What would be the point of it? Do you enjoy such things?"

"Pray, do not toy with me, Miss Bennet."

"And do not make assumptions about me." She brought her foot down sharply.

He smiled broadly. It was an attractive, if wholly irritating expression. "Ah, the lady does have a spark after all. Do go on."

"Do not presume to know what I do or do not appreciate, or what I do or do not want. Do not presume you know me at all."

He rose and approached, slowly, deliberately. "It would seem I do not."

"Few do, if any, and I am decidedly tired of those who insist they do and make decisions on my behalf because of it."

"So then you did not mind being the brunt of Collins' temper? You would rather have been left there to absorb his whims of displeasure?"

"What does it matter? It seems you have already decided—"

He grabbed her wrist, not painfully, but insistently, and pulled her close. "Do be reasonable. I saw the look on your face when you thought no one was looking. I know the meaning of that look."

"Do you? Do you, indeed? Tell me then, for I should like to know what I have inadvertently revealed whilst being spied upon."

"I did not spy upon you."

"Did I invite your company?"

"It is my estate and my land. I have free rein here. You might be construed to be the one intruding upon me." His eyebrow rose over very fine, if a little playful, eyes.

"Indeed, you are correct. I shall remember that in the future. Perhaps you should tell me where I am permitted in this house as well. I would not wish to be accused of trespassing here. Shall I keep to my rooms, or am I allowed to the hallways as well? Shall I use the servants' stairs that I might stay out of your sight and mind?"

He dropped her wrist and held up open hands. "Enough! I did not call you here in order to fight with you."

"Then why did you call me here, like a servant in your home?"

"You are not a servant. You are a guest—a welcome, invited guest ... one to whom I owe an apology. I asked you here to tell you I am sorry for acting like Darcy and determining what should be done with no reference to your wishes." Something in his expression was utterly and completely sincere, even a bit pleading.

"I do not imagine you offer many apologies. It shall be interesting to hear how you might deliver one."

His eyes bulged. "And that is not what I would have expected from a woman about to receive an apology from a man unaccustomed to delivering them."

"You assumed I would be meek and appreciative, deeply grateful for the gift you were offering?"

He snorted. "Perhaps a touch."

"Then you think well of yourself, do you not, and little of the one against whom you may have transgressed. It seems this encounter is entirely about relieving your discomfort and entirely disconnected to mine."

He dragged his hand over his face. "What discomforts have you? Is not Rosings superior to the vicarage? After all, Collins is not here."

"No, sir, he is not. But Mr. Collins is not the only bane of my existence."

"Do tell me. What else proves a bane to you?"

"We might start with your aunt. She will be insisting upon my constant company during all her waking hours. In fact, she already has. Your staff believes I am the resident expert in all things regarding Lady Catherine. I have already been consulted four times on that point by different upper servants. Moreover, I have put a stop to at least two maids' plans to flee the estate; that is probably a good thing all told."

"Well then, I thank you for your interventions." His eyes twinkled. Was he enjoying this conversation?

"You will have a great deal more to thank me for, then."

"Do illuminate me." His eyes crinkled as they would have had he been smiling—which he was not, but seemed to be, anyway.

"In my 'office' upstairs, I now have all the household ledgers. Parkes assumes I shall study them and advise her. Cook expects I shall review her menus and come up with some plan to meet Lady Catherine's demands and maintain the budget available to the kitchen. Somehow, I am to figure out how to purchase what is possible and create suitable substitute menus and, if that were not enough, manage to distract Lady Catherine from reacting to the fact that her table does not contain what she required."

"Parkes and Cook?"

"Even your valet has been to see me."

"My valet? You have gone too far. That is absurd, wholly and completely." He scratched the side of his head violently. "Stop, pray stop. I do not wish to know why my valet saw fit to consult you on anything! It sounds like the entire household has descended upon you like a cloud of locusts."

"More like lambs separated from their shepherd and hopeful they have found one again."

"But why would they be turning to you?"

"Because of Lizzy." Gracious, that came out rather more bitter than intended.

"I had an inkling that she was more integral to the running of this house than anyone really knew. But this is far and away beyond what I would ever have expected." He sat lightly on the edge of his desk. "So, despite my attempt to do a service on your behalf, I am to see that you are the one doing me a service."

She nodded.

He covered his eyes with his hand, his shoulders sagging. "I had absolutely no idea my staff would be turning to my guests for assistance. Why would they not come to me?"

"Women run a household, not men. They would no sooner turn to you than to Mr. Michaels. Now that you have had my answer, I would insist upon one of my own."

"I suppose you are entitled."

"Why did you involve yourself in the matter despite my request that you not?"

He stared at the ceiling, the only place in the room not cramped and cluttered. "Would you believe me if I told you it was out of fear Darcy would find out about your treatment at Collins' hand? It is something he would not tolerate, and he would hold me accountable for it."

"That does not ring true. I cannot imagine you have ever allowed Darcy to bully you. You are not afraid of him. You respect him, but you do not fear him." What was it about Colonel Fitzwilliam that urged her to such boldness? Was it simply that he did not dismiss her out of hand, that he seemed to listen when she spoke?

"I cannot tolerate a coward, and any man who must hit a woman in his household is a coward. I will not permit such a cur to win in his petty power plays, particularly not when he holds a position of influence over others on my estate. I have a responsibility to protect these people from that sort of man …"

"Beginning with me?" She stepped very close and peered up into his eyes.

They were steel blue, the color of gun metal.

He swallowed hard. "Yes, beginning with you. You are, after all, family to me now. Who else should be first to enjoy the little I have to offer?"

"And you did not expect Mr. Michaels to perform the office to your satisfaction?"

"Were you planning to make him privy to the situation, or simply pacify him with a clever explanation of this?" He stroked the crest of her cheek with the back of his knuckles.

She closed her eyes. Who would have thought callouses could be so gentle?

"Forgive my familiarity." He pulled his hand away, and she stepped back.

"You are most thoughtful. Pray excuse me. I spoke thoughtlessly, and I should never have—" She turned away.

He caught her hand, just briefly. "Not at all. It was, in truth, rather refreshing. There are not many who will speak frankly to me. I give you my permission to continue to do so as long as you remain at Rosings."

"You will regret permitting such an extravagant liberty. I give you leave to change your mind, and I will not think less of you for it."

"That sounds like a challenge, Miss Bennet. I like a challenge."

Her cheeks flushed. Oh, the way he was looking at her!

A soft rap at the door made her jump. "Pardon me, sir." Mrs. Jenkinson peeked in. "Lady Catherine is asking for Miss Bennet."

"Pray excuse me, sir. My hostess calls." She curtsied and followed Mrs. Jenkinson out.

Mrs. Jenkinson did not hurry, so neither did she. The wide, relatively dim hall enveloped her with the artificial sense of being alone. False though it may be with servants about and stern de Bourgh ancestors staring down from their portraits, it was enough for a moment's contemplation.

Her cheek burned where he had stroked it. She pressed her palm to her face, but the cool touch did nothing to alleviate the sensation.

Insolent, arrogant, disagreeable man! How dare he touch her like that, uninvited?

Family he might be, but truly this was too much. It would be entirely proper, even justified for her to demand her things be packed and leave. Perhaps, that might even teach him something about propriety and restraint. She was not the kind of woman to whom he was accustomed, if he thought that was appropriate treatment.

Was this the beginning of what Charlotte feared might happen? No, he had not been suggestive or demanding in any way. Only tender and considerate.

Still, Charlotte would argue that is what he would want her to believe in order to lure her into … something. No, this was not about seduction, just the lack of suitable boundaries.

But those were important. Maybe, she should go.

Where though? After Colonel Fitzwilliam's show of dominance, she could not return to the parsonage, at least not so soon. Collins' temper would be worse, if anything, not better.

She squeezed her eyes shut as the echoes of Collins' voice and the sharp smack of the back of his hand across her cheek seared through her. She blinked away the burning in her eyes. This was not the time to rehearse those memories. Foolish girl.

Why should she be so fragile now? He was not the first man to treat her thus … and he might not be the last, but his hand had been unexpected. She had been guarded at home, but fool that she was, she had dropped her defenses at the vicarage. Without opportunity to steel herself against the outburst, it had affected her as Father's never had.

Must put that out of her mind now. She needed to gather herself for the trial waiting ahead in the small parlor.

Lady Catherine proved tired and a bit whiny, like a child in need of a nap, requiring only a little encouragement to take to her rooms for a rest. It seemed almost too easy.

Mary returned to her chambers, asking not to be disturbed until dinner. Would anyone honor the request, though? It seemed likely; who was left that had not already visited her?

She paced the perimeter of her bedroom and the adjacent dressing room. Unlike at the Collinses', these were not the most modest quarters in the house. Nor were they royal chambers for titled guests—but that was a good thing, too; such a place would never have been comfortable.

The rooms were pretty, larger and better appointed than any she had ever enjoyed before. Pink floral paper hangings with curtains and bed furnishings to match, a walnut bed with carved posts and slender lines, tables, and a chest of drawers all welcomed her. All the furniture fit in the room without impinging on the walking space. That alone felt like real luxury.

She did not absolutely need a dressing room, but the sunny little space with a soft armchair and stool that invited her to read by the window was an extravagance she could hardly complain about. And the full-length mirror beside the well-appointed dressing table—indulgences like that might well spoil her.

Would it really be such a trial to stay here?

No. But that was not the point.

She pumped her fists at her side. How dare Fitzwilliam take away all her choices? What right had he to make decisions for her? Imperious, pretentious, domineering popinjay! If only she could escape Rosings as Lizzy had.

She sat on the edge of the mattresses piled high on the bedframe. Was the top one down? She fell backwards, embraced by the indulgence.

How dramatic she was being! Her and Lizzy's situations were hardly similar. Lady Catherine was a different woman then—angry, and vengeful, but she no longer held such sway.

Still though, Lizzy was fortunate.

When Lizzy went missing, Darcy turned into a desperate madman; no one would get in the way of his quest for her. He had to be all but tied down to prevent him from going out sick and in the rain to continue his search. He was a force of nature who would stop at nothing, absolutely nothing, to find and protect the woman he adored.

That sort of intensity was not Michaels' way. A precise, well-ordered man, he would do things with planning and control, but little passion.

She wrapped her arms around her waist and rocked slightly.

Enough! Enough! He did not deserve such doubt!

She pushed herself to her feet, nearly dragging the counterpane with her. Blast and botheration! It struggled within her grasp as she fought to restore it to its formerly tidy state.

What point was there in driving herself to misery this way? Comparing Michaels to Darcy was as ridiculous as comparing herself to Lizzy. It was foolish.

But how could she not compare herself to the one person who had what she most wanted …

She clutched her temples and groaned. One more ugly truth. Yes, Lizzy had what she wanted, but what was that, precisely?

 To be loved passionately? To be recognized as strong and competent? To be respected? To have the power of choice? What was it that she was really looking for?

Did she have any right to hope for it when she was so plain and ordinary and had little expectation of being otherwise? Heroines were all beautiful, gay, and sparkling. Like Lizzy and Lydia.

And now she had a headache. A thundering, bone-shattering, knee-weakening headache, a battle of Napoleonic proportions playing out in the confines of her skull.

She fell headlong on the bed and sank into the many mattresses. What perfect justice to be meted out for her uncharitable thoughts. She pulled a feather pillow over her head and fell asleep.

✣Chapter 5

FITZWILLIAM SCANNED HIS walnut-paneled room. Thanks to his valet's efforts, the chaos of the study did not extend here. The large green upholstered chair and oak side table near the window were devoid of any journals or stray papers.

He stood in front of his mirror in his dressing room and watched his valet from the corner of his eye. He was fussing with something in the closet. Again. But what was he doing?

Ever since yesterday when Miss Bennet complained the man had been sought her advice, Fitzwilliam could not shake the question from his mind. What would the valet require from her?

The mahogany shaving table and wash stand on the opposite wall were exactly as usual, impeccably clean and smelling of Fitzwilliam's own soaps. The inlaid satinwood tall boy and clothes chest beside it with gleaming brass handles seemed freshly polished, but otherwise undisturbed. Perhaps he should go through the drawers. The only thing remotely unusual was the lack of any garments on the clothes rack near the mirror, but even that was not entirely peculiar.

The valet wandered out of the closet, holding up his hunter green jacket, waiting for an approving nod. He hung it on the rack and began to brush it vigorously.

"Wait, no. Is that the one with the ink stain?" Fitzwilliam reached for the right sleeve. He had dragged it across a still-wet letter, ruining the letter and in all likelihood the jacket as well. It was the last thing he should be seen wearing to dinner.

"Yes sir, but the situation is remedied now." The valet handed it over.

Fitzwilliam inspected both sleeves. No trace of ink remained.

"Do you approve, sir?"

"Indeed, but I understood the stain to be irreparable."

"It was, sir. The sleeve cuffs were replaced, as was the collar, in a contrasting fabric. The look is quite fashionable if I do say so myself." The man looked a little too pleased with himself.

Fitzwilliam held it at arm's length. The cuffs had been changed to a black velvet sort of affair. Not only stylish, but it would hide further ink mishaps.

Probably on Miss Bennet's advice.

He slipped the garment on and tugged his shirt sleeves into position. The jacket was smart, much more so than in its original incarnation—and no doubt the repair much cheaper than acquiring entirely new apparel.

Was there anything that Bennet women did not have a useful opinion about?

He trotted downstairs. With Lady Catherine's state, it fell to him to be available to entertain Rosings' guests in the gold parlor before dinner. Granted, it was only Michaels and Miss Bennet, but still he should keep up appearances.

And if he failed to appear, it would give Aunt Catherine one more reason to become agitated. Something none of them needed.

Miss Bennet stood near the windows, one hand resting lightly on the dark gold brocade curtains that ran from ceiling to floor, peering toward the lane that led up to the manor. Fitzwilliam paused just inside the doorway. She favored Elizabeth in her profile, just a little bit. Her expression was not wistful as she waited, rather a tad impatient.

Her face was always more agreeable with just a bit of fire in her eyes.

Odd how well she looked in the room, even in a plain gown of puce linen or muslin or some such. Whatever it was, the color was pleasing in the candle-light, against the deep ivory painted walls and golden-yellow upholstery of the four matching couches near the small pianoforte. Any other woman he might have accused of doing it intentionally.

"Good evening, Colonel." She turned and curtsied.

He bowed slightly. "Good evening, Miss Bennet. I trust you are feeling better this evening?"

They met in the middle of the room, just beside the inlaid card table already set with matching wooden chairs in case they chose cards as their evening's entertainment.

"I am, sir, thank you. Pray forgive my missing dinner last night."

"There was little to miss, truth be told. The conversation was sparse, and Aunt Catherine carried most of it herself. Not that it might be considered a bad thing. Usually if she carries both sides of the conversation herself, she finds it quite agreeable and little troubles her."

The corners of her lips crept up. "Indeed, I have found it so. It is a small enough thing to give her comfort. And if other conversation is desired, it is easy to make opportunity for it elsewhere."

"Is this a gentle effort to tutor me in the ways to live peaceably with my aunt?" He wrinkled his lips and raised his brows.

She looked at him, a tiny glint of mischief in her eye. "What need has a decorated officer to be tutored in the ways of peace?"

He rolled his eyes. "Are you suggesting that an education in the ways of warfare is an insufficient foundation—"

"I have said no such thing, sir. Perhaps, though, your conscience is speaking for you?"

"You think my conscience guilty?"

"I know of no one without something to repine." She turned away from him, her voice trailing off into a tight, high note.

Why did conversations with her so often turn serious? He ran a finger around his collar and tugged. What could a sheltered gentlewoman know of a troublesome conscience? What did she suspect of him?

Small Tom appeared in the doorway. "Mr. Michaels, sir."

Michaels strode in with his precise, measured

steps. Good Lord, the man might be drilling with a regiment for the exactness of his stride.

"Good evening, Colonel." Michaels bowed and turned to Miss Bennet. "Mary."

His eyes turned up a bit at the corners. Was that all the passion he could muster for the woman to whom he was betrothed?

Miss Bennet stepped toward him and curtsied, but her smile did not reach her eyes. "I am pleased you have joined us." She glanced back toward the long-case clock in the far corner of the room.

As if on her command, it chimed half past six.

The dinner invitation had been for six o'clock.

"Forgive me, Colonel. My sincerest apologies. There was a something of a to-do about fields and fencing among the northern tenants." Michaels peered at Miss Bennet, his expression halfway between annoyed and conciliatory.

So, she shared one of Darcy's peculiarities, a penchant for living by the clock. How odd, but it was somehow comforting to know her in possession of a genuine flaw.

"Think nothing of it. I have no doubt my best interests are your priority. Surely the tenants are more significant than dinner."

Miss Bennet bit her upper lip and looked away. It was probably unkind to tease her that way. Mealtimes might not be important, but her sensibilities were.

"Besides, Aunt Catherine has not yet—ah, here she is."

Mrs. Jenkinson, with Aunt Catherine—dressed for a state dinner—on her arm, slipped through the doorway.

"It is good to see all of you assembled. I do find it

so unmannerly when guests are late. Shall we to dinner then?" She swept out of the room, feathered headdress bobbing and burgundy taffeta crinkling.

A brief conversation of glances and raised eyebrows passed between Michaels and Miss Bennet as he offered her his arm.

Fitzwilliam swallowed back a smirk. It was nice to watch someone else be on the receiving end of such looks for a change. He followed them out.

Michaels leaned a little closer to her, voice muted. "You are bruised. What happened?"

"It is nothing, merely my own clumsiness." Miss Bennet turned her face aside.

"It is not like you to be ungainly."

"I was … I was having a … conversation with Mr. Collins. I was not watching where I was going. I … I ran into a door that unexpectedly opened as we passed."

"A conversation? I hardly think that likely. He is not one to promote a mutual discussion."

"Perhaps I was being kind."

"As you always are." He patted her hand as they entered the dining room.

Was that all he would say on the matter? Did he not notice that the marks were nothing like what a door would leave in its wake? Could he not see what was in front of him, or did he not wish to be bothered with what might prove inconvenient and uncomfortable?

Fitzwilliam grumbled under his breath and took his place at the foot of the oblong table in the small dining room. It would seat as many as eight comfortably. With only five it felt a little barren.

Fewer candles than usual lit the walnut-paneled

space, perhaps a quarter less, but an additional mirror on the opposite wall caught the light and made the space virtually as bright as usual. The distinct odor of tallow lingered at the edges of the mealtime scents. Somehow, Miss Bennet had seen to it that nearly half of the remaining candles were switched from wax to tallow. How had she effected the change so quickly?

Aunt Catherine announced the dishes—fish, soup, poultry, and vegetables—fewer than usual. He bit his lip and did not correct her as she got several of them wrong. She did not seem to notice that the sideboards on either side of the table held empty covered dishes, and he was not about to inquire as to their presence.

Miss Bennet cast a demure glance his way and offered a long, slow blink of approval.

The expression should not have excited the warmth in his chest that it did, but there was no stopping it.

Small Tom poured wine, an appealing, but lesser vintage than was usually set before guests. Soup plates were served—that wrinkly white vegetable; yes, it was cauliflower, not turtle—and Aunt Catherine launched into conversation. "The sermon last Sunday was quite pleasing, was it not?" She settled back into her chair, chest puffed. "I had the final reading of it, you know. I think Mr. Collins did a creditable job in his presentation of the matter."

"It was wise counsel, indeed, your ladyship. The parish is in your debt for insisting that men be reminded of their role in the family." Miss Bennet dabbed a drop of soup from her chin.

"I am certain it is necessary, for they are quite apt to forget, you know." Aunt Catherine tossed her head just a mite, like a bird done with its preening.

Fitzwilliam clenched his fist under the table. Aunt Catherine knew nothing of what was right and proper. She herself encouraged Bennet to be everything that was despicable in a man. She would probably approve Collins' behavior as well.

"And who better to deliver such a message than one who sets the model for the rest of the parish." Michaels murmured, not looking up from his dinner.

Fitzwilliam choked on the bite of bread that had sopped up the last of his soup.

"Exactly why I chose Mr. Collins. He shows such attention to all those details." Aunt Catherine waved her hands for emphasis, nearly knocking over the glass nearest her plate.

"I suppose him an excellent resource in teaching men the correct ways to manage their tempers?" Fitzwilliam muttered through clenched teeth.

"Many men have foul tempers. It is unseemly to display them. It is necessary to instruct them in how to regulate their animal spirits." She struck the table with her knuckles.

"And you consider Collins the man to do such a thing?"

Aunt Catherine leaned forward, her elbows braced on the table. Her face screwed into deep lines and knots.

Miss Bennet shook her head and mouthed *no*.

"Have you considered the man's temper, Aunt?"

"His temper? He has no temper. He has never shown me any temper."

"Of course, he would not do such a thing to his patroness. It would be unseemly. But when I served in the army, it was a well-known fact that if one wanted to learn about the competency of an officer, looking to those who served below him was the surest source of information."

"What has that to do with Mr. Collins?"

"Have you ever asked Mrs. Collins about the nature of her husband's temper?"

"Why would I ever do such a thing? What is her opinion in any of this?"

Miss Bennet ground her teeth as the tablecloth bunched in her hands.

Perhaps she was right. Only she was actually listening to him, and she already understood what he was trying to communicate.

Fitzwilliam dipped his head and leaned back. "Of course, you are correct, Aunt. There is no reason her opinion should be of any consideration at all."

"I am glad you agree." Aunt Catherine rang for the second course.

The servants removed used plates and platters and replaced them. Some dishes were new, those nearest Aunt Catherine. Several were different to what was normally served at Rosings: inferior cuts of meat, vegetables that Aunt Catherine considered more appropriate for the peasantry; all those were carefully placed farthest away from her. A few offerings had already been presented and were merely placed in new serving dishes. Those were positioned nearest Fitzwilliam.

Miss Bennet caught his eye with a narrow glare. On this point she would brook no interference. He pressed his lips hard and managed a fractional nod. Her expression eased, and she exhaled heavily.

It was a clever plan; he had to give her credit for that. Certainly, one much less confrontational than insisting on changes in the menu. Though Aunt Catherine muttered about the quality of the venison, which was in fact mutton in a cauliflower, cabbage, and beetroot cream sauce usually served on venison, she did not seem to notice the substitutions. Good thing that he did not abhor disguise the way Darcy did. Sometimes it was entirely necessary.

After dinner, they withdrew to the gold parlor where Aunt Catherine decided they should play cards. Fitzwilliam dealt a hand of whist, but she kept forgetting the rules. Her agitation increased until Miss Bennet declared that Aunt Catherine had won the hand and perhaps upon that triumph, should retire for the evening. It took a bit of effort to secure her agreement, but at last, Miss Bennet and Mrs. Jenkinson escorted her to her chambers.

The relative silence and the dim light from limited candles lent a private air to the room, one conducive to important conversation. Best not to waste it.

"A glass of port, Michaels?" Fitzwilliam headed for the decanter on the far side of the parlor.

"A small one. Thank you."

Fitzwilliam handed him a crystal glass and sat back down at the card table.

Michaels saluted him with the glass. "I was rather surprised to hear that you had invited Mary to stay in the manor. She does seem well able to manage Lady Catherine's needs, though."

"Indeed she does. I hope she will be able to impart her expertise when we find a long-term companion for my aunt. In just the day she has been here, the house is already far more peaceful." Fitzwilliam looked squarely at Michaels. "I think it more peaceful than most of the houses in the parish now."

"That is a change indeed, considering what things

were like even a week ago."

"I hope Miss Bennet finds it pleasant to be in a household more peaceful than the vicarage."

Michaels leaned forward on his knees. "Whatever do you mean? I have never noticed any disharmony there."

Finally!

"I do not imagine a well-mannered household would be prone to demonstrate discord to visitors."

"Then how would you—"

"I am apt to observe things that most would disregard. One must if one is to stay alive in time of war. Have you never seen how Mrs. Collins always stands beyond arm's length from her husband? Or the way she twitches and flinches when his voice rises, even in services?"

Michaels pulled his chair a mite closer to Fitzwilliam's. "I have never made note of any of that."

"I have found the reactions of one's subordinates to be telling of a man's character."

"You do not approve of the man. I know you have never liked him." Michaels stroked his chin. "With his recent inheritance in Hertfordshire, it is possible to see him away rather quickly."

Fitzwilliam blinked and twitched his head. Agreeable as the notion was, this was not the point he was trying to make. How could he be so blind to the safety of one whom he should be dedicated to protect? "Has he pursued finding a curate since our last abortive discussion of the matter?"

"Not to my knowledge. I think he was rather put off by Lady Catherine's dramatic reaction. But I know of several reputable young men seeking a curacy of whom we might make inquires. I think it would be wise to discuss with Collins a proper salary for the curate, though. He seems to be the type who would readily insist a curate try to live and maintain the parsonage on but fifty pounds a year."

Fitzwilliam snorted. "He would deny the man the use of the parsonage altogether if he could. Send out the inquiries. I have no problem selecting a curate for him and informing him of the choice."

"Perhaps, Mary will assist us in dealing with Lady Catherine's concerns in these matters."

"I should think Miss Bennet will not repine Collins' departure."

"It is difficult to have her father's relation living so close. I do not think she prefers his company." Michaels' voice deepened into something resembling a growl.

Perhaps the man did have a bit of a spark after all.

"Darcy hates the sight of Bennet and barely tolerates Collins. I have to think that Bennet's disagreeable nature must be common in the family."

Michaels rubbed his fist across his chin. "That is awfully harsh, do you not think? I prefer to believe Bennet a rare aberration."

Fitzwilliam sighed. Perhaps the spark was the aberration.

Maybe Miss Bennet was right to just allow the issue to lie quietly. Especially now, when she no longer needed to live with the Collinses.

A fortnight later, the initial flurry of busyness settled down into something much more routine. Each morning, Mary met with Parkes and Cook to discuss household matters. Occasionally Small Tom would call upon her as well. After that, she would take breakfast with Lady Catherine and Mrs. Jenkinson, suggesting plans for the day in keeping with Lady Catherine's health. Some days it was more successful than others—one day Lady Catherine dissolved into what could most rightly be deemed a full out temper tantrum that lasted half the day, but that was an exception. Most days involved only a little discussion and negotiation before Lady Catherine was satisfied. After breakfast, Mary would have a few hours to herself, often spent reading from Rosings' surprisingly extensive library, writing letters, or walking the grounds.

In the afternoon, Lady Catherine invariably required further attentions, but it usually ended with assisting Mrs. Jenkinson in helping Lady Catherine to bed for a several hours long nap. Most days, Mary called upon the parsonage during that time, generally welcomed by Mr. Collins because she brought fresh news of Lady Catherine's condition. Such an attentive vicar he was. Most evenings Michaels would call, after the day's work had been accomplished, often having dinner at Lady Catherine's table.

Colonel Fitzwilliam seemed quite content with the situation, allowing her to take charge of Lady Catherine's needs as she saw fit. He even went so far as to hold his tongue when he disagreed with his aunt and avoided correcting her obvious errors and confusion. Clearly, it was not easy, and was sometimes a very great trial for him, given the deep furrows in his brow. He was not always entirely successful, but he was putting forth a genuine effort. There was an excellent chance he would be able to manage well enough on his own, once a proper companion was installed.

Mary saw Parkes out of the sitting-room-cum-office and closed the door behind her, pressing her back against the cool wood. It felt good to stand after too many hours in the arm chair behind the desk. It was a comfortable chair, but the navy brocade now held a divot shaped very much like her backside, and her back was suffering for it.

A soft breeze rustled the heavy curtains as it whispered through the open windows, wafting in the scent of fresh grass with a hint of sheep. How delightful it would have been to sneak out and run through the breezes, bonnet in one hand, her spencer in the other, sunshine kissing her cheeks and wind rushing against her ears.

If only she could. But there was too much to be done.

In a week, she would be married and managing her own home. Rosings needed to be prepared for that. It was time for breakfast with Lady Catherine, after that she would review several responses to the inquiries sent to find a companion for Lady Catherine. Later in the day, she would begin working up menus and shopping lists that would see Rosings through the next month.

The faint sounds of the front door opening drifted through the paneled door. Was that Collins' voice? What was he doing here—probably just could not resist the opportunity to come to Rosings and see Lady Catherine himself. Wait, Michaels had mentioned they had received some letters regarding the curacy. Collins must be here for Colonel Fitzwilliam, not her.

While that was, a good thing, in and of itself, it did

add a layer of complication to the morning. That conversation must not—

Shrieks pierced the air.

Lady Catherine's.

She flew down the stairs at a pace only possible on a well-designed staircase, with a secure banister to cling to. Had this been the parsonage, she would have surely broken her neck. She followed the screeching to the colonel's study.

Lady Catherine stood in the middle of the wide hall, half in shadow, half in light that streamed through the study door. Regal in her full glory: gold silk gown catching the afternoon sun, ostrich plumes bobbing over her head, she shouted, mostly unintelligible accusations and mutterings, some to people not even there. It was never a good thing to see her dressed for evening so early in the day.

Collins, Fitzwilliam and Michaels lined up opposite her, near the study door, courtiers waiting their turn to attend their royal patron. While the colonel's expression was decidedly irate, Collins seemed mildly terrified, wringing his hands like a washer woman at her craft.

"No, no, no! I did not give permission for hiring a curate! I selected Collins for the parish, and with the parish he shall remain." Lady Catherine's heel clattered against the polished marble, and she shook her fists at her sides.

"Your opinion does not matter in this circumstance, Aunt." Colonel Fitzwilliam rolled his eyes, voice deep and level, barely one step down from the command tone he resorted to when truly infuriated.

Foolish, stupid man.

"Lady Catherine, pray understand," Collins edged

half a step forward and bowed from his shoulders.

"My understanding is not at fault. I understand perfectly well what is going on. You are trying to betray me." She shooed him back with her fan.

He minced back, nearly stepping on Michaels' feet. "Nothing could be farther from the truth, Madam. I am solicitous of all your wishes and desires."

"I do not desire a curate. That is my final word on the matter. You will do exactly as I say." She poked Collins in the chest with her fan to punctuate the final three words.

Colonel Fitzwilliam interposed himself between them. "Enough! Stop your blithering. The issue has been decided. Leave it to us. Trouble yourself with it no further."

"You have no right to speak to me that way, nephew! I think it is time for you to go back to Matlock to relearn some manners. Get Long Tom. I want him now. He will see you are removed at once." She looked over her shoulder, scanning the hall.

"I live here. This is my home." He pulled his shoulders back, seeking to tower over her. Why did he try? Intimidating her always failed—usually spectacularly.

Mary edged between them, applying her elbows to Colonel Fitzwilliam's shoulder and chest as necessary. "Pray, Mr. Michaels, get both these gentlemen out of here at once."

Colonel Fitzwilliam loomed over her, glowering like an officer. She rose on tip toes and returned the expression.

His eyes widened, and he backed away.

She took Lady Catherine's arm. "Mr. Michaels has this matter well in hand. Do not worry."

"But I do not wish the parish to have a curate."

Mary encouraged her to take a step down the hall and another, toward the front hall. "They are well aware of your wishes. You know you can trust them. They are all loyal to you. You have nothing to worry about."

Behind her, Michaels' hushed voice urged the men back to the study. He shut the door and the hall dimmed considerably. Why had he not stepped in sooner? He knew better than to allow the colonel to antagonize Lady Catherine.

Lady Catherine paused, blinking and searched for the missing light. Her forehead knotted which usually presaged an outburst.

"Perhaps you would like a walk outside?" Mary led her toward the garden doors just outside the small parlor.

"I have not had my walk today, have I?" She squinted, staring at Mary.

"No you have not. You do so enjoy your flowers."

"You are a thoughtful girl, Miss Bennet. Which one are you? There are too many Bennet girls."

"I am Mary." She held the door open and helped Lady Catherine down the three polished stone steps on to the well-maintained sandy path that led to the main flower garden.

"That is a good, sensible name, Mary. I approve of it, you know."

"I am glad to hear that, madam. My mother will be pleased to hear it. I shall write to her directly and tell her."

The flowers enveloped them on all sides, as tall as their shoulders in some places, as low as their ankles in others, the air laden with a heady mix of floral perfumes so thick one could almost taste it. Abundant blossoms in pinks, yellows and whites, entertained bees—so many that the air hummed and buzzed around them.

"Oh look, the peonies are blooming. When did I order them planted here? I do not recall." Lady Catherine paused and pushed her face into a mass of pale pink blooms.

They had the same conversation yesterday.

"The gardener says that you ordered them changed last spring. So, this is the first time they have bloomed."

"Well then, I made a very good decision, did I not?" Lady Catherine pulled her face back, several petals clung to her left cheek.

"Yes, you did." Mary took her arm and helped her stand.

"I make good decisions." Her cheeks grew tight and expression dark. "I do, do I not, Miss Mary Bennet? My decisions are right and good."

"You have made many decisions throughout your life, so very many. Perhaps you are tired from them, just a bit?"

Lady Catherine shrank into an uncertain old woman. "I am weary at times. It tires me to think so hard these days."

"Of course it does. After all that you have done for Rosings Park and its people, it is only right for you to be tired. Would it not be pleasing to have someone else to make some of those decisions for you? So that you might rest and enjoy Rosings as you ought?"

Lady Catherine rubbed her bottom lip with her fingertips, stretching it down, revealing yellowed teeth. "What an odd idea. I never considered. Would it be right and proper to just allow someone else?"

"Not just anyone, but one of your line, whom you could trust. That would be agreeable, would it not?"

"I suppose so ... yes, perhaps ... possibly." She blinked hard. "That might be a very good notion. I will have to think on the matter further."

They continued along the path to where it met another leading to a simple white gazebo in the shade of three mature dogwood trees, still bearing white blossoms.

"One cannot be expected to make such a significant decision so lightly. It is good for you to think on it. In the meantime, perhaps you would like to tell Colonel Fitzwilliam that he may begin with some small decisions to help you see how wise and conscientious he might be."

"Wise? Fitzwilliam? He is not wise. He is lonely, very lonely. He needs a wife. Mrs. Collins can help. A vicar's wife is good for introductions. Does she know any heiresses? That is what he needs, you know. So he can live in the manner to which he is accustomed. You help her, and we shall find him a good wife."

"I am sure he will be glad of it." It was hard to get the words out and maintain a proper expression of decorum. "Would you like to sit on your favorite bench? Look, I think Mrs. Jenkinson is there, in the gazebo."

"I would speak with her now. There are things I need to tell her about Anne."

Mary beckoned Mrs. Jenkinson, and she hurried to meet them. "Lady Catherine would like to speak with you."

Mrs. Jenkinson took Lady Catherine's arm and led

her toward the gazebo, under the bower of dogwood branches.

Mary turned towards the house, detouring through the rose garden, sedate and understated. Bees zipped back and forth along the path, but paid her little mind, far more intent on the flowers than her intrusion. Roses, especially the way their sweet balm hung in the air, reminded her of Mama and the roses that she grew. They were not nearly so abundant or as spectacular as those at Rosings, but Mama had a way of coaxing them to bloom where no one else could. She was stubborn that way.

Not unlike the denizens of Rosings. Why did Colonel Fitzwilliam choose now to be so obstinate? If only he would be a little more patient and not insist he get his way immediately. Commands and orders were not the only means to get something accomplished.

Next Saturday could not come soon enough.

Michaels met her amongst the roses, calm and level as he always was, offering no clue as to how their discussion proceeded in Lady Catherine's absence. "Did you take her back to her room?"

"No, she is in the gazebo with Mrs. Jenkinson. Being out of doors soothes her. What is more, she is slowly becoming reconciled to allowing someone else to make decisions."

He offered his arm. "I do not know how you do it, Mary. You have a way with her unlike anyone else. I am glad to hear you are making headway with her. The colonel's patience with her is running thin."

"Has it ever been anything else?"

They walked on toward the house, sand crunching softly under their feet. Tall rose canes waved in the breeze beside them, occasionally catching their clothes and releasing them, as if to urge them not to walk too fast.

"Officers are not known for their forbearance, you know." Did he know how high-handed he sounded now? A little too much like Colonel Fitzwilliam.

"Well then that is a flaw which needs to be addressed. If he does not change his ways with her, I swear to you, disaster will ensue."

"Is that not a bit dramatic?"

She stopped, counted to ten, and turned on him.

Oh, the look on his face!

She balanced her fists on her hips. "Are you suggesting that I do not know what I am talking about? Or perhaps that an old woman whose wits are failing is incapable of causing great damage. Or perhaps—"

He threw up open hands, snaring his jacket cuff on a thorny cane. "Please, Mary, calm down. You are taking offense where I assure you none was intended. Perchance dealing with her is wearing on your patience as well?"

Or maybe it was dealing with stubborn men that had her worn threadbare.

"Mayhaps you are peckish? I expect you missed breakfast altogether this morning. The colonel has invited us all to share his table. How does that sound?"

Condescending and conciliatory.

But Michaels' expression was sincere. He was trying to be helpful and deserved to have the effort credited to his accounts. While not perfect, it was something, and she should appreciate it for what it was.

She slipped her hand in the crook of his arm and allowed him to escort her back to the house.

ᴥᵂᴥChapter 6

FITZWILLIAM STRAIGHTENED HIS jacket—the one with the cuffs replaced on Miss Bennet's suggestion—and followed his guests from the dining room to the gold parlor. Michaels and Miss Bennet talked softly, probably about something polite and proper. It was difficult to imagine them at anything else. Behind them, Collins nattered to his wife—so big she looked like she might well explode—about the good taste and elegance demonstrated in the portraiture hung in the dimly lit hallway.

It required every fragment of self-control he could muster not to tell them those were Aunt Catherine's least favorite paintings—ones she hoped to remove.

Aunt Catherine's absence at dinner aided his digestion considerably. Unfettered conversation, without the worry of unexpectedly upsetting his aunt, even if it centered on the business of finding a curate and a companion, was a rare blessing these days.

The sofas in the gold parlor were arranged around a low table for tea and biscuits and possibly a board game after that. Enough candles to permit the activity—and no more—lit the room, held in ormolu candlesticks backed by mirrors, some from other rooms, to maximize the light.

Fitzwilliam smiled to himself. Miss Bennet was diligent about their practice of economy.

Collins planted himself in the center of the sofa nearest the pianoforte, eyeing the instrument insistently. When that failed to produce any result at all, he badgered Miss Bennet until she played for them, ignoring his wife's pleas otherwise. It was unfortunate for all. Miss Bennet was an indifferent player, and none would have suffered to miss her concerto. Unfortunately, it provided Collins with another victory over his cousin, reinforcing—in his mind at least—the power he wielded over his family. That alone was nearly insufferable. But worse still, it seemed no one but himself recognized the discomfiture on Miss Bennet's face.

How could Michaels be so unable to recognize it? Everything in her bearing spoke misery. Though she made efforts to hide it, it was clear, and painful, nay nauseating to watch. The poor woman clearly wanted deliverance from the spectacle, but was only met with further demands for her to perform.

The final notes of her song faded away. Collins drew a deep breath.

Fitzwilliam jumped up. "Perhaps, Mr. Collins, you might be prevailed upon to read to us."

Mrs. Collins pinched the bridge of her nose and shook her head.

Collins' chest inflated as he squared his shoulders. "I should be honored sir."

Miss Bennet lost no time in leaving the pianoforte, moving toward the bookcase, away from the group. The slump in her posture had lessened. That must be a good sign.

"What would you like me to read, sir?" Collins rose, settling into his best vicar's posture.

Insufferable, proud …

Small Tom burst into the room, eyes wide, panting. "Colonel!"

Fitzwilliam, alert and battle-ready, bolted toward the butler.

"Sir, there is a fire in the main barn. Mrs. Jenkinson cannot find Lady Catherine and fears—"

Michaels and Miss Bennet were at his sides.

"I will send the scullery maids for the farmers." Miss Bennet pointed at Small Tom. "Marshal the footmen and the hall boys." She dashed out, pelting toward the kitchen.

Fitzwilliam charged out, Michaels and Collins on his heels.

By the time they pounded out of the nearest side door, his heart thundered in his ears, pulse fast and furious. They sprinted alongside the house which stood between them and the barn. Sand and gravel churned from his boots and his toes dug deep into the slightly damp path, lit by silvery light from the full moon.

His nose burned, and his throat threatened to close against the acrid, smoky fumes assailing him on the winds. They rounded the corner. An eerie crimson glow backlit the barn. Men's shouts and burgeoning chaos surged around him as men gathered from all directions.

The ghosts of cannon fire and rifle reports rang out. So much like France. So much.

No! Not now! He could not afford it now.

A horse screamed, and another.

Just as his had when it was shot from under him.

He stumbled. Michaels grabbed his elbow, keeping him upright. They skidded in the deep gravel near the barn's front doors. His eyes stung and watered in the billowing smoke.

Grooms struggled to manage pawing, skittering horses. They were too near the barn. Damn it all! They needed to get the beasts as far away from the fire as possible, not be milling around in the midst of all the confusion!

"I'll manage the grooms," Michaels called from somewhere that felt very, very far away, and dashed off into the commotion.

Fitzwilliam paused, frozen. Flames licked at the open windows. The building was not entirely engulfed, not yet. But neither had been the house at the edge of the battle field …

"Colonel!" A woman nearly tripped as she came to a stop beside him.

He jumped and stared at her. She was not the girl from the French cottage, burned and dying. He peered at her through the blinding haze.

Miss Bennet. Yes, it was Miss Bennet.

"The first of the farmers have arrived. But Lady Catherine is missing."

Lady Catherine? What was she doing in France? She had not followed the drum with him. He blinked hard and squinted.

"Colonel, you are needed here!" She grasped his shoulders and shook him.

Perhaps. But he was required in France too … He pulled away and turned aside.

She yanked something from her waist and held it under his nose.

Gah!

He staggered back, choking on the pungent smelling salts.

She caught him before he fell. He clung tightly to her arm.

"Are you well?"

Such concern in her dark eyes. He could get lost in them.

"Colonel?"

"Yes … yes, thank you." He gulped in a deep breath. But the air was neither cool nor sweet.

"The staff is organizing buckets and wet sacks. The farmers are arriving. They need you to coordinate their efforts." She pointed toward the stone well near the barn.

"Of course, of course." He shook his head again. "I am well now." He sprinted twenty yards to the well, his head clearing with each thundering step.

How had she known what was happening, what to do?

Two burly farmers with empty buckets shouldered past him, nearly knocking him over.

The chief groom pelted up with an armload of feedbags and dropped them near the well. "There are two horses still inside. Don't know how—"

The farmers doused the sacks until they were sopping. Several maids rushed in to carry fresh wet bags to those battling the blaze.

Fitzwilliam jumped aside for the running girls. "How is not the concern. Get axes and open that far wall. See if you can get them out that way."

Michaels appeared at his elbow, a young groom with him. "The boy thinks he saw Lady Catherine."

"Speak!"

The boy leapt back, stammering. "I cannot be certain, sir. I was in the hayloft, asleep as the chief groom bid me. Someone came in with a candle, calling for a carriage to be readied. I did not see who it was, but it were a lady's voice, sir. Then I saw the straw coming to blaze, and that same voice screamed."

"No one has found her—she must still be inside!" Michaels looked over his shoulder toward the barn.

"Lady Catherine, inside?"

When had Collins joined them?

"We must rescue her!" Collins ran pell-mell, arms flailing, toward the burning building.

Fitzwilliam glanced at Michaels.

"Soak your cravat in water and tie it around your face first." Michaels borrowed a bucket from the well.

Fitzwilliam wound and tied the cravat as he loped for the barn. This was too bloody familiar!

He could not … yes he could. He had to!

The heat struck him first—searing, red, singeing hair, pungent, vile—then the noise. Fire made a distinct sound—crackling, popping, roaring—as it consumed, ravaged, devastated …

Smelling salts … remember the sharp, burning, bracing smelling salts.

He ducked his head and plunged inside.

Smoke, choking, blinding smoke burned his eyes, his face. He crouched lower, into air a mite clearer.

"This way!" Michaels called over the fire's rumble from somewhere to his right.

A flash of white—that must be him.

Fitzwilliam staggered toward it.

Pounding and shouting on the other side of the wall.

Horses shrieking.

Flames flared—yellow and orange, angry—posturing, threatening.

"Here, I have found her!"

He hauled himself toward Michaels' cry.

A trembling, sobbing body fell into him. Deadweight, covered in far too much fabric. A singed ostrich plume dangled in her face. He grabbed her and dragged her toward a break in the wall. Perhaps a window? But smoke rose and fought him for right of passage.

He dropped the simpering body near the wall and thrust his hands through the opening—a window too small to climb through. Damn it all!—waving and screaming with what little voice he had left.

Somewhere behind him, heat surged. The fiery roar redoubled.

He choked and coughed, throat raw. This was the fate he had cheated on that French field. The one they said it had been a miracle to escape. One did not cheat death for very long. No, it would make a claim that no one could elude.

Not even an officer of His Majesty's army.

How did one prepare to meet his Maker? Was there a prayer, some confession he should offer?

Someone outside clutched his hand and held it tight—a soft, small, strong hand. A woman's voice cried something that sounded like his name. Other words became lost in smoke-induced choking.

Other voices gathered near the woman's. Thumping and pounding on the other side. They called to him, words he could not make out.

Cannon fire—what else could that be—echoed behind him. Sparks flew. Crunching, crashing.

His vision narrowed into darkness.

Mary clutched Fitzwilliam's hand—it was too large and scarred to be Michaels' or Collins'—as men feverishly pounded beside her to break open the wall near the window. Heat radiated from wallboards, too hot to touch now. Smoke rasped her lungs and threatened to blind her.

His fingers went slack in hers, but she clung to them. How was it possible that the distance from one side of a frame wall to the other could be so far?

Someone pulled her out of the way and three men tore through the remainder of the wall. Smoke poured out like roiling flood waters, even as the rescuers rushed through the gaping maw.

Mary met them as they dragged out two limp forms. She directed them to a grassy spot away from the barn.

"Water! I need water!" She knelt between Fitzwilliam and Lady Catherine.

They were motionless in the moonlight, covered in soot and singed fabric. If only there was more light!

Lady Catherine coughed, weakly, but with growing force. Mary rolled her to her side. She waved a girl over to attend her.

But Fitzwilliam was still.

Deathly still.

She leaned over him, her ear very close to his face. Nothing.

No! Not acceptable. He had squeezed her hand back just a moment ago. He could not leave her. Not yet.

She pinched his nose, covered his mouth with her own and blew hard. Her father had tried to breathe life into one of her brothers that way, not knowing that she had watched. He had not succeeded, but that was no reason not to try now. What other alternative was there?

The midwife who had taught Papa the practice called it the "kiss of life." It was improper, totally improper, frowned upon for the intimacy it implied.

She pulled back. His chest fell, but it did not rise on its own.

His lips were still warm—death had not claimed him yet. She puffed breath into him again.

And again.

His cheek twitched, and he coughed. Weakly at first, pawing at the ground with one hand.

She rolled him to his side and pounded his back. He hacked and gasped for breath, spitting foam and phlegm on the grass.

Behind her, gasps and cries, and someone clapped. Others added to the applause that mingled with the surrounding din.

Rosings had not lost its new master. Not yet. Its people approved.

"It is going down!" a ragged voice screamed from near the barn.

Where was Michaels? She sprang to her feet and cast about. Even in the midst of the moonlit chaos, his distinct form should be obvious in the crowd.

No … heavens no!

She pelted toward the blaze.

A groan, deep guttural and desperate, tore from the barn—a dying gasp from timbers nearly consumed. The barn's frame slowly crumbled in on itself in a shower of sparks and flame.

A burning sliver of timber smashed against her upper arm, knocking her to the ground.

Hot, so very hot—searing pain. Flames licked at her sleeve and crept toward her shoulder.

Someone threw a wet sack on her and patted her down with it.

Better now, much better.

She dismissed him—or was it her—and they ran back to the chaos.

She peeled back the sodden canvas feedbag. Her sleeve hung in sooty tatters, singed and black in places. She tore the fabric, peeling it away from the blistered skin beneath.

"Miss Bennet." Parkes touched her uninjured shoulder. "Pray, can you come?"

She accepted Parkes' hand up.

It should not be so difficult to stand.

Parkes picked her way through the throng. Mary staggered along behind, losing sight of Parkes twice.

"Here, Miss." Parkes knelt beside a badly burnt man, his face charred, halfway down his chest.

Mary half-crouched, half-fell beside him. He was so badly burnt. She placed her hand on his chest, still as death.

She blinked hard and pulled the remains of the cravat from the less injured side of his face, his empty eyes half-lidded.

Collins.

Dead. His skin was already cooling, too far gone. No kiss could save him.

"Keep Mrs. Collins away from here. I shall ... I shall tell her." Oh, Charlotte!

But, where was Michaels?

"Miss Bennet!"

She turned toward the voice. Parkes hauled her to her feet, steadying her as her knees threatened to give way.

Two men dragged a third, hanging limply between them, toward her.

Michaels.

Parkes—bless her—helped her to them.

They laid Michaels on a grassy patch. She fell to her knees, landing almost the same time as he. He coughed and sputtered, his breath fast and ragged. Burns covered the left side of his face, trailing down to his chest and along his shoulder. Singed clothing stuck to the blistered and charred skin. He opened his eyes, just a sliver, and groaned.

She clutched his hand. "I am here."

His lips worked, but no words came forth. Only a thin, bubbling froth.

"Lady Catherine and Fitzwilliam have been recovered."

His head twitched in something like a nod.

Parkes hovered over her. "Miss, you have been burned too. You need help, let me—"

"No, no, there are others far worse than myself. You must send for the surgeon and the apothecary." Mary braced both hands hard on the ground as hot winds abraded her wounds. She gritted her teeth and squeezed her eyes shut until the wave of agony passed. "Call for Mrs. Anderson, the vicar's wife from the next parish, Mrs. Hughes and Mrs. Leighton, their housekeepers as well. See that the injured are taken to the manor—set up the servants' hall for them. Check the stores. We will need lime-water and oils—linseed and sweet—yellow basilicum ointment and—"

"I am not sure what we have in the stores." Parkes crouched beside her and steadied her. "I am certain we have no yellow basilicum."

"Set one of the girls to make some. We will need it in great amounts."

"I am not even sure how to make it."

Mary slapped her forehead and sat back hard. She clenched her first and sucked in several deep breaths, counting until far too many harsh words on her tongue subsided.

Not everyone had lived with a physician who pontificated loud and long on preferred remedies and formulas. And the need to be prepared for the vicissitudes of life.

Apparently, those of high enough rank did not need to anticipate vicissitudes. She clutched her temples. Impatience with Parkes would serve no one well right now.

"Have you a copy of Buchan's *Domestic Medicine* in the house?" Pray let at least that much be available.

"I am not sure. Lady Catherine has had a physician in attendance for so long that –"

"I see. Now is not the time to go digging about the library for one. I know there is one in the mistress' parlor of the parsonage. Send someone to fetch the Collins' housekeeper and have her bring it to me. After this is finished, you will make certain that there is a copy kept in your office. I will return to the house now and check the stores and still room myself."

"Yes, of course." Parkes waved down a young groom who looked anxious to be away from the dead and injured. Then she took a pile of wet sacks from a young maid and directed her run back to the manor with Mary.

"Start moving the casualties to the house immediately." Mary called over her shoulder, forcing herself into a trot back to the house.

How was it possible that a place as large as Rosings could be so ill-prepared for such an event? Truly, it had nothing to do with adequacy of resources, and everything to do with the mentality of its mistress. It was one thing to rely upon the physician she patronized for major issues, but there was no reason the household should not be prepared to handle more mundane crises. No wonder Lizzy had always seen to the needs of the servants. How many of those needs could have been addressed by a simple copy of Buchan's text? How much unnecessary expense at the apothecary's could have been spared by preparing remedies at home?

The waste!

They entered through the kitchen and lit a candle from the fireplace. Half eaten platters and dishes from dinner were scattered along the work tables, left where they landed when the kitchen staff answered the call of "Fire!" Empty halls echoing with unnatural stillness provided an eerie foil to the bedlam outside.

"Do you know how to make limewater?" Mary scanned the stillroom for quicklime.

"Yes, Miss, and poppy tea, too."

"Good, good, we will need that as well. The quicklime is near the empty jugs on the floor there, the filter paper is in the drawer of the work table, and the poppies are in that basket on the shelf. Get them while I find the things for the yellow basilicum." Mary jogged to the back of the stillroom and up a short ladder. From a high shelf she retrieved a box of yellow wax, one of white resin and a jar with frankincense. Those would be sufficient for the time being.

The maid met her at the base of the ladder and took the supplies. "What am I to do with these?"

"In a large pan, melt one part yellow wax, one of frankincense and one of white resin together then add it to four parts of melted lard. Can you remember that?"

"I can, Miss. My brother is one of the ones hurt— pray, you will help him too?" Tears pooled in the girl's too-big-for-her-face eyes. Poor child, could not have been more than twelve.

"Of course I will." She patted the girl's shoulder. "Now get started. We will need it all as soon as it is ready."

The maid scurried off to the kitchen as Mary wound her way through the narrow passages to the servants' hall.

Chapter 7

LOUD VOICES AND groans greeted her as she approached the servants' hall. How many were injured?

The long rough-hewn table that seated nearly all of Rosings' lower servants had been shoved against one wall, chairs stacked atop it. Lingering odors from their past meal still hung in the air, quickly being replaced by smoke, burnt flesh, and blood. Candlesticks cast their glow from each corner, but the room still seemed more in shadow than in light. Pallets—six, no eight of them—were laid out along the floor, straw mattresses pulled from unused beds and covered in old sheets.

Just inside the door, Parkes caught her arm. "Lady Catherine and the colonel are being taken to their chambers. Mr. Michaels is in a guest room near yours."

Mary scanned the dimly lit hall. Several grooms —

one of them looked like the young maid—a footman, two sons of a tenant farmer …"Very good. And Mr. Collins?"

"Laid out in the downstairs sitting room."

"Mrs. Collins?"

"She is upstairs, resting in one of the guest rooms. I have a maid keeping watch with her." The drawn lines beside her eyes suggested Parkes dreaded the possibility of a birth tonight as much as she.

"I will see to her." Mary slipped out.

What would she say? Lizzy always knew what to say.

The main hall glowed with candles carried by servants buzzing about. An ungainly form pressed through the throng. Mary trotted to meet her.

"Where is he?" Charlotte peered over Mary's shoulder, trying to see down the dark hall. "The news, is it …"

Mary tucked her arm around Charlotte's back just in time to keep her from falling, bearing most of the weight on her own burns.

She should not think of herself at such a time when Charlotte was suffering so much more. A junior footman rushed up with a hall chair—generally thought to be more for decoration than for actual use—and they helped Charlotte to sit.

A full quarter of an hour passed before she regained enough strength to make it into the sitting room.

Cold, dark and still. Somehow the door seemed to stop all the noise from outside. Fitting, but eerie.

Two meager candles lit the room, both near the doorway, casting long somber shadows on the bodies. The faintly bacon-y scent of the tallow masked the odor of death that would soon overpower them. Flowers would have to be brought in soon. A prim little settee and matching chairs had been pushed aside and a pair of low square tables placed in the middle of the room. A shaft of moonlight shone directly on the tables, illuminating the remains of Collins' face.

Charlotte staggered to him, barely skirting the bodies of the two stable boys lying on blankets near the tables. Even in death, Collins' rank was acknowledged. Charlotte touched his hand, tears streaming silently down her cheeks. She half-fell onto the settee beside him.

A tiny sob burst forth. Mary rushed to her side.

Charlotte clung to her neck, sobbing into her shoulder—the injured one. Heavens above! Scorching pain shot through Mary's core with each shuddering gasp.

"What am I to do? What am I to do?"

Mary bit her tongue. This was not the time for advice.

"Where am I to go? The babies? The midwife says there are two! I—we—have no home! Where are they to be born? Where am I to raise them? How will we live?"

"You will stay here, near me, until the babies are born and you are churched."

"Then what? To go from the chapel to the workhouse? I have nothing! My dowry was but fifty pounds! We cannot live on that."

Mary pulled away—that might have been worse than allowing Charlotte to continue leaning on her—and clutched Charlotte's shoulders. "Your son will inherit Mr. Collins' estate. You will see—"

"And if they are but daughters? Even if there is a son, he may not live—you know how dangerous it is when there are two—" An hysterical edge crept into Charlotte's voice.

"Have you forgotten your family in Meryton? They will not turn you out."

"My father was so glad to be rid of me, to see me out of the house. My brothers, so relieved that I would not be a burden to them. To return Lucan Lodge, with infants? They will blame me for being a bad wife! Pray write to them for me. Tell them what has happened; that it was not my fault; that I have been a good and dutiful wife to him …" She dissolved into incoherent cries.

Mary held her close again and rubbed her back. What must it be to lose a husband at such a time? Surely Charlotte's family could not be so hardhearted. Papa might be, but he was by no means typical, was he?

"I will write to your family directly. It will be well. I am certain. Let me take you upstairs and give you something to help you sleep."

Charlotte sniffled and nodded, allowing Mary to guide her out. Near the stairs, she caught the same junior footman who brought them the chair. "Go to the parsonage and fetch Mrs. Collins' maid to come attend her mistress."

He bowed sharply and ran off, probably relieved to have a task that would take him out of the chaos in the house.

"Miss Bennet!" Parkes trundled up, Mr. Peters, the surgeon, and Mr. Lang, the apothecary, in her wake. "They wish to discuss the injured with you." She waved them forward, a little relief in her eyes. "The ladies you summoned have arrived as well with supplies."

"Lay the provisions out in the kitchen. Wait for me. I will be there soon."

Parkes curtsied and hurried off.

Both Peters and Lang wore an air of offense, drawing breaths they no doubt intended to use to give it voice. Offense seemed their favorite hobby. Someone ought to recommend they take up the velocipede instead. "I have much to attend. Pray, tell me directly what you have to communicate." Best set the tone immediately, lest they forget they were dealing with a Bennet.

Did they realize they edged back in tandem or how ridiculous they looked side-by-side: Peters, a great lanky bird of a man next to Lang, a short, stout earthenware teapot?

"Do you intend to keep the injured here, at Rosings?" Mr. Peters pulled back his shoulders and fluffed his feathers like a stork settling in to wait for prey.

Now was not the time to roll her eyes. "They were injured here; they should be tended here so as not to be a burden to their families."

"I am not certain Lady Catherine—"

"She is no longer mistress here. I am quite certain Colonel Fitzwilliam will accept my advice on the matter." She folded her arms over her chest. Botheration! That hurt!

Mr. Peters glanced at Mr. Lang and cleared his throat. "In that case you may instruct the ladies who will be working with you as follows: for the first two days let the burns be frequently anointed with a mixture of lime-water and oil. Apply poultices of bread and milk, softened with fresh butter, to the affected parts, to abate the heat and inflammation. Keep the injured on a strict cooling regimen, giving them a saline solution with small doses of nitre. When the inflammation begins to abate, dress the wounds with yellow basilicum. Where any black spots appear touch them with the tincture of myrrh; to prevent their spreading, provide doses of Peruvian bark. On the third day, I will return to determine which of them are ready to return to their homes. For those with high fevers or who have become costive, I will bleed them and administer an emollient clyster."

He looked at her as though he expected her to be impressed. But why? Those were essentially the same recommendations that Papa made the time when Kitty had spilled the boiling tea kettle over her arm.

Arrogant, self-important, overbearing—

Mr. Lang pulled his shoulder in front of Mr. Peters, an ungainly move at best with everything about Peters so much longer than Lang. Would they never stop posturing? "I am, of course prepared to supply whatever Rosings may need for the comfort of the unfortunates."

Mary grumbled under her breath. Condescension was offensive, not helpful. "Mr. Peters, see to Lady Catherine, Colonel Fitzwilliam and Mr. Michaels, then report to me. Mr. Lang, go downstairs and look in on the injured there. Attend me in the kitchen with a report on your suggestions."

Their eyes widened; they glanced at each other.

She clapped sharply and they jumped. "What are you waiting for? If you cannot follow simple directions you are dismissed. You are not the only medical men in the region."

They stammered and stuttered. "Yes, Miss Bennet." With matching bows, they hurried off.

A scullery maid waited in their wake. "Mrs. Parkes—"

"I am on my way directly." Mary dragged her hand down her face. No, no time for reflections now. She trudged—albeit quickly, but still trudged—to the kitchen.

More work tables had been brought in to hold the additional supplies. Someone had strained the lime-water and finished the yellow basilicum as well. Good, at least one of the matrons knew what she was doing.

Mrs. Anderson, Mrs. Hughes, Mrs. Leighton, and their housekeepers proved invaluable. Their examples seemed to inspire Parkes' confidence in her own judgment, increasing her own activity and energy.

How had she missed the damage Lady Catherine had done to the woman's pride in her work?

Mrs. Leighton, a compact woman with the force of a summer thunderstorm, ushered the staff and volunteers out to tend their charges. Silence, cold and aching, descended on the kitchen drowning out the old food and medicinal scents in the air. Mary staggered to a chair abandoned near the wall, dragged it near the fire, and sank down into it.

In the quiet, the throbbing pain in her shoulder grew too loud to ignore. Probably should deal with to that. She could not manage the household if her own wounds festered. But that could wait a moment or three, until the strength returned to her legs.

The medical men would barge in soon, demanding she attend to their expertise with proper feminine grace and appreciation for all they knew. Where was she going to find the wherewithal for that?

Yes, they were helpful and had some useful knowledge. But was it possible they could do so without the arrogance? Their attitude provoked a contrary side in her that few had ever seen. It would be best to keep it that way, but it required such focus to keep it under control. How would she find that now?

If only Lizzy were here. She always seemed to know what to do, how to handle the most difficult of people—even Papa. This would be easy for her—foolishly, ridiculously easy. Not mind-numbingly confusing and draining. Why could she not be more useful, more compassionate, more comforting? Lizzy made it look so easy. It should not be so demanding, should it?

She rubbed her temples and squeezed her eyes shut. Maybe with a few more moments of quiet—

Heavy foot falls clomped just beyond the door. That would be the men. Probably for the best. These reflections were not at all helpful now. She sucked in a deep breath and arranged her face into an imitation of calm. They would never look at her closely enough to tell it was a façade, so it would be good enough for now.

The next two days passed in a blur of poppy tea, bandages, lime-water, and oil washes. Two grooms had recovered sufficiently to return to their families. The rest remained in the servants' hall. Mrs. Leighton was certain the farmers' sons would be able to go back to their homes in the next day or so and was working with Parkes to prepare an unused servant's room to take the remaining four after that. It would help the staff to have their hall and much of their regular routine, back.

Late in the morning, well past the time she should have eaten breakfast, Mary, still in a rumpled morning gown, staggered out of Lady Catherine's room and fell into a blue velvet armchair placed just outside the door. The soft rounded back welcomed her, embracing her weariness and offering rest. Yes, it looked entirely out of place there in the corridor, clashing with the ivory paint and dark paneling. A hall chair should have been used, but the armchair was far more comfortable, and everyone dealing with Lady Catherine needed an extra measure of comfort now.

Lady Catherine remained in her stuffy, darkened room, refusing to tolerate sunlight or fresh air, convinced they would usher in the Angel of Death. Each time the door opened and someone walked in, she panicked, thinking the Angel was coming for her.

Anointing and bandaging her wounds, difficult at first, had grown even worse since she had developed a fever and cough. Just the sight of bandages and lime water were enough to send her into histrionics. Poor Mrs. Jenkinson was exhausted beyond words, so Mrs. Hughes and Mrs. Leighton took turns sitting with Lady Catherine.

The matrons were the embodiment of patience and grace, tolerant of the quirks and infirmity of the Queen of Rosings Park in ways that Mary simply could not be. At least not now.

She would have to tell Colonel Fitzwilliam to invite those families to dinner very often after this was over.

Assuming, of course, he did not succumb to his own injuries. His burns were not as extensive as some, but the fever and deep wracking cough that developed just a few hours after the fire and shook him to his bones sounded almost like consumption and could prove as deadly.

The surgeon would arrive soon to ply him with clysters and poultices, and to bleed him. The apothecary would offer any number of decoctions, syrups and pills to abate the cough and improve his strength. Hopefully some of them would be more helpful than harmful. If he did not recover, the estate would probably not either. Even Mr. Michaels' expertise could not save it then.

Michaels.

She dragged her sleeve across her eyes.

"Miss Bennet." Parkes appeared at her right hand, again. How often had she seemed to appear out of nowhere these past few days? "He needs you."

Mary pushed herself up and followed Parkes to Michaels' room. It was not as though she did not know the way on her own. She had spent nearly every moment she could steal away from Lady Catherine there. But the gesture of support was kind.

He stirred, groaning softly, as she entered the room. Sunlight filtered through partly drawn curtains, fluttering in the soft breeze that whispered through the slightly open window. Sandy-colored paper hangings brightened the room without being garish, allowing the simple oak furniture to stand out. The bed furnishings were pulled up and away, revealing a lonely figure, swathed in so many bandages he nearly disappeared against the bed linen—only his eyes, mouth and one hand were visible.

Even with the fresh air, the putrid odor of festering flesh assaulted her first step inside. The scent had grown more powerful in the last few hours, now nearly overpowering.

His chest rattled as he breathed.

She gulped and pulled her shoulders back. This was not the first time she had done this and would probably not be the last.

She could do this. There was no choice.

"You have come," he whispered, hoarse and effortful.

"Of course I have. You know I shall always come when you ask."

"I know. You are such a helpmeet to me. You always have been." His rheumy eyes caught hers, implying so much that had never been said.

She sat on the bed beside him, swallowing back the stench-induced bile in the back of her throat. "What can I do for you?"

"I am so very tired. Lay here beside me and sing to me. Help me to sleep." He patted the coverlet beside him with a shallow movement of his fingertips.

She stretched out on her side next to him and laid her hand over his uninjured one, their fingers twining. "What shall I sing?"

"You know my favorite lullaby."

Why? Why must it be that?

She blinked rapidly and drew as deep a breath as her constricted chest would allow.

"Sleep my love and peace attend thee, all through the night,
Guardian angels God will send thee, all through the night,
Soft the drowsy hours are creeping, hill and vale in slumber sleeping,
I my loving vigil keeping, all through the night.

While the moon her watch is keeping, all through the night
While the weary world is sleeping, all through the night
O'er thy spirit gently stealing, visions of delight revealing

Breathes a pure and holy feeling, all through the night.

Love, to thee my thoughts are turning, all through the night
All for thee my heart is yearning, all through the night.
Though sad fate our lives may sever, parting will not last forever,
There's a hope that leaves me never, all through the night."

Sometime between the third and fourth repetition the rattle ceased, and his fingers went slack. She sang it through twice more as his fingers cooled against hers.

Her chest tightened, squeezing the air from her lungs. His pain was over now. He was at peace. That was good; he deserved that. She could not be so selfish as to want him to linger, not in such agony. This was a mercy.

For him.

Was it—could it have been her fault? She had paid too much attention to Fitzwilliam, not just during the accident, but before, too? Was it for her ingratitude that Michaels was taken away now? Had she brought this on herself? She curled into a tight ball, holding her breath to still the shuddering sobs.

What was she to do now? Where was she to go? Without a husband, she would have no home. And with Collins gone, too—would Father take her back? Certainly no one else would ever want her the way Michaels had.

He had been a good man.

And now he was gone.

Heavens above, he was gone.

"Poor dear lamb." Parkes' calloused hand lay heavy on her back.

Strong, steady hands helped her up and held her until she was sure on her feet. Another—or was it the same one?—held her arm and took her to her room, plying her with tea that tasted suspiciously of laudanum.

Pray not that, she needed her head about her. There was so much yet to be done. So many injured who needed tending. But she could hardly do that when her eyelids were so heavy and her limbs so slow to move.

Perhaps it would not hurt to rest, for just a moment. To close her eyes for just a breath. Then she would get back to work.

Sunlight, harsh and demanding assaulted her. First, bright barbs scorched her eyes, then burning heat on her face. Would it not stop? Calling birds added insult to injury. How could they be about so early in the day? Mary forced her eyes open.

The angles of the light in the window and the shadows on the floor chided her. It was not early; not at all. The rose-painted porcelain mantel clock declared it sometime past midday, but her vision were too blurry to be certain just how far.

How could the clock be so unrelenting, so unwavering when everything had just changed? Irrevocably.

He was gone.

She was alone now. More so than she had ever been before.

She rolled up to sit on the edge of the soft bed. So comfortable—it called to her, beckoning her back for just a little more oblivion. Would it really be so bad?

No, but neither would it change anything.

Someone must have helped her into a nightgown and tied the rose-colored floral bed curtains securely out of the way so they would not accidentally brush up against her shoulder. The wounds bore fresh dressings and she could smell yellow basilicum underneath. Would the world ever stop smelling of it?

Heavens above, her shoulder hurt. And her body ached deep to her bones: legs, back, even her hands throbbed. A burgeoning headache crept along the back of her skull, teasing with a promise of hitting her full force when it was least convenient.

How fitting.

How did one begin the first day of an entirely different life? What did one say? Wear? Do?

Lizzy and Lydia had done it, but they knew what their new life should look like as married women. Even Charlotte had some model to follow, some identity in society: a parson's widow.

The knot in her stomach tightened, and she hunched over, burying her face in her hands. She fell back onto her bed, on her side, curling in on herself.

There was no name for what she was now. No means by which her loss could be recognized. Once more, she was lost, somewhere betwixt and between. Neither this nor that, neither bride nor widow.

Forgotten.

She wrapped the soft linen sheet tight around her and pulled the down pillow over her head. If she could just stay here. No one would notice, no one would even care.

No one ever did.

Unless there was something to be done. Then she was essential.

Her eyes burned, but she scrubbed it away with the sheet's embroidered edge. Was it really so bad to be needed, in a practical and real way?

There were things to be done, important things to be done. Things that could not be delegated to servants.

At least for a little while, she had a purpose.

She forced herself to sit up, slowly shedding the warm cocoon around her. The cool air should have braced her, but it chilled the emptiness within instead. She ducked into a sunbeam near the window that had warmed a swatch of rich carpet underfoot. How soft and warm and welcoming it was, tickling her toes and inviting her to linger. Not everything was cold and ignoring her.

Somehow that seemed very significant right now.

She turned her face into the sunshine, closing her eyes and letting her head fall back until her burns pulled. Those caressing beams had followed her inside her room, seeking her out to comfort her, not waiting for her to seek them in the fields.

It was good not to be entirely alone. He would have wanted that for her.

Once the sunbeams had thoroughly warmed her, to the point of leaving a fine sheen of sweat on her forehead, she dressed. The plain old drop-front gown had once been Jane's. Some days that was an unpleasant reminder because it was really too large and had never been altered, but as she eased it over her bandaged shoulder she was grateful.

Still, it was a rather brutal process, but it was bracing. Nothing like a solid pain to help one refocus.

That was positively maudlin.

But who had a better right to be so now?

Charlotte.

She half-walked, half-staggered to the dressing room. A maid would probably be available to help her pin her hair if she called. But the maid would chatter as she always did, asking questions Mary had no desire to answer, offering opinions she would not want to hear.

Best manage the affair on her own. She sat at the dainty oak dressing table laid with an embroidered cloth and her personal items, and gingerly reached for her hairbrush.

Oh, that bloody fool sleeve! It rasped against her burn, threatening to torture her all day. Hell and damnation!

Gracious what language! She dragged her hand down her face.

Fitzwilliam's influence for certain. Pain and laudanum had loosened his tongue to the point where it mattered not who was in his hearing. Servants, ladies, the surgeon, all were treated to the same vulgar effusions when his burns were washed and dressed.

Still, it was no excuse for her to pick up his habits. Especially around Charlotte.

Where would she be now? Parkes would know.

Mary tucked in a final hair pin and stole a final glance in the looking glass. Dark circles beneath her eyes, pale gaunt cheeks, traces of soot still lingering around her jaw. She really looked as different as she felt.

No one was likely to notice though. Probably better that way though, it was not time to talk about her grief, not yet.

The bright wide corridor outside her room was empty, save for a young maid who disappeared behind a servants' door almost as soon as Mary spotted her. Was that intentional, or had she actually been heading there? To the main stairs then, surely the entire household could not be hiding from her.

She grasped the sturdy banister with her uninjured arm. The graceful marble staircase seemed much longer than usual. Halfway down, a black-draped blur rushing past knocked her off her feet. She fell hard to sit upon the steps.

"Mary!" Charlotte grabbed her arm—the wrong arm— and knelt beside her. "You must—pray, I cannot. I simply cannot!"

Mary blinked away the stars and extricated her arm from Charlotte's grasp. The mourning veil made Charlotte's red puffy eyes stand out from her white face.

Parkes trundled up behind Charlotte, her voice sharp. "Miss Bennet! You need not be out of bed. You need to rest, too."

"But I cannot do this! I have already sat vigil all night. I can do no more. You have not sat with them at all. It is only fitting that you manage this. Pray, you must! You are a paragon of good sense and will know what to do. I trust you completely."

"What—"

"Thank you, you are a true friend." Charlotte pushed up and waddled up the rest of the stairs, huffing and puffing the entire way.

Parkes helped Mary to her feet—a slow, laborious process. Next time, she would simply slide down the rest of the way like a child. That could not possibly hurt worse.

"What is wrong with Charlotte?" Mary clutched the bannister. If only the stairs would stop spinning beneath her.

"To start, she is resentful she has had to keep vigil with the dead all night. She is increasing and needs to sleep, you know." Parkes pinched the bridge of her nose. "I am sure she is exhausted, but I have only just got a girl free from other tasks to take her place. She does not understand that even an increasing widow has many responsibilities. Now, the Charon twins are here, and it is too much for her, it seems."

Mary squeezed her eyes shut, pressing them with thumb and forefinger. Was Charlotte really beyond choosing the funeral arrangements for her own husband?

Parkes' voice dropped to a whisper. "They will need to speak to you as well."

"Of course. In the colonel's office?"

"Shall I send some chocolate to you there?"

"No, I would rather have coffee, with cream and sugar."

Parkes' eyebrows rose, but she nodded and hurried off.

Chocolate was too much of a luxury, and something she liked too well to associate with the task she must face. A bitter, black beverage seemed all the more fitting.

How Colonel Fitzwilliam would tease her if he knew. He was a confirmed coffee drinker.

The Charon twins rose to greet her as she entered the study. Parkes must have sent someone in to tidy it. The chaos seemed confined to a pair of tables flanking the wide desk. The piles of books and paper were hardly neat, but they were not in immediate danger of toppling over. Dirty dishes were nowhere in sight and all the furniture had been returned to its appropriate places, out of the room's main path. Truthfully, it was hardly presentable, but it was such an improvement from the last time she had seen it, the transformation seemed incredible.

It was hard to remember the twins' real names— they had been called by the name of Hades' ferryman so long it just seemed to belong to them. They were identical in every way: long, lean men, with pronounced cheek bones and toothy smiles—the pleasant variety, not the hungry kind. Bushy brown hair and red cheeks kept them from looking skeletal. Still, it was hard not to sense a chill in the room whenever they were about. They wore black suits that hung a little loose on their boney frames with starched white cravats, tied with neat but simple knots.

The only difference between them: one carried a small portfolio—he was the undertaker, ready to write notes about the arrangements they decided upon. The other's hands were calloused and rough from building coffins.

They had served Rosings for years, with Lady Catherine's full approbation. Her approval often meant that a tradesman was merely appropriately humble and flattering, but the twins were also known for their honesty and fairness, the sort of men with whom Mary was willing to do business. A small blessing for which to give thanks.

"We offer you and Mrs. Collins our condolences." The undertaker bowed slightly.

"It is Mrs. Collins who has suffered the greatest

loss."

"Whilst that may be true, we acknowledge yours as well." The coffin-maker bowed exactly like his brother.

Though kind and sincere, their similarity made their sentiments eerie.

"Thank you for your kindness. Mrs. Collins has charged me with making the arrangements for Mr. Collins." She sat down behind the desk. Colonel Fitzwilliam's chair was too tall for her, only her toes touched the floor.

It would have been more appropriate to invite them to sit near the fireplace on the sofas there. But she had not the energy for social niceties, only enough to get the necessary tasks accomplished.

"One in her condition probably should not be burdened with such decisions." It was to the coffin-maker's credit that he did not look upon it as an opportunity to press a grieving woman into spending more than she should.

"Do you prefer to plan two funerals, or to do them jointly?"

She swallowed hard and gripped the bulky chair arm. "If the vicar, Mr. Anderson, agrees, I think it best to plan for a single service." There, the first decision had been made. She could do this. It would be well.

Almost on cue, Mrs. Parkes brought a tray bearing coffee and toast with butter and jam. Dear woman, trying to keep up her strength. She really was a gem.

Mary sipped her coffee, laced with barely enough sugar and cream to cut the bitterness to tolerable levels, as the undertaker, the more vocal of the brothers, discussed coffins and preparing the bodies for viewing, which shrouds would be preferred, which attendants to hire and how to transport the deceased to church and graveyard. And of course, funeral favors.

Why did there have to be so many decisions to be made, so many things to be done and none but her to do it?

Rosemary sprigs for remembrance, tied with black ribbon would have to do for favors. The still room could supply the rosemary, and black ribbon was within their means. As for the rest, coffins had to be purchased—renting them might be economical, but both men deserved better. Still though, they did not need to be lead-lined.

Fitzwilliam's valet could wash and dress the bodies and a maid could be spared to sew the shrouds. They might not be fine work, but it would be sufficient. Enough genuine mourners from the estate would be present that others need not be hired. Mr. Collins might have liked to have them and Lady Catherine would have required them, but Michaels would insist that the estate bear none but the absolute necessary expenses for such an event. In that she would honor him. Few would understand, and some might even call her a skinflint for it, but it was a fitting tribute.

.

Chapter 8

Fitzwilliam propped himself on his elbows, groaning. Hazy purple-blue rays of sun peeked past his curtains. Was it morning or evening? The fool mantel clock was no help in discerning.

Bloody bother!

How long had he been in bed? He pulled himself up to sit, the soft mattresses conforming beneath him. Stiff muscles screamed as loudly as the burns coursing down his legs and chest. Surely, he must have been here at least a month.

He smacked his lips against the dry cotton-wool of his mouth. Was there anything to drink in the room—anything not laced with a potion to make him to sleep again?

How much brandy and laudanum had they poured down his throat to make the last days—or was it weeks?—bearable?

He swung his legs over the edge of the high bed, then slid off to stand——feeble as an old woman. But he managed to find the chamber pot in the dim room and use it on his own. How low had he sunk that doing so should feel like an accomplishment?

He paused near the window, flipping the curtain aside. The sun was sinking behind the western fields. So it was evening. He had slept another day away.

The comfortable wingchair near the dark fireplace seemed at least a mile away, but somehow he made it that far and slowly lowered himself into it, permitting himself a string of epithets he hardly ever used as a reward for the effort. Soft, quiet darkness tucked in around him like a blanket, heavy, comforting.

Perhaps he would sleep in this chair—maybe stay for several days. No civilized being would ask him to move again, at least not tonight. How his body ached!

Laudanum. Yes that would be the thing right now. A bit of oblivion would sate the nagging hunger that tickled the back of his mind and erase the pain.

Yes, a very good notion.

He leaned into the chair's embrace and closed his eyes. A gaunt, skeletal image of Andrew, staggering about in an opium-induced stupor, taunted him, beckoned to him.

Join me. It is so easy. You cannot resist.

Perhaps Andrew was right. The pain ... he was so tired ... so weak. And Rosings? After this, what point was there in soldiering on?

He glanced over his shoulder. A fading sunbeam glittered across the dark laudanum bottle on the bedside table. Just a few steps would bring relief.

Perhaps he could reach it without standing. His hand hung midair, the bottle still well beyond his reach. Strong, slim fingers grasped his hand … no wait, there was no one there. What?

But the sensation was strong. A memory, or was it a ghost?

Those were Miss Bennet's fingers, clinging to him keeping him focused as blackness came over him. What had been her fate? Was she a ghost that now took his hand in the twilight?

He screwed his eyes shut and squeezed his temples.

The servants' door in the dressing room squealed and two sets of soft footsteps approached.

What were the maids doing at this hour? Probably tending the bloody fire. Best pretend he was asleep and let them manage their task quickly. He allowed his head to loll to the side and he closed his eyes.

"Oh, good, he's sleeping. I heard they's been giving him laudanum. He won't wake up for anything." The girl spoke in a low, throaty whisper.

"What a relief. I heard one gets an earful around him, especially when bandage changing is due."

"I'd gladly take that to dealing with that trollop on the other end of the hall."

What trollop? He peeked on eye open. The two girls knelt before the fireplace. Whatever they were doing was lost in the shadows.

"You mean Miss Bennet?"

"Of course I mean her. What other woman here was a'kissing the master in front of everyone while her own betrothed were being burned to death in the flames. It's not decent!"

"Hush! Mrs. Parkes says you must not speak that way. None of us should. That was not a kiss, not in the regular sense. I heard it called a 'kiss of life'. Miss

Bennet breathed life back into him when he was dead. We should be grateful he is alive. We would all be without work soon if he were dead."

It had not been a dream. She had been there, hovering over him as though she had kissed him. Cold prickled coursed down his spine.

The smaller of the two girls folded her arms over her chest and huffed. "You can say that all you like, but I won't believe it. One moment she's kissing the master and then two days later she's lying in bed beside her dying man, singing him to his final sleep. It ain't decent, I tell you. And I won't be serving her, I can tell you that. I may just be a maid, but I got standards."

"Be careful, Mrs. Parkes will sack you if she hears that. Miss Bennet has been good for Rosings. I do not much like hearing anything against her, either."

"Your father would whip you if he caught you kissing a man not promised to you. It's just wrong and you know it. What makes her so high and mighty that it shouldn't matter if she does it?"

"Because it was not a kiss!"

"I saw it, you didn't. I know what I saw."

"Fine, go about your way then, but do not come crying to me when Parkes casts you out." The taller girl tossed her head and tiptoed back towards the servants' door.

"It ain't me that's gonna be thrown out. Miss Bennet's ruined and she'll be pitched into the hedgerows soon enough." The smaller girl trailed after her.

The door clicked shut.

The kiss of life? He had heard of it—one of the army doctors had spoken of it. It was controversial and improper. If Miss Bennet had indeed done that for him, her reputation would be completely compromised if word got out.

Fitzwilliam drew in a deep breath and another. Though his chest ached, and he coughed violently at the deep breaths, the material issue was that he was still breathing, still living.

Thanks to her.

Damned, bloody hell!

How much talk had already gone on about her actions? Even if the servants held their tongues—as well they should in appreciation for her efforts—if the news got out, there would be no end to the gossip's spread.

He knotted his fingers in his hair. Were there not enough concerns for him to deal with, without having the burden of Miss Bennet's reputation and future?

Gah! That was monstrously ungrateful. Something Andrew would have said.

Was he becoming his brother?

You think you are better than your elder brother—the heir to Matlock? Your father's favorite? You have never been more than me, and you never will be.

Andrew's bitter laugh burned his mind.

Fitzwilliam pushed against the chair's arms and rose, inch by agonizing inch, until he stood somewhat upright. He grabbed a banyan left hanging off the bed post and shrugged it on.

Dear Lord that hurt!

He had been a colonel in His Majesty's service. He had stood against Napoleon and returned. Rosings would not conquer him. Laudanum would not conquer him. Not today.

The servants' door was closer than the other door, so he shuffled toward it. Not nearly as dignified as a firm march, but it was away from the laudanum bottle.

Another string of epithets—more vile than the first—rewarded his arrival at the bottom of the stairs.

The corridor proved nearly as dark as the servants' stair—a quiet, unnatural dark. Occasional moonbeams through the windows broke the darkness, casting irregular shadows on all they touched, draped like specters haunting the manor.

Perhaps that was to be expected. Who would inhabit the downstairs rooms at this hour with himself and Lady Catherine injured? Still though, it was unsettling, so different from the place he visited as a boy.

Why was the door to the sitting room ajar?

He trudged to the room, hand against the wall for support.

A young maid, more girl than woman, jumped to her feet, clutching her apron to her cheeks. "Mrs. Collins and Miss Bennet needed to sleep, sir." She glanced over her shoulder into the dimly lit room.

Heavy drapes on two windows were tightly drawn against any marauding light—sun or moon. Two candles flickered light and shadow toward the center of the room. Coffins, two of them on low tables, occupied most of the open space. Fresh flowers—so many vases lined the room—and fresh-cut coffin wood— neither masked the fetid odor of death.

So much death.

But who?

He covered his mouth and nose with his banyan. Two steps closer revealed the faces.

Collins on the right, Michaels on the left.

Bile filled his mouth, and he fled. What would the maid think to see him cast up his accounts here?

He made it to his study, to a chamber pot, before dry heaves overwhelmed him. He spat sour bile but nothing else.

How long had it been since he had eaten?

He shoved the chamber pot aside and panted until the roiling in his belly stopped.

Moonbeams streamed bright through the window, onto his desk. It was so tidy. Who had been working there? Michaels—no that was not possible.

What was he going to do without Michaels?

His knees softened, and he half-fell into the chair behind his desk.

Damn it all! He needed to move more carefully!

What were those? He shuffled through a small stack of papers in the center of his desk. A bill from the Charon twins—was that all that was planned for the funerals? It was barely decent. But it was affordable.

Farther down the stack, a letter to Darcy, explaining what had happened. One to Collins' solicitor regarding the estate whose fate was in limbo, awaiting the birth of Collins' baby. Another to Michaels' brother. All brief and business-like—written in a precise, neat hand. Surely it must have been Miss Bennet's.

She had already been running the household. Was she now sitting in for Michaels, too? Great heavens, did she never stop? Darcy thought Elizabeth a force of nature, but it seemed this Miss Bennet was something even beyond that.

What was that? A soft stirring from the far corner of the room? He squinted into shadows near the fireplace.

A dark form curled on the sofa in the corner near

the far window. The profile of a face, the line of a feminine figure.

It was her.

How long had Miss Bennet been here? Had she just finished those letters, stopping to rest a few minutes before soldiering on to the next task?

She stirred and muttered something.

He held his breath.

"Need to tell Parkes … assign another maid … no regrets …he lives … rosemary … Mrs. Collins will tie ribbons …" She scrubbed her face with her hand, stretched one leg and whimpered—how seriously had she been injured?

Her breathing settled into a deep regular pattern.

Thank heavens!

What could he say to her? What should he say? Should he thank her? Apologize? Assure her that Parkes had orders to sack the judgmental wretch of a maid?

Whatever it was, here and now, alone and in the dark, was not the time for it.

He dragged himself from the study and to the main stairs. Sleep, he needed sleep now. Then he would decide how to manage the coming storms … and Miss Bennet.

The next morning a somber haze hung in the air as Mary stared at herself in the full length dressing room mirror, smoothing the black bombazine skirt one more time. The deep black mourning fabric clashed horribly with the delicate floral paper hanging behind her. Not unlike the way it looked on her. The subtle diagonal ridges of the wool were so different to what she normally wore—such fine material, cut into a dress she would never have chosen—nor have been able to afford—herself.

The gown did not fit well, binding in some places—especially across her burns—and too large in others, chafing overall. A little like her grief—there was no prescribed way for her to wear it. It was not designed for one such as herself. She could only muddle through to do the best she could.

Parkes had brought it in just an hour earlier, telling her Colonel Fitzwilliam had insisted she find Miss Bennet something suitable to wear amongst Anne de Bourgh's old things. It was gracious, if a little high-handed of him. Best focus on the gracious.

It was not time yet, so she sat in the soft chair near the windows. Fog hovered low to the ground, embracing the fields with a sort of mourning veil of its own, painting the window panes with tiny teardrops. How very gothic sounding.

The mantel clock chimed. She rose, no point in procrastinating.

Fitzwilliam and Charlotte greeted her in the sunlit small parlor, each a bit off color and wobbly on their feet. The open coffins were laid out on a high table—thankfully out of the sun. The settee, chairs and tables were all draped in the same somber black crepe that covered the pale yellow brocade curtains. A large willow basket full of rosemary bundles tied with black ribbons occupied a black crepe-swathed chair near the door.

She covered her nose and mouth with her handkerchief. The funeral should probably have been conducted several days ago.

Not probably. Definitely.

Why had no one thought to open the windows?

She shuffled to the far window, fighting to kick the slightly too-long, too-full skirt out of her way as she did. A young maid and the colonel joined her efforts, just a few steps behind. Soon a soft, moist cross breeze helped clear some of the most fetid vapors.

But not nearly enough.

"Take another maid out with you and gather more flowers." Mary pointed toward the girl then the door.

The maid scurried out with a tiny curtsey and a look of great relief.

Fitzwilliam muttered some complaint under his breath.

"Seeing the entire house readied, and a meal prepared whilst not disturbing her ladyship is no small undertaking." That was probably far more curt than necessary.

He bowed his head and sighed. "Forgive me."

Something about the uneasy lines around his mouth— "You are correct, though. The smell is particularly distressing. I am sure Mrs. Collins suffers cruelly for it. Perhaps you might escort her outside for a few minutes, before the mourners arrive?"

He looked up, a flicker of gratitude in his eyes. "And would you not benefit as well?"

"I have only just arrived. I shall be fine, thank you." It was only a small lie. For now she could rely on her constitution—and empty stomach—to carry her through. Someone needed to remain here in case mourners arrived.

He bowed from his shoulders and returned to Charlotte's side. She took his arm, and they disappeared down the hallway toward the garden door.

Mary arranged her face into something somber, but calm and drew in a deep, death-tainted breath. Her tears would wait until no one would be troubled by her outburst. She would remain all things that were right and proper for a woman until then.

Michaels would be proud of her.

Later, perhaps in the days to come, she would indulge in a brisk run to the tumbledown shack and the well, where she could give voice to violent sensibilities. Some time when Fitzwilliam was well-occupied and no one would come looking for her.

Parkes appeared at the doorway. "Mr. and Mrs. Barrow to pay their respects."

Of course, the first mourners should arrive whilst Charlotte and the colonel were outside. No, that was ungracious, blaming them when it was her idea in the first place.

Mary picked up a black-ribboned bundle of rosemary from a basket. She knew what to say, had rehearsed it a hundred times in her mind already. It had only taken the first fifty to be able to get through it without her throat closing or her eyes burning. She would be able to do this.

Fitzwilliam and Charlotte returned not long afterward, to take their places greeting mourners, looking a touch chagrined at their tardiness. Little matter, really. There was a steady enough stream of mourners to keep them all occupied.

Soon enough the longcase clock near the great stairs chimed, and the pall bearers entered. Fitzwilliam had graciously offered his services as one, but his injuries were still too fresh to permit it. It was an honor that he offered, though. But now was not the time to think of it.

The pallbearers placed the lids on the coffins and lifted them to their shoulders. In perfect step they marched in single file from the sitting room to the hall and out of the front door, into the lingering fog and to the wagon waiting to carry the coffins to the church. The mourners followed in a slow, dignified procession

Colonel Fitzwilliam lingered back and approached Mary. "Is there anything you need? Have the staff been properly attending to you needs?"

What an odd look—what had he heard? What did he know? The blood drained from her face and she broke eye contact. "Thank you for asking. Everything is well."

His forehead creased and the lines around his mouth tightened.

Pray let him not pursue this, not here, not now!

He nodded, slow and somber, and followed out after the mourners.

Mary and Charlotte looked at each other over the nearly empty basket of rosemary bundles and yards of black crepe, the only tangible remainder of their losses. Could silence echo? Sonorous, even thundering, pulsing against her skull, right behind her ears. She tried to press it away with her fingertips, but it only drove the ache deeper, until it wrapped itself around her lungs, threatening to steal her breath.

Was it as the lower maid had said? Might she have been able to save him, had she not been busy with Fitzwilliam? Could her efforts have pulled him free just a few moments sooner, before it was too late? She wrapped her arms around her waist. Was his loss her fault?

And if it were, what could she do now?

A low moan cut through the silence, gently like a hot knife through a jelly. Charlotte doubled over, her face knotted with a faraway expression.

"Are you having pains?" Mary rushed to her side.

"It is nothing. They are the same ones that have come and gone for days."

"I am not so certain." Mary slid her arm around Charlotte's shoulders.

"It will be well. Do not worry on my account." Charlotte murmured through gritted teeth.

That was easy for Charlotte to say. She might be the one near her time, but Mary would be the one needed to manage everything when it came.

Another ungracious thought. Mary dragged her hand down her face. She really needed to work harder at her attitude. Gratitude and graciousness were what she needed today. Bitterness served none well.

Charlotte panted, hard and a little frothy, like a horse run too hard.

No! No! No!

What child chose to be born on the day of his father's funeral? What kind of twisted humor would choose now to bring life into the world?

"Oh, oh! Mary, I do not think I can do this." Charlotte wrapped one arm across her belly and clutched at the seat with the other.

"Neither of us have much choice in the matter. We will endure what must be." She probably ought to be more comforting …

"But the dinner guests, when they come, they will hear my travail!" Her words ended in a wail. "A woman should be silent at such a time, penitent—"

"Stop—I want no such rhetoric." Mr. Collins was not going speak from the grave before he was even buried. "If you need to cry out, so be it. Collins never had a right to try to govern such a time as this."

"But Lady Catherine—"

"Will have a suitable dose of laudanum to keep her quiet and comfortable for as long as is necessary. She has no place to dictate how any of this is to go, either."

"But it is her house!"

"Charlotte, that is entirely enough. I have never known you prone to hysteria. I will not stand by and allow you to take that path now. Take a deep breath, like that, and another. Find that well of good-sense I know you have and dwell there. You have an heir to birth, one who will take on his father's legacy." And if she were wrong, they would deal with that when it came. For now, Charlotte did not need another worry or distraction.

And neither did she.

Chapter 9

PARKES—BLESS HER foresight—already had a remote chamber prepared for Charlotte's lying in. The small room had no paper hanging, only light blue paint on its walls, with faded darker blue curtains that had probably started out in another room. The plain oak bed had no bed curtains and only a few mattresses. A press, dressing table, chair, washstand and a cradle, all plain and serviceable, accounted for the rest of the room's furnishings. It resembled a room at the parsonage more than one at Rosings. But, situated at the far end of the guest wing, it offered as much distance from both dinner guests and Lady Catherine as possible. Charlotte babbled her gratitude for that fact as they settled her within.

Parkes closed the windows and pulled the curtains shut. Darkness settled over the room, with only slivers of light peeking around the curtains. Though it was what was done in preparation for a woman's travail, it still felt just a bit ominous. A maid scurried in to lay a roaring fire. It would not take long for the room to grow uncomfortably warm.

So this was how she was to spend the evening, and conceivably the next day or even two. Could Charlotte do without her long enough for her to change from her borrowed mourning gown? This could not possibly be the appropriate thing to wear for a lying in, could it?

Was it wrong to feel the loss of the company at dinner tonight?

Of course it was. It was wrong and petty and self-ish. Charlotte's needs were far more urgent than her own, and a proper and decent friend would know and feel that.

At least that is what Jane would have said at such a time.

Maybe Jane was right. At least a little. If nothing else, she should definitely stay until Mrs. Grant arrived and took over. She pulled a chair close and sat beside Charlotte, holding her hands as each pain washed over her.

Mrs. Grant arrived in short order, all bustle and authority, and began arranging everything to her liking, even bringing in a birthing chair. How pleasing it was to let someone else take over the situation.

Charlotte's waters broke, and she was gripped with the first all-consuming pain of her travail. Her composure shattered in a wrenching scream that lingered in the dark stuffy room until the next pain over-whelmed her.

One of the upper maids slipped into the room and minced to Mary's side. "Forgive me, Miss."

"Has Mrs. Jenkinson sent you?"

The maid curtsied.

Mary leaned close to the bed. "Charlotte, I must attend Lady Catherine for a moment. I will return soon."

Charlotte clutched her shoulders. "No, pray do not go! You promised me you would stay with me!"

"I also promised you that Lady Catherine would not come in and make demands of you. To fulfill that promise, I must go, but only for a short time. Mrs. Grant will be here, and all will be well."

Mrs. Grant patted her shoulder and edged between Mary and the bedside. "Take a deep breath, Mrs. Collins and gather your wits. Nothing has befallen you that is not common to all women. You cannot allow yourself to falter so soon. You are strong enough for this. I expect you to show me that."

"You have no idea …"

Mary slipped out before another pain seized her.

Cleaning Lady Catherine's wounds and then medicating and dressing them required a full hour. When at last Lady Catherine slid into a laudanum induced sleep Mary ducked out and ran for her room. Time to finally shed the bombazine.

A maid intercepted her halfway there. "Mrs. Grant says you are wanted most urgently."

"Has something gone amiss?"

"No, Miss. Mrs. Grant says it is nearly her time."

"It is not possible. It has not been that long."

The maid shrugged. "Mrs. Grant says that sometimes it goes that way."

Of course it would. Perhaps it was for the best, though. Even it if were not, it was not as though she could affect any of it. Mary jogged the breadth of

Rosings manor again.

Mary plunged into Charlotte's stiflingly hot, dark room. She stood beside her bed as Charlotte screamed—a gut wrenching, visceral cry.

Mrs. Grant supported her on one side and pointed to the birthing chair. "Help me!"

Three pains came and went before they were able to situate Charlotte in the birthing chair.

Mrs. Grant crouched before her as another pain began. "I see the head, Mrs. Collins. You must push now."

Mary gripped her hands and whispered encouragements as Charlotte bore down and screeched.

"There now! You have a daughter, Mrs. Collins." Mrs. Grant caught the mewling infant in a cloth and handed her to Mary while she dealt with the afterbirth.

"She is lovely, Charlotte. She looks like you." Mary stroked the crying baby's cheek. Her cries were strong and she waved her spindly arms with vigor.

She really was a dear wee thing, small, but not frighteningly so, her head not squashed as other babies' often were.

"There now, take her to your breast." Mrs. Grant did not look up from her duties.

"To what end?" Charlotte moaned, writhing. "We are homeless and near penniless. What mercy is there in prolonging her suffering?"

"Charlotte Collins, what are you saying?" Mary shoved the baby at her. "You have far greater sense than this! I will hear no more of this nonsense. Take care of your daughter this moment."

Charlotte cried out and clutched her still-distended belly.

"It is as I thought; there is another. Put the infant in the cradle, Miss Bennet. Mrs. Collins still requires you."

Mary tucked the squalling infant into the cradle near the bed. Pray she would quiet soon. The sound would do nothing for Charlotte's nerves. Or hers.

Several more pains seized her, but really not that many, and Charlotte was delivered again. The newborn cried.

Thank Providence for that.

"And? What is it?" Charlotte, pale and sweaty, pulled forward, trying to see it for herself.

"It is a boy, Mrs. Collins."

"Bring him to me. Bring them both to me."

Mrs. Grant swaddled the boy and placed him on Charlotte's breast. Mary helped her take her daughter on the other side.

"He looks like his father. Can you see? Mr. Collins' eyes. But how will I ever manage two?" Charlotte gazed down at the sucking babies.

"The Good Lord gave you two bubbies which is entirely enough for two babies. But you must have help, and you must rest and eat properly." Mrs. Grant trundled to the washstand and washed her hands.

"Mary, you will write to my family and tell them of my news? And the solicitors! They must know of my son's birth, that the estate is to go to him. Perhaps my father—"

"I will write the letters and get them in the post as soon as may be. Perhaps your father might come with your mother or sister to take you back to Meryton and help you settle into your new home."

Mary swallowed hard. It was a good thing, a very good thing. As long as her son lived, Charlotte would have a home of her own. Even in her widowhood, Charlotte was very, very lucky. Mary dragged her sleeve across her eyes.

"I can manage from here, Miss Bennet." Mrs. Grant whispered in her ear. "You might still see some of the guests downstairs?"

"Yes, thank you. Colonel Fitzwilliam should know the news." Mary dipped in a weak curtsey and left.

Fitzwilliam closed the massive front door behind the black-garbed couple and leaned wearily against the carved mahogany. Damn, that shoulder still hurt. A great deal. That was the last of the guests, who had descended upon the funeral dinner like a cloud of locusts.

No, that was not fair, not at all. Many, if not most, had been genuinely sorrowful and respectful—despite their healthy appetites. And with Miss Bennet's efforts of economy, the meal should not render them limited to meatless tables the remainder of the—what period did those budgets run on, a week, a fortnight, a month? Whatever it was, they would still be able to eat, and that was a very good thing.

Small Tom stood back and gave him a queer look. He was probably right, since sagging against the front door as though keeping wolves at bay was an odd posture for the master of the manor to take. But what about this day had not been decidedly odd?

He dismissed the butler with a wave and shoved himself off the door. How tired could one be and still walk?

Apparently the answer was soul-crushingly tired.

He forced his feet to move, stopping in the dining

room to pour two glasses of wine—not the best Rosings had ever served, but it was in the stores, so it would do. He had eaten little at dinner, and Miss Bennet had eaten nothing at all—maybe nothing all day. Hopefully she would still be in the drawing room when he returned. They both deserved a few moments of relaxation.

She had moved from the small, hard chair beside the pianoforte to a generous, plush wingback near the fireplace. Half the candles in the room were extinguished—her doing no doubt. A low fire flickered, its light only reaching halfway into the room. Shadows danced and reached, trying to obtain the corners, barely failing their attempts.

Her legs stretched out in front of her on a low tufted stool, ankles demurely crossed. She had a well-turned ankle, but they were mostly hidden by far too much black fabric—whatever the disagreeable stuff was called.

The color did not suit her at all. Far too severe for her delicate features and coloring. Nymphs did not dance about in black and neither should she. How long would she wear it? There was no prescribed period for mourning one's betrothed. What would seem appropriate to her?

He dragged another wingback near hers, handed her a glass, and sat down. "No arguments now. You ate nothing at dinner. You should enjoy this much at least."

She sighed softly and sipped the wine.

Good.

Truth be told, he had not the energy for an argument. What parts of him that were not weary ached with a bone-jarring throbbing he thought he had left behind in France. He mimicked her posture and tasted his wine.

She glanced at him. Something that might have been a sort of half-smile, played about her lips, though she said nothing. There was a great deal to be said for silent companionship.

The mantel clock chimed some small number of chimes. She rolled the stem of her empty glass between her palms, staring into the dregs of the wine.

"Do you want more?"

"Thank you, no. I do not know that I should have had this. I feel quite warm and muzzy."

"Enjoy it. You deserve to be a bit muzzy."

"How does one earn muzziness?" There was something so earnest and little-girlish in her voice.

"How do you do it, Miss Mary Bennet? I have not worked you out at all."

"What is there to work out sir? And why would you care to?" She did not look at him, just stared into that spinning glass.

"A great deal, madam, a very great deal."

"Do not trouble yourself with such nonsense. You have far more important concerns."

"Not now, I do not. I can hardly think of a puzzle I would more like to solve." He set his glass on the floor and twisted to face her, elbows planted on the chair's arms.

The firelight highlighted her profile.

He could not tear his eyes away. Botheration.

She was not classically pretty, not at all. Technically, she was as plain as he. But there was something in the fine details that was attractive, captivating even. Once one really looked at her, it was difficult to stop.

"What are you about, sir?" She turned just enough

to reveal her eyes.

Those were easily her finest feature. Penetrating, seeing more than they revealed, like Elizabeth's. Still, they had a compelling quality all their own, shining in their gold-flecked hazel depths.

"About? Why must I be about something?"

"You have had too much wine."

"That I am looking at you means I have had too much wine?"

"Generally, sir, yes, it does." She rolled her eyes.

So superior, so matter-of-fact. So very, very amusing. He chuckled.

She set her glass aside, planted her feet, and folded her arms over her chest. "And now you laugh at me, sir. I think that proves my point."

"You misunderstand me, Miss Bennet, misunderstand me entirely."

"What do you think I understand—or rather, do not?"

Oh, that smug look on her face was not to be borne!

He sat back and stared into the fireplace. "You see me as the rest of my family does. The spare to the heir who will inherit the fortune. I am a convenient plan in reserve who will ensure Matlock does not leave the family line should anything happen to Andrew—who seems bent on trying as hard as possible to make that happen whilst my father, and yours, as a matter of fact, do everything they can to prevent such a tragedy."

"There is bitterness in your tone."

"Bitterness? Indeed? Are you surprised? Would you not entertain just a touch of bitterness yourself, being relegated to second-rate in everything you do?

The middle child, good enough to serve His Majesty, but hardly useful for anything else."

She rose with all the grace and dignity of a nymph-princess and strode to the fireplace as if to emphasize her royal bearing. Ever so slowly, she turned to face him.

He gasped. Oh, the fire in her eyes, on her face!

Had there ever been such glorious indignation? Fury rising up glowed, literally glowed, shone through the fiber of her being. No longer a nymph, the fire birthed her into her true form, a fiery goddess—perhaps one never seen before.

Spectacular.

Glorious.

Furious.

A chill coursed down his spine.

"Consider yourself fortunate you have a role, no matter how small. And you could augment that with something truly smart in the King's service."

He knotted his fists and rose. "Smart, is that what it seems to you? Surrounded by explosions and muck, covered by blood and brains not your own?" He stood close to her, too close, breathing heavily, teeth clenched to the point of pain.

She leveled those remarkable eyes on him and held his gaze. Unflinching.

He leaned closer and narrowed his eyes.

She matched his posture.

What? No one dared—

"Yes, sir, by all common understanding, it is a smart profession."

"For one who loves death."

"It is a profession and an honest one for which you might be respected and earn the title of gentleman."

"A profession I have long detested."

She tossed her head in positively elegant disdain. "At least you had the opportunity for a profession to hate in the first place."

"So you think it a privilege?"

"One I would happily trade places with you for."

"You may have it then! What privations shall I take on in your place?" He threw up his hands and stalked three paces away, her fury too much to bear.

She cocked her head. Something feline—or was it just predatory—crossed her features. "I shall not ask so much of you. You may continue on as the middle child. I would not dare take from you your most notable, defining trait."

"How gracious of you." His lip curled back as he snorted his appreciation.

"But as the third daughter, you will be relieved from all illusions of usefulness, or desirability. After a man has two daughters, he places great stock in the possibility his new wife will produce for him a son. When she does not, there is profound disappointment. At least the older two, with beauty and wit— and a far better dowry—have hopes of marrying well. Perhaps the younger ones as well, with beauty and vivacity to their credit. But with neither to your account, you will be overlooked everywhere you go, only noticed to the extent that you might be useful to someone. Even that is not worthy of notice; after all, a servant could easily suffice for the task. That is all you have to look forward to, for there is no useful occupation to which you can apply yourself and remain respectable. Unlike gentlemen, ladies have few options. As soon as we leave our home to take on some form of work, our reputation becomes suspect and unrecoverable."

"Surely you exaggerate."

She snorted and turned her shoulder to him, her light ripping away from him with an agonizing tear.

He staggered, catching himself on the mantel.

She strode toward the dark window. "When have you been in company, and no one remembered to introduce you? When has your name been left off an invitation because someone forgot you had been born? When have you sat through an entire assembly with not a single partner willing to dance with you? Did you learn to play pianoforte so that you would not have to face the ignominy of having no partners at private gatherings?"

How could she say such things as though she were talking about the weather and nothing more? He approached her, his steps soft, slow and measured. Close enough to feel the heat from the fire still radiating from her skin, he stopped.

"They are fools."

"I hardly expect anyone else might agree."

"But they have not seen you, really seen you."

She turned again, fury returning. "And what do you think you have seen?"

Heavens, she was stunning! "I do not know how you have done it."

"Done what?"

"Everything. Absolutely everything."

She rolled her eyes.

He took her shoulder—the one without the bandages—in his hand. So much strength in such narrow, soft curves. "If you do not wish to be dismissed, then do not dismiss me, either. I have seen powerful commanders who have not managed what you have with such poise and grace. And somehow you have not drawn attention to yourself for it."

She lowered her gaze.

"No, you will look at me when I speak." He tipped up her chin, aching to see her eyes. "I asked for your help in handling Aunt Catherine whom you well know is beyond what I can do. Not only have you done that, but you have managed everything so efficiently and easily that no one has noticed what you have done. No one but me."

"It is nothing."

"Stop." He brought his boot down firmly. "I do not appreciate false humility."

"There is nothing false—"

"Indeed there is. You would not tolerate another's efforts being ignored in such a way. There is no harm in recognizing yours."

She flinched like one struck. "Perhaps there is."

"Tell me he did not."

"It does not signify."

"Yes, it does. To me it does."

"Pray leave it."

"No, I insist you hear me." He resisted the urge to shake her. "You are without a doubt the strongest woman of my acquaintance. How you succeeded in carrying off a viewing, a dinner, attending to a birth and caring for a madwoman all in a single day, I cannot fathom. How are you still standing, and so calm? My sister lost a suitor once, not even a betrothed, and she—"

"You think I have no feelings?" Her voice thinned to something razor sharp and pointed, slicing through his sentiment. "Just because I can master them when needed—you are just like the rest assuming that I feel nothing, that you might say anything you like to me, like a dog or a horse, and I will have no reaction. Nothing ever bothers Mary!" She tossed her head and stepped around him. "You are no different from the rest."

He grabbed her uninjured arm and nearly jerked her off her feet. "Trust me. I have not made that mistake. I am privileged to see your fury."

"You have a decidedly odd taste if you consider that a privilege."

"Perhaps I do." He could not contain the smile. "Will you slap me if I tell you are one of the handsomest women of my acquaintance?"

"I should. I have been warned you might say such a thing in the hopes of having some of your baser needs satisfied."

It probably was inappropriate to laugh, considering the look in her eyes, but it would not remain contained. "If I were trying to seduce you, that is not what I would say."

"Of course not. There was good reason I told Charlotte she need not worry."

"So, she is worried for your reputation?"

"It is her role as a married friend." She held her ground, true soldier that she was.

"If I were going to seduce you," he leaned close, so close her warm breath tickled his cheek. "I would tell you that at first I thought you plain, but have since discovered that is a cloak you wear to repel the insincere. But I have seen you without it. That day at the well, in the sun you revealed yourself: a woodland nymph, a rare creature few men see, much less capture. One that transformed in the firelight tonight into—"

"Pray stop! It is—"

"Entirely true. I cannot look away. I am mesmerized—"

She pushed his chest with a strength that would have been surprising in another woman, but seemed right from her.

"You have gone too far, sir, and I implore you to stop. I will not be mocked." She looked toward the door.

He caught her elbows and ducked to catch her gaze. "Michaels never told you such things?"

She drew in a sharp breath and swallowed hard.

"Fool! Idiot, taking you for granted like the rest."

"Do not speak of him so. He was a good man."

"Indeed he was. The best of men, but not one up to the fire and the passions that are in you. You deserve more."

The sob was soft and dainty, ladylike at first, but as it grew, it seized her with trembling that threatened to knock her off her feet.

He pulled her into his chest, wrapping his arms tightly around her. What else could he do?

Warm and soft, strong and supple, she leaned into him, a storm of wracking, wrenching cries pouring over her. He pressed his cheek to the top of her head.

She smelt of flowers.

Flowers bending in a summer storm. They would raise their heads again, sturdy, proud, and beautiful. The tempest took nothing away, only proved their strength.

"I have seen you for what you are, Miss Bennet. And I will never forget what I have seen. But, if you wish, I promise, I shall keep my peace. It will be our secret."

She hiccupped and nodded into his chest, clinging to him.

A woman so strong, pressing into him for strength. Had he ever been so highly regarded?

❧ Chapter 10

SEVERAL DAYS AFTER the funeral—or was it a week? Recently, it was so difficult to tell—Fitzwilliam staggered into his study, candlestick in hand. He was scarcely decent for company with his dark jacket shrugged on over his barely tucked shirt and cravat just wound around his throat without a knot. But no one should be about downstairs after ten o'clock— Miss Bennet tended to keep early hours—so who would there be to shock or offend? At least it was better than padding about the house in a banyan tied over his nightshirt.

Besides, it was the best he could muster under the circumstances. Who would have thought a funeral, interment and ensuing dinner could be so taxing? Mr. Peters had warned him not to exert himself too vigorously or there would be a price to be paid.

He leaned against the doorframe, panting. Someday the stairs would not render him breathless, but how long would it take? The flickering candle revealed that the room remained tidy—Miss Bennet's work no doubt—even tidier than the last time he had been inside—yes it was a se'nnight ago. Papers and books were now confined to the desk and bookcase behind, in orderly stacks, all the corners lining up. All the furniture was where it belonged, even the wingchair Michaels had used was returned to the side of its mate near the fireplace.

Damn it all.

A wave of vertigo struck him full force. He hung in the doorway until it passed. At least the spells were not lasting very long any more.

Peters had been right. Exhaustion, fever, pain and all manner of digestive ills rose up to thank him for his efforts in the role over the funeral proceedings.

Somehow it was fitting; the first social event he would preside over was a funeral. Mother would probably have a fit over how bad an omen that was.

What did it mean that a birth, two in actuality, should immediately follow?

Strange times, these. Very strange indeed.

He tumbled into the chair behind his desk. Surely there had to be a more comfortable chair to be found somewhere in the house. Bloody thing was too short and too narrow ... wait, this was not the right chair in the first place.

What was his desk chair doing across the room? He shoved the offending piece of furniture aside. He would have his proper chair. Why did forcible cursing and creative epithets not cajole it into?

He fell into his seat again. Much better. There was a great deal to be said for a chair that was tall enough to fit one's legs.

Brandy would be welcome right now. Or port. Or even gin. He squinted toward the liquor cabinet.

Naturally, all the decanters in the room proved empty.

He clutched his temples. Had Michaels allotted any funds for him to restock the cellars? Where were those books?

Neat piles of papers and ledgers lined his desk along both sides. Behind him, the lower shelves of the bookcase contained more tidy stacks between neatly lined-up journals intermingled with reference books and the newest volumes of the *Agricultural Review*. No doubt a hint that he should be reading those, soon.

But with whom would he discuss them?

Fitzwilliam dropped his head into his hands, elbows braced on the desk. Damn, the burns along his arm still hurt. Two decent men had been lost that day—well one decent man at least—and two stable boys; two infants were now fatherless; and Miss Bennet's best, and perhaps only, hope for a future apart from her family was gone. How many others had been injured? How close had he come to losing his own life?

Closer than he had ever come on the battlefield. And he could not fault Napoleon or his cronies this time.

He had only himself to blame.

Miss Bennet had warned him, adamantly, vociferously, that he should handle Lady Catherine carefully. That she was capable of causing a great deal of harm, quite without intending to, but incredibly capable nonetheless. Miss Bennet had been right.

Perhaps if he had not been so forceful with the old woman, had coddled and cajoled her as Miss Bennet had insisted, he would have still got his way. His pride might have suffered, to be sure. But that would likely have been all. The estate—the families, the animals, the structures, would not have.

The hard callouses on his palms raked across his face and his fingers knotted in his hair. He was responsible for this tragedy and for everything that happened at Rosings. Utterly and completely.

If this was the kind of responsibility Darcy bore, no wonder he was such a stiff-rumped old stager, so stiff and proud, wandering about as though he knew everything.

But he did know a great deal. Like how to manage his people. Darcy was far from perfect, though. There was some consolation in that. He made his fair share of mistakes.

But he always faced them head on and confronted them, corrected them. That was what set him apart from Father and Andrew. Darcy did not run away.

What will you do?

He sat up straight and scanned the room. No one was there. But the voice was clear, clear as if Darcy were standing there himself, scolding.

What would he do?

He pushed up from his chair and stood, leaning hard over the desk out of breath and sweating. It would pass soon, it would pass.

What were all those letters, there on the far corner of the desk?

To Michaels' brother, his solicitor, Longbourn's solicitor, Mrs. Collins' family, and several more. All in

Miss Bennet's nearly perfect hand, most waiting for a signature from him.

Things he needed done, but never asked for help with.

Beside them, lists and sheets of notes, familiar-looking. Wait, they were based on Michael's recommendations for the estate, but condensed into specific, actionable points, on a timetable.

Damn. Damn. Damn! He bounced his fist on the desktop. That woman was more efficient than most of His Majesty's army. When had she done all this—not to mention how? Women were not trained for this—were they? Certainly his sisters were not.

How much did he owe her now?

He sank back into his chair. A stack of unopened letters caught his eye, one bearing Father's handwriting. Father's secretary wrote most of his correspondence. When Father himself wrote, it was usually because it was a private matter and he was very upset. What joy was to be his?

He snatched up the letter and broke the stubborn seal—stubborn as Father tended to be. Another delightful omen.

Thin, spidery handwriting done with a sharp pen, so quickly the letters were faint in some places. Father must have been agitated when he penned it.

F,

A letter came from the vicinity of Rosings Park with news that I can hardly fathom. Am I to understand that you are unaware of the entire situation? That is what this person implies. But I cannot believe even you would be so obtuse not to recognize the grave nature of your situation.

Had someone uncovered more debts of which he

was unaware? But who would be in such a position to do that? Had some crime been perpetrated by one of the denizens of Rosings Park, and now they were accused of harboring a fugitive?

The local surgeon has written to me with news of a serious fire… damage to the barns…death of livestock…injuries…to Lady Catherine and yourself…

But he did not mention the deaths of Collins and Michaels? Did his informant fail to mention those points?

I have been told, in some great detail, of your injuries and ensuing rescue…

Ah, there it was, the being taken to task for the indignity of being injured whilst dirtying his hands with trying to stop the fire. Father was nothing if not true to himself. Or perhaps it would be to blame him for not managing Aunt Catherine well enough to prevent her injury. Slight difference, but still very much in his character.

It is bad enough that Darcy got himself tangled up with that Bennet woman. I have been forced to admit her into my family. You cannot possibly expect me to accept another one.

He dropped the letter. What? No, that was not possible!

That conniving woman planned this, I am certain. You owe her nothing. Do you understand me? Absolutely nothing.

Do not allow her to manipulate you with the notion of compromise. It was entirely her own fault, her own actions. She took advantage of you whilst you were incapacitated. You are not responsible for that.

I know the Bennets can be devious—the man himself is nigh on intolerable. Were it not for the efficacy of his treatments to your brother, this would be the final straw, and I would dismiss him altogether. As it is, I avoid having him at my table— only makes his ambition worse. He cannot seem to understand that I am not my sister.

Be careful of the scheming wench. Anyone clever enough to make such a show is not to be underestimated. Pay her whatever is necessary to keep her quiet and send her far away. Scotland would be agreeable. Andrew has inflicted enough damage upon the family's reputation. We do not need any new addition to it …

Fitzwilliam's hand shook. Surging energy poured through every vein, every sinew, and if he did not expend it soon, it would explode. He locked the door and barred the servants' door with a chair. Now was not the time to be walked in on.

He stomped from the desk to the fireplace and back until he lost count of crossings. That surgeon would pay for this and pay dearly. But why had he written such a letter? What was to be gained from it?

Men like him did not trouble themselves simply for the amusement in it. No, there was some gain to be had—

He slammed his fist into his palm. Of course! He hated Bennet and this was too ripe a means of exacting revenge to pass up. Discrediting the daughter would not necessarily discredit the man himself, though. He would do that on his own, trying to use the situation to his own benefit.

Clever, neat, and despicable. All with so little expense or risk to his own reputation. Peters was smarter than Fitzwilliam had given him credit for.

But was he astute enough to understand the reasons when he discovered that he was no longer welcome inside the borders of Rosings Park, or when he was branded as the worst sort of gossip? A small suggestion that his local rival surgeon was a man of greater discretion and skill would make him feel the weight of what he had done.

That would indeed be entirely satisfying.

But not sufficient, not at all.

None of that would have any impact on the true victim of his machinations, Miss Bennet. After losing so much, she now stood to lose even her good name. Her father would never accept her back into his home, not after such an accusation. Darcy might take her in, probably would, he was dutiful that way. She would certainly want for nothing.

Except to be out of her sister's shadow. No doubt she wanted that as much as he wanted to be out of his brother's.

How dreadful it would be to have to live under Andrew's roof with no other choice. Elizabeth was hardly like him, to be sure, but still …

He would escape with the life she had given him back and all the possibilities it held, while she would be stripped of her future. Bloody unacceptable.

He owed her too much to turn away from her now, whether she knew she needed his help or not. Her situation was his responsibility, and he would find a remedy. Somehow, Miss Bennet would not suffer for what she had done for him.

But how? A young woman's reputation, it was said, was as brittle as it was beautiful, and once shattered, all but impossible to repair. There had to be a way.

He needed help—and he knew where to find it: Mother.

She was brilliant, utterly brilliant at such things. Father might think himself a master in society, but it was Mother's machinations that enabled his political career. Any influence he had was due to Mother's efforts. She would find a way to salvage Miss Bennet's reputation.

He reached for pen and paper.

Wait, no, this was not the sort of thing one should write in a letter. Too much discretion was required. He would have to go to Matlock.

He would not have to stay long, just a few days. His valet could pack for the journey in an hour—he could leave at dawn.

He paused just long enough to sign the letters Miss Bennet had left on his desk and leave her a brief note of explanation. Just as well she was not about. It would be difficult to explain his abrupt departure to her face without revealing too much.

She would probably be displeased that he left before totally recovered, but it would be all made up for when he returned with one of Mother's brilliant schemes in hand that would make everything right again. Miss Bennet would definitely forgive him them. Maybe even offer him one of those rare, delightful smiles of hers.

She really was very pretty when she smiled.

Before breakfast with Lady Catherine, Mary made a quick detour to the study. With any luck, Colonel Fitzwilliam would have signed the letters she had left for him, and she could get them out along with the ones she had written this morning.

The study was empty. He had been there, though. Papers were laid out, neatly, along the desk, not the way she had left them. Several journals were open and two volumes of the *Agricultural Review* were missing from the shelf. A few candle drips decorated the desktop, but no other debris had gathered. He must not have been there very long, probably late last night.

A note addressed to her lay atop the pile of letters she had penned.

Most urgent business takes me to Matlock. The entire resources of Rosings are at your disposal whilst I am gone. I expect no more than a se'nnight spent at Matlock. Assuming good weather and favorable roads, I anticipate returning within a fortnight. Pray forgive the abruptness of my journey. I shall explain everything when I return.

He would explain when he returned. How nice for him.

She fell into his too-large chair, her feet not quite reaching the floor. It should not be irritating that he would return his chair back to its rightful place, but it was.

How easy it was for him to just run off and leave the problems of Rosings Park squarely upon her shoulders. At least he had signed the necessary letters.

And he had given her a time frame in which to expect him. Nothing compelled him to do that—or to promise a full explanation when he returned. Perhaps this was his—albeit imperfect—attempt to be considerate. No doubt a man of his standing might have had little practice with such things—which should make this mean even that much more.

But what did it mean?

What could it mean?

She ran her fingertips along his handwriting. It felt no different from any letter written on good quality paper. Still though, it brought a warm flush to her cheeks.

Foolish girl!

His feelings could only be appropriate consideration and appreciation for the services she had offered him on behalf of Lady Catherine.

Of course, that was it.

Surely, that was all.

Over the next ten days, Charlotte began to leave her lying-in rooms for brief periods and Rosings settled into a predictable routine. She, Charlotte, and Lady Catherine enjoyed economical meals, taking their modest entertainments—simple games, cards, reading, and music—early in the day to save on candles. Was it wrong to take such pleasure in so quiet a lifestyle?

Michaels would have approved. It was the sort of course that would set Rosings back on its feet. A fitting memorial to him. Far more fitting than continuing to wear ill-fitting black bombazine.

She had returned the mourning gown to Parkes and resumed wearing her own familiar plain but comfortable gowns. Charlotte noticed, and disapproved but gave up the fight rather quickly. Without a wet nurse to help, most of her energies were taken up by the babies. It would be impolitic to express her gratitude for that, though.

Nuncheon had just been set out in a little-used sitting room—Mary called it the rose room because one wall, almost completely of windows, overlooked the rose garden. Mary and Charlotte had taken to sitting there in the afternoon whilst Lady Catherine and the babies napped. The windows faced full west, making it unpleasant to Lady Catherine, at least during afternoons. The intense sunlight had faded the paper hangings and upholstery to nearly white, a little stark against the dark walnut of the furniture. Perhaps that was the charm of the room, golden glows, warmth that penetrated the bones and the faded scent of roses that lingered in every corner.

Charlotte moved gingerly from the food on the sideboard –cold meats, cheeses, bread, pickles, and fruit—to the couch, balancing a full plate in her hand. Several extra pillows had been laid out for her comfort. "It seems I do nothing but eat these days."

"With two babies to feed, it is not surprising. You are not following the midwife's suggestions as to your diet, though." Mary filled her plate and followed her.

"Gruel and tea? I cannot possibly survive on that. Why would I be so hungry if I were not meant to eat?" Charlotte took a generous bite of cold chicken. "Do I look unhealthy to you?"

"No, I suppose not. And the babies are happy, so that must be a good sign."

"They are lovely, are they not?" Charlotte got a little misty-eyed.

"Have you settled on names yet?" Mary nibbled on a pickled carrot.

"He shall be named for his father, William Lucas Collins. That is an honorable name, and one which his father would have approved, I am sure."

An itchy prickle raced across the back of Mary's

neck. It was not right to think ill of the dead, but did she really have to name the boy for him? "And your daughter?"

"Catherine Anne. Do not look at me that way. It is what he would have wanted, and I cannot deny him a last wish." Charlotte shrugged and returned to her plate.

Mary pushed up from her chair, leaving her plate behind in favor of the glory of the roses through the windows. Their fresh perfume wafted through on the soft breeze.

What point in discussing the matter? Catherine Anne was a good enough name for a girl, an excellent one for an infant who was little wanted and would wither in the shadow of her all-important brother.

No. That was uncharitable and unfair. There was no assurance that Charlotte would ignore her daughter in favor of her son—and no guarantee that she would not, either. The boy's life was her guarantee of a home and an income. If there were any reason for favoritism, would that not certainly be one?

Charlotte's underlying nature was kind. Perhaps in the absence of Collins, the children would reflect her more than him. Little William might be a thoughtful and generous brother, fond of his sister and solicitous of her well-being. It was not unheard of. Darcy took excellent care of Miss Georgiana, or so Elizabeth said.

It would be years before it might be known either way. But it was a far more charitable thought to be sure.

"Miss?" Parkes appeared at the door, looking positively flabbergasted.

"What is wrong?" What new tragedy could be inflicted upon Rosings Park?

"Sir William and Lady Lucas, and Miss Claremont have arrived."

With no word of warning and with a guest? "You may show them in. Charlotte, it seems your family is impatient to greet the new arrivals."

Charlotte sputtered and stood. "What did you write in your letter to them?"

"Excuse me?"

"I should not have spoken so. Pray forgive me. I do not know what came over me." Her expression suggested her apology was somewhat less than sincere

"You asked me to write those letters for you, and refused to read them before they were posted."

Charlotte stared at her hands. "You are right of course."

Yes, she was. But no point in belaboring that issue.

A stout, ruddy man in a tight cravat and a woman who looked like she belonged with him shuffled in. A young woman, in a pale muslin dress followed in their wake.

"Sir William, Lady Lucas, and their niece, Miss Claremont." Parkes curtsied and ducked away.

"Oh, my dear Charlotte!" Lady Lucas rushed past Mary to clasp Charlotte's hands. "Imagine our surprise to hear you had already been delivered!"

Sir William bowed to Mary. "We had only just written to Mr. Collins to tell him of our plans to be here a fortnight before the … ah … expected events."

"I had no idea." Mary cocked her head at Charlotte. Slapping her forehead would be in poor taste. So would rolling her eyes. "We are so glad you have come. You are welcome to stay here at Rosings to be near Charlotte."

"Are you sure? Colonel Fitzwilliam is not here—"

"He has authorized me to offer such an invitation in his absence." Her voice was probably a touch more severe than it had to be, but really, Charlotte was being most vexing.

"We are most honored." Sir William bowed again.

Heavens, he had an alarming similarity to Mr. Collins.

"If you will excuse me, I shall have rooms made ready." Mary curtsied and slipped out.

With Parkes' assistance, she assigned the Lucases and Miss Claremont chambers at the farthest end of the guest wing near Charlotte's lying in room and well away from Lady Catherine.

Of course, Lady Catherine would be all perverse surprise and randomness: today she was calm and relatively lucid. She was certain she had written to the Lucases herself and invited them to come and visit. It was right and proper that they should be at Rosings and even more pleasing that they brought along Mrs. Collins' younger cousin. No doubt it would be a most improving experience for Miss Claremont.

Who was she to question her good fortune? One must relish it when it came.

Dinner was held in the somewhat dimly lit small dining room with Lady Catherine commanding the event from the head of the table. How happy and in her element she seemed, gold silk taffeta rustling and ostrich plume bobbing over her head.

Sir William sat beside her, at her behest, privy to the bulk of her conversation. His similarities to Mr. Collins actually seemed to soothe Lady Catherine's nerves, and the good man had judgment enough not to correct her when she twice slipped and referred to him as Mr. Collins. The Lucases also failed to comment upon the misnamed dishes on the table. One might wonder if they even noticed that it was mutton, not venison on their plates. Or perhaps they were just naturally very gracious.

Either way, it seemed a good thing that they had come.

Miss Claremont, sitting between Mary and Charlotte, was in too much awe of Lady Catherine to notice much. Poor girl kept reciting Lady Catherine's advice under her breath, probably in hopes she would not forget it, just as Lady Catherine admonished.

Why Charlotte had married Mr. Collins had always been something of a mystery, but now it made more sense, if only just a bit.

Lady Catherine fell asleep in the gold parlor shortly after they withdrew, but Charlotte and her family were tired too, so it was just as well that they all tiptoed out and retired early.

Except Mary.

With Mrs. Jenkinson's help, she put Lady Catherine to bed and wandered, candles in hand, into the study, now well-ordered and presentable. How many hours had she spent in that room recently—not just tidying it, but working there? One might think too many, but they had been purposeful hours when she had felt useful and needed.

She peered at the desk and the bookcase behind it. So much work yet to be done. Journal entries needed to be made and checked in several different accounts in the red, green and blue bound notebooks lined up exactly behind the desk chair. It probably would not hurt to read the newest edition of the *Agricultural Review;* the one Fitzwilliam had left behind, just to the journals' right. Not exactly touted as feminine reading material, but considering autumn harvests were not that many weeks away, it could prove essential to understanding Mr. Michaels' plans.

But first, she should deal with the post already piling up on the desk, at least the business letters and those addressed to Michaels. Personal correspondence she would avoid.

She scooped up the letters, lit several candles on the mantle, and settled into a wingback chair near the fire to open the one in Fitzwilliam's handwriting.

M,

Did that stand for Michaels, or perhaps Mary? What a silly reason to smile, but there it was, and little she could do for it.

Those I needed to speak to have been away and the weather conspires against me. I will be delayed another fortnight.

F

She folded the letter into its original creases and returned it to the small pile. It was unfortunate, but such delays happened all the time. They were nothing to be upset by. Certainly nothing to take personally— and he had written to tell her, a consideration Michaels had never offered her. She closed her eyes and leaned her head back.

It was not as though there was urgent business here for him to accomplish. The farm could continue as it was until harvest time. She could tend to what was needed in the meantime. Besides, his return would probably mean a disturbance in their quiet routine. How pleasant it would be to hold onto it a little while longer.

Still though, his opinions on the Lucases would be

fascinating to hear. He would most likely deem Sir William ridiculous. If nothing else, he would find a way to draw some kind of interesting conversation out of them. At least, Miss Claremont would laugh at his good humor and stop her incessant stammering at Lady Catherine's presence. Fitzwilliam was good at making people feel at ease, welcome in his presence— a skill she totally lacked. A gentlemanly trait to be sure.

And he did play a mean game of commerce, particularly now when confits were all he was permitted to bet. Somehow the lower stakes meant he had to increase the general level of hilarity, and he did it admirably. Though as a rule she did not like cards, commerce with him was an exception. A trip to the confectioner for more confits would be necessary before he returned.

How empty Rosings felt without him.

Well, he would be back soon enough, back to his old tricks. Running roughshod over preferences and doing whatever he pleased.

Until then, though, it would be rather lonely.

﹇ Chapter 11

RAIN—TORRENTIAL, DELUGING rain—started on his second day out, delaying his arrival at Matlock by several days. Just enough that he managed to miss Lord and Lady Matlock's departure to Pemberley by six hours.

Under other circumstances, he would have simply continued on to meet them there. Spending time alone with Andrew held little appeal. Decidedly little. But his valet had been right when he had suggested that perhaps Fitzwilliam might not be up to the rigors of travel just yet.

By the time he reached Matlock manor, a racking cough had settled in his chest and a persistent fever set every muscle in his body to aching. A solid night's rest would bring him to rights. He could be on the road the next morning.

Or not.

Three days later, Andrew sauntered into his room, still gaunt as a broomstick. Midmorning sunlight highlighted the hair that stuck out like dry straw. His color was—well whatever it was, was not quite right. Still though, it was far and away an improvement from before Bennet began treating him. That in itself was a little frightening.

"So, the conquering hero has deigned to return to his ancestral home." Andrew pulled a small chair across the dark carpet alongside Fitzwilliam's bed and dropped into it backwards, dangling his arms over the scrollwork wooden back. He must not have fully regained his strength; he chose the smallest, lightest chair in the chamber.

The room had not changed much since Fitzwilliam had officially taken up residence at Rosings Park. Naturally mother would have not had the time to arrange for the deep blue walls to be painted some fresher color. But, she had talked about changing the worn gold wool drapes with tiny moth holes and fraying fringe for something smarter, and removing some of the scarred furniture to lesser guest rooms. Apparently she did not want the family reminded of the scuffles he had with his brother in that room. Maybe sentimentality had overwhelmed her redecorating fervor, as neither of those projects had been accomplished.

"I expected you would prefer to keep to your own estate, now you are master of Rosings Park." He cocked his head and lifted his brow, but something in his eyes—

Fitzwilliam propped himself up on his elbows and pulled several extra pillows—lovely down ones—under his shoulders. "You do not like that I am now a landed gentleman."

Gaunt shoulders shrugged as sparse eyebrows rose. "The idea does take a bit of getting used to."

"My having Rosings takes nothing away from you." Unless one considered being the only landed Matlock offspring among Andrew's possessions. He leaned back into the pillows. At least they welcomed him.

"It was surprising to learn Anne's will named you as heir." Andrew's lip curled back revealing stained and missing teeth.

What was that supposed to mean? He sucked in as deep a breath as his aching lungs allowed— Oh, Andrew's breath was foul!— and held it until the urge to voice sharp words passed. "She never said anything to me of it. I should have thought it would to go to one of her de Bourgh cousins."

"Rightfully it should have. Absolutely. For an estate to leave the family hands—it is a disgrace."

Fitzwilliam scooted higher in the bed. "It sounds as though you begrudge me this opportunity to establish myself."

"It is not what you were raised for. The army was always your destiny. I find it odd that you would abandon it so easily."

"My destiny has always been to linger around as a spare in case your plans of self-destruction finally came to fruition."

Andrew laughed—bitter and hoarse. "Always so touchy, little brother. Such a hot-head. It is no wonder Father shipped you out to the army. You would have made fools of us all had you gone into the church."

As if Andrew had not already done so himself.

"Why are you here?"

"I think the more relevant question, is why have you come? I have heard some very interesting rumors—"

"None of your concern." Fitzwilliam struggled to sit up. The dizziness passed quickly. That was a good sign.

"So it is true. You did get yourself tangled in a compromise and now you are going to seek Father's help out of the situation. The one thing you promised you would never do—ask Father to bail you out of unpleasant circumstances. Yet here you are." Andrew leaned back and stretched his long legs, trousers hanging loosely from them.

"You have no idea of what you are talking about."

"Perhaps not. But, I thought it only fair to warn you; Bennet is coming today. I am sure he will demand an audience."

Fitzwilliam clutched his temples. "Turn him away. I have no wish to see him."

"And deny myself the entertainment? I hardly think so. You think yourself so clever where women are concerned, to have never caught yourself in a scandal. And so damn proud of it. I shall enjoy this very much."

"Get out."

Andrew laughed the same derisive cackle he had always used to remind Fitzwilliam of all the privileges of the eldest son.

Fitzwilliam swung out of bed and towered over him. Even in the grips of a fever, he could best Andrew physically. And he would.

"Truly, Fitz? You would—"

He reached for Andrew's arm. "Get out, now, or I

shall help you out."

Andrew pulled away and raised his hands. "So touchy, little brother. So sensitive. You used to be able to take a joke." He ambled toward the door. "Enjoy your audience with Bennet."

The door banged shut behind him.

Fitzwilliam rang for his valet and staggered for his clothes. If he could stand, he could get himself in a carriage. That would be enough. Elizabeth would surely allow him to recuperate at Pemberley in peace.

A double knock at the door—why was his valet knocking?

"Come."

"Mr. Bennet, sir." His valet tried to stand in the doorway blocking the entrance.

Bennet, in a fine black suit, white silk cravat, and mantle of self-righteousness, shouldered his way in. "Colonel."

"I do not recall inviting you in. You may leave." He turned his back on Bennet and nodded at his valet. "Pack my things. I wish to leave for Pemberley immediately."

"I believe we have business to discuss, Colonel." Bennet stood between Fitzwilliam and his valet and folded his arms over his chest.

Pompous, arrogant fool. Did he think that indignant posturing meant anything?

"I have nothing to discuss with you."

"I must insist. You have compromised my daughter. I intend to see reparations made." Was that a predatory look in Bennet's eyes?

"You daughter is not compromised."

"That is not how I understand it. I have had letters from Peters at Rosings. You mean to tell me you did not kiss her, soundly and publicly, after you were pulled from the remains of the burning barn?"

Fitzwilliam laughed so hard that it turned into a coughing spasm. "Hardly."

"But you were seen by many in an intimate embrace."

"You daughter breathed life into my unconscious body, sir. That is hardly an intimate embrace."

"I hardly know anything more intimate than the creation—or restoration—of life." His brows twitched in a far too suggestive way.

He deserved to be shaken. One more remark like that, and he would be.

"As I understand, it was something she learned from you."

"I assure you, I have taught my daughters nothing of the sort."

"Then your daughter is a particularly brilliant woman. I am alive today because of her intervention."

Bennet smiled as though he had just gained an advantage. "Even more reason why you should be concerned with the great harm you have enacted upon her. What will become of her now? It was not as if she was highly marriageable before. Now, having lost her betrothed and her reputation, what will become of her?"

"She could live with you."

"I have an unmarried girl yet at home, I can hardly risk her prospects for a wayward daughter." Bennet lifted an open hand.

"Wayward? You call her wayward?" Fitzwilliam clenched his fists—better to clench them than use them, at least for the moment.

Bennet shrugged. "What amends will you offer her?"

"What do you want me to offer her?"

"Certainly not marriage, if that is what concerns you. With the state of Rosings, you cannot throw yourself away upon a plain, penniless girl. You need an heiress—I full well understand that. Mary's needs are simple enough. A few hundred pounds a year would set her up for life and adequately compensate her ruination."

That amount would be enough to allow her to support her unmarried sister and mother, too. How convenient for Bennet. Bloody bastard.

"She is not ruined!" Fitzwilliam stomped. Too bad he was not wearing his boots. It would have been a far more impressive show.

"Would that the rest of the world agreed with you, sir. It would be far better for us all. But that is hardly the world we live in. Is it now? If not to her, you owe it to Darcy to make it right."

"How is Darcy to be affected by any of this?" Did the man have no shame?

"His wife is Mary's sister. She would be distressed by her sister's fall, and by extension, he."

"So now I owe it to Darcy to make an offer—"

Bennet drove his fist into his palm. "I have told you already no one expects you to marry the girl. Just see to it she is not a burden to anyone! You owe us that."

"Get out."

"Excuse me?"

"Get out. Go attend my brother if you will, but get from my chambers. Never impose your company on me again, or I will set the footmen on you."

"Good day, then." Bennet straightened his lapels and sauntered out as though leaving of his own accord.

Utterly insufferable—he was no gentleman. It was truly a testament to Miss Bennet's character that she was absolutely nothing like her father.

After saving his life, she deserved more than to be sent away into the country somewhere to live the life of an unwelcome spinster, banished from all good society.

There had to be another answer. If Mother did not have one, then perhaps Darcy and Elizabeth would. He would see them this afternoon.

But perhaps just a brief lie down first, just to regain his equanimity.

The brief respite became several more days spent abed with his valet stationed at the door to repel unwanted guests. On the fourth day, he emerged near dawn, strong enough, at last, to continue on to Pemberley, with only a misty fog to hamper his travels.

He arrived at Pemberley before breakfast, nerves tense and plucked thin, as though ready for battle.

Mrs. Reynolds greeted him at the great paneled mahogany door. The woman was tiny, but a force of nature to be reckoned with. Fortunately, he enjoyed the woman's favor. She promised to bring Darcy word of his arrival. He would call upon Darcy soon, but first, he had to talk to Mother.

She was an early riser and liked to walk in the morning. A creature of habit, she had her favorite paths at Pemberley. With any luck, he would be able to intercept her on one of those for a private discussion. No doubt she had been mulling over his situation for days now and would have sorted it all out. She always did, for his sisters, for Andrew, even for Father. She would not fail him.

A light rain fell in a soft grey mist. Mother would probably prefer the east walking path through the old hardwoods. The canopy would afford a little defense from the rain. He hurried off toward the woods.

A mix of sand and loam muffled his brisk footsteps as the densely overhung footpath welcomed him. Tiny raindrops pattered on the sheltering leaves, imposing on the trail's normal quietude. They apologized with a fresh green smell that reminded him of early spring. The entire scene bore a great deal of similarity to Rosings' haunted path, without the tumble-down shack, well-spring and ghost stories to make it irresistible to young boys. Still though, these woods somehow felt more mature, even serious.

"Colonel?" Elizabeth approached him, the shoulders of her rust-colored spencer glittering with a fine coating of mist. The edge of her matching bonnet was framed with pearly raindrops

"Good morning." He bowed. "Have I not asked you to call me Richard?"

"Indeed you have." She paused alongside him, looking up with a not-quite smile in her eyes.

He gestured down the narrow trail and they continued on, falling easily into step with one another. Her skirts swished in time with their steps.

"I cannot tell you how pleased we are to find you in a far better state than we were led to expect."

"Peters wrote to you, too?"

"It seems he was a rather active correspondent." She cocked her head and quirked an eyebrow, probing, not quite demanding. Yet.

"So it seems. He corresponded with your father and my parents as well."

"Your parents came to compare notes with us. I do not think they were impressed with what my father had to say to them about the situation."

"I had the pleasure of his company at Matlock before I left." He laced his hands behind his back.

"We all have relations whom we would rather not have credited to our accounts." Elizabeth laughed. How much she sounded like her sister. They looked a bit alike too, particularly around the eyes.

"To be fair, the transformation in my brother is rather remarkable. Granted, he was still more wraith than man, but it was a dramatic improvement."

"Lady Matlock has mentioned something similar. I am glad for your family. How is Mary?"

"A paragon of virtue. Truly, she has been indispensable. She is uniquely able to manage Aunt Catherine. The entire household depends upon her."

"Mr. Peters said that she had been injured?"

"She suffered burns, but has had a good recovery, as far as I know. I am ever in her debt, as they were acquired in her efforts to rescue myself and my aunt."

"So what Mr. Peters says is true?" Her voice thinned and tightened—the sound of dread.

"That she breathed life into me when I was at death's door?"

"That her reputation …"

"That is what I am told as well, though little word of that has been spoken at Rosings. There she is far too well-respected—and necessary—for anyone to dare speak against her. I do hope to have remedy for the matter soon."

She chewed her lower lip. "A remedy? There are

few ways in which a young lady's reputation can be repaired. Darcy and I will—"

"No. I appreciate the offer, but this matter is not Darcy's …"

"Richard!"

The hair on the back of his neck rose—a childhood reflex.

"Good morning, Lady Matlock." Elizabeth curtsied, but there was a subtle edge to her voice.

"I am hardly surprised to find you treading Lady Anne's favorite paths. It seems only fitting that you should enjoy them as well as she." Mother approached with all the grace and confidence—and none of the easy comfort—that Elizabeth carried. She wore a fashionable walking ensemble in silver-blue that matched the gloomy skies. Matching her clothes to the clouds was exactly the sort of thing that Mother might do. But the feathered affair she wore on her head was a poor choice, the misty rain left the feathers droopy and plastered against her head.

"Indeed, I find them very pleasing. I am grateful to find our tastes so similar." Tight little lines formed alongside Elizabeth's eyes.

Mother strode toward them and slipped her hand into the crook of his arm. "Will you forgive me, dear? My sister's condition is so complex—it is scarcely something that can be conveyed in infrequent letters. There is a great deal my son and I need to speak of."

"Of course, I understand. Do excuse me." Elizabeth curtsied and turned away, not surrendering any of her confidence to Lady Matlock. Few women could survive an encounter with Mother so unscathed.

A little of the tension slipped away as Elizabeth disappeared around a sharp bend.

Mother sniffed. "Well, I will confess that Catherine was entirely wrong. Miss Bennet—"

"Mrs. Darcy."

She cleared her throat. "Mrs. Darcy has not polluted the shades of Pemberley after all. She has wisely made very few changes to the house or the grounds. I am sure it was Darcy's suggestion that she keep things the way dear Anne settled them, but it is to the girl's credit that she would listen to advice."

As catty as it all sounded, Mother really was bordering on absolutely cordial—for her anyway. It was equally clear, though, Elizabeth's standards of cordiality were a little different, and she did not appreciate Mother's efforts nearly as much.

Mother tugged his arm, and they set off in the opposite direction from Elizabeth.

"I have heard Catherine is not improving and is not likely to." She harrumphed under her breath. "She always has been so high-strung. We have warned her all her life that giving in to such extreme sensibilities would come back to plague her. Moderation is the thing. But did she listen? Can you ever imagine Catherine listening to anything she did not wish to hear? I am told that some become docile in their dotage. It somehow does not surprise me that my sister would have none of it."

He snorted and bit his tongue. It was one thing for Mother to disparage Aunt Catherine, but quite another for him to do so.

"However, Catherine's situation is not what I wish to talk about. We have far more serious circumstances facing us right now. You received your father's letter, no doubt?"

Excellent, excellent! It was as he hoped. She had thought out the matter. His answer was moments away. "I did. I confess I am all astonishment at it. I have heard no word spoken of it." At least no word spoken openly.

"I suppose that is a good thing, all things considered. It would be best to contain this as much as possible. First, I must know, is the report true?"

"That Miss Bennet saved my life, yes, that is entirely true."

"And she used that means by which to do it?" Mother turned on him that look of scrutiny he often suffered as a boy.

He grumbled under his breath. "I was not conscious at the time, so I do not have firsthand knowledge of the event, but the housekeeper tells me that it is so."

"That is unfortunate."

He turned his face away and rolled his eyes. "Thank you ever so much."

She slapped his arm—his burned arm. "You will not take that tone or that expression with me. I will not have it."

He pulled his arm away from hers. "And I would thank you to not to harass burns that are still healing."

She gasped and stared at him, jaw gaping. "I had no idea." At least she had some shame. "So then, the girl has compromised herself."

"Her name is Miss Bennet, and I would thank you to use it. She is after all, Darcy's sister now."

She brushed the thought away. "I am loath to admit the connection. The father is a horrid creature."

"He refreshed my memory whilst I was at Matlock."

"I can only image what he had to say to you. What did he demand?"

"That I set her up with some yearly sum, far away from Kent."

She heaved a deep sigh and stared into the dripping, leafy canopy, squinting as droplets hit her cheeks. "I am thankful to hear it. He has so much audacity in him, I was certain he would insist you marry the chit."

He stopped and stood before her, towering over her. "Let us be entirely clear on this point, Mother. Miss Mary Bennet is no chit. She is everything that is proper and admirable in a woman."

She smiled a tight, sarcastic smile. "Which is why she compromised herself."

"In order to save my life. Why does that point seem lost on everyone? Or is it only of significance to me?"

"Do not be so dramatic. I would have thought you far beyond that."

"Do you really consider my life and breath such a trivial thing?"

"Now you are being just silly. I will not dignify that with an answer."

How very dear.

"In any case, it is good that Bennet has not set his sights to try to wrangle a marriage out of this."

"No, he did not."

But perhaps he should have.

His jaw dropped. Why had the thought not come to him before? Perhaps he was as dull as Father had always accused him of being. Marriage would indeed solve this issue. If she would have him.

How had that not been his first thought?

"Even he realizes you must have an heiress. That is the only solution for Rosings."

It was a solution, admittedly one he had often thought of, but hardly the only one. "Darcy and my steward suggested economy and updated farming techniques."

The corner of her lips pulled back. How she resembled Andrew when she did that. "Of course, he would suggest that. But he has never faced the realities of debt. Those kinds of solutions always sound better to those who are not in the midst of such trying times."

"Is that your way of saying that they take too long?"

"A decade is a long time to live like a pauper."

"Even with the late steward's plans of economy, I would hardly suggest I am living like a pauper."

"But certainly not in the standard to which you are accustomed."

Was that a challenge in her eyes? Did she think him unable to endure privation? "It is far and away better than the way we lived on the continent."

"Do be reasonable, Richard. Pray, just once. This is far too important to be ridiculous about." She pressed his uninjured arm.

"Should I not be the determinant of what is an unacceptable way for me to live?"

"Whether or not you like it, society has a great deal to say about it. An heiress, particularly one whose family is prepared to turn her fortune over in total at the time of the marriage, will solve everything. I have taken the liberty of exploring the marriage mart, and I have discovered several young women who would fit the need rather nicely. There are three whose fortunes exceed Rosings' debt and who are from merchant families anxious for connections to an old and landed family. They all have brothers who could benefit by the association with the Matlock name. One of them should prove agreeable enough. I think we could have the matter settled by Christmastime—a lovely time to plan a wedding."

"You have a wedding already planned on my behalf? How thoughtful." How controlling. Just like every other aspect of his life she thought she could manage.

"Just settle the issue at hand as cheaply as possible, and I will arrange for the introductions."

He grunted, rather more loudly than he had intended.

"I am only being practical. The less you spend on Miss Mary Bennet, the better. But if necessary, your father is prepared to step in and help. How much do you think it will require to send her away to some corner of the kingdom, never to be mentioned again? Her father suggested a few hundred pounds a year?"

He raked his hair. "That will not do at all."

"You think you owe her more? Yes, you are grateful for her saving your life. But really, you would hardly pay a surgeon more for the same service."

"But he would be benefited by having done so, and his career improved for it. The same cannot be said for her."

"You are really far too sentimental. It will not serve you well."

"And if I do not wish to send her away?"

"It sounds as if you have some attachment to her."
She chewed the inside of her cheek, lips pursed to
one side. Her planning face. "That changes things. I
suppose you will need to set her up nearby and keep
her under your protection. That will be more expensive to be sure, but it can be done. If you have
developed some fondness for the girl, it would be acceptable. And perhaps, it would be less expensive
than other similar diversions. It is not the first time
you have talked of setting a woman up that way—
What is wrong? The look on your face—I do not like
it at all. What are you thinking, Richard?"

"I never considered taking her as a mistress."

"No! You cannot mean to marry her! It was entirely bad enough to have Darcy marry an unconnected
woman with no fortune and little beauty. But he
could afford it. You cannot. I absolutely forbid it."
She stopped short, hands on her hips.

He was not a small boy anymore, whether she understood it or not. "I will do just that. I am a fool for
not thinking of it myself—utterly and completely a
fool. It is exactly the answer I needed."

She grabbed his forearms and shook them. "Un-
questionably not! Your father will prohibit it. You can
expect no help from him if you pursue such a ridiculous venture. It will ruin you, ruin Rosings. What will
be left for your sons?"

Was that a ray of sun piercing the clouds and
branches to shine on him? Probably not, but it
seemed as though there should be one. "I do not intend to ask Father's help. I never did."

"Darcy is not in favor of such a match either. We
have discussed it at length."

"So, you came here to discuss my problems with

him and solve them without any involvement on my part."

"Clearly you are well beyond both your expertise and your means."

He turned so sharply, his heel dug into the soft ground.

"Do not turn your back on me. Where do you think are you going?"

"Away from here." He stormed away.

"You are acting like a child. Come back here!"

At least she had given him the answer that he had come for. He should have seen it himself—it was so clear. So bloody, astoundingly clear!

She was the elusive, impossible woman he had always desired, fiery and practical, an ethereal beauty with wit, temper, and tenacity, who would not wither before him. What good was an heiress when there was such a woman? How could he have failed to see it?

But now that he did, not even Darcy best dare stand in his way.

Chapter 12

AN UNEVENTFUL FORTNIGHT passed in the Lucases'
company. It seemed the whole family was as quiet
and retiring as Charlotte. Even Lady Catherine improved in their presence, readily employing herself in
the improvement of Miss Claremont, who relished
the attention.

Perhaps it was the Lucases' propensity to routine.
They naturally did everything at the same time every
day without looking at a clock. Even the babies fell
into a schedule quickly. The house radiated a calm,
quietude that might grow dull over the long term, but
for now, was a needed relief from the intensity of the
prior month.

At exactly ten o'clock, all the Lucas clan descended
the grand stairs in the same order they paraded in every day on their trek to the spacious morning room.
They sat in exactly the same order around the round
table: Charlotte with the windows on her right where
the light was best for sewing, her mother on her left.

They skipped a chair—ostensibly for Lady Catherine—then Sir William and Miss Claremont near the inlaid sideboard where breakfast was laid out on silver and china serving dishes, wafting tempting fresh-baked scents through the room. The three ladies requested chocolate while Sir William preferred tea. They all liked toast, very brown, with jam and clotted cream. Though the routine was soothing, it also bordered on the ridiculous.

Mary sipped her coffee—a bad habit definitely gleaned from Colonel Fitzwilliam—enjoying a friendly sunbeam that insisted on making its way past the curtains. Dust motes played along its length, a romping sort of game, like children in the spring fields, too long cooped up over winter.

Much like Charlotte. She had recovered well from her travails and was growing impatient to be out and about once again. It was nearing time for her churching. Perhaps she should call upon Mr. Anderson who had been filling in for Mr. Collins.

Or should they wait until Colonel Fitzwilliam returned?

She chuckled at herself. Why would he be interested in such a thing? Conceivably, if it were his wife, but for a guest? No, he would just as soon have the matter handled decently and without him.

"What do you think, Miss Bennet?"

Mary jumped and blinked. What had Sir William just asked?

"Woolgathering, Mary?" Charlotte snickered, settling her chocolate cup into its saucer with a soft clink. "But no, I know you better. You were planning something—you always are. Papa wanted to know your thoughts on his ideas."

Sir William cleared his throat. "Ah yes, we had been discussing Charlotte's future, you see. Rosings is quite lovely, and the hospitality has been truly grand, but mayhap, it seems that we are approaching the time, I think, if you agree—"

Mary bit her lip. Interrupting him would not make him get to the point any faster. She had tried.

Lady Lucas laid her hand on his wrist. "I believe what my husband is trying to say is that it seems we are near the end of Charlotte's confinement. We do not wish to trespass upon Rosings' cordiality. Longbourn is ready to receive its new family."

"Are the babies not very young to make such a journey?" Mary refilled her coffee cup.

"It is only eight hours by carriage." Charlotte murmured, a little defensively. "With my mother and cousin to help I think it will be quite manageable. Mrs. Grant suggests that the babies should be strong enough for traveling in another fortnight or so."

"Shall I speak to the vicar to see you churched before you go?"

Charlotte laughed. "That is what you were planning, was it not?"

Sir William chuckled low in his belly. "She is just as you say, Charlotte. What is the saying? Still waters run deep?"

"You will be greatly missed." It was entirely true. Charlotte was the last real friend she had at Rosings, other than Fitzwilliam of course.

When had she started thinking of him as a friend? He was though. One of a precious few with a glimpse into who she really was.

"About that…" Charlotte glanced at Lady Lucas who blinked at Sir William.

"Yes, with regards to that. We were discussing, that is, we talked amongst ourselves. The question came about ..."

Lady Lucas tapped his hand. "Though Lucas Lodge is not far from Longbourn, Charlotte will be there all alone. We thought that, perhaps, given the circumstances here, you might like to join her."

"Live at Longbourn?"

Charlotte nodded a bit too vigorously. "Yes, exactly. I have come to depend upon your company so much over the last months. I do not know what I shall do without you—"

"Without Miss Bennet?" Lady Catherine swept into the room, a fury of icy blue taffeta and feathers.

Dressed for evening first thing in the morning? This could turn bad, very quickly.

Mary jumped up and took Lady Catherine's arm. Mrs. Jenkinson cowered behind Lady Catherine, like a dog that had just been kicked.

"Would you like a cup of tea, Lady Catherine, or coffee? I can get you wine if you prefer." Mary ushered her toward her favorite chair.

Lady Catherine yanked her arm out of Mary's grasp. "Why would I want tea or coffee? This is not the drawing room. Why is dinner being served in the morning room? Where is Parkes? Surely she is going mad."

"I shall see you have some wine, then." Mary waved Mrs. Jenkinson into action. "Pray sit down. The sun ... sunset ... is most agreeable."

"I do not wish to sit. Why do I care about the sun? What I want to know is what you were talking about? I must have my share of the conversation."

Mary sent the Lucases a warning glance. "Churching, Lady Catherine. We were discussing churching."

"Whatever for?"

"Charlotte, your ladyship." Lady Lucas hovered between sitting and standing.

"Why? Are you increasing?" Lady Catherine rapped the table hard enough to rattle the china.

"Ah, your ladyship …" Sir William straightened his labels as he rose.

Mary gestured for him to sit. "We were simply discussing the practice."

"Should not Mr. Collins be a part of the discussion then? Is it not his job? Where is he? He knows better than to be late for dinner. I have told him most strenuously. It is abhorrently rude to be late. I insist on knowing where he is!"

Charlotte pressed the back of her hand to her mouth.

"He is away at present." Mary took her arm again.

"I did not give him leave to travel. Why is he gone? He should be attending to his duties. I have not given him permission."

"This trip … it is in relation with … a service he has done on your behalf." Mary bit her lip.

"When? I did not authorize—" Her eyes narrowed. "You are lying to me, Miss Bennet!"

"No—"

"Yes, you are. This is about that estate, Longfarm, the one I did not give him permission to inherit!"

The Lucases gasped and huddled closer together.

"You see, it is! How dare you conspire to conceal things from me? I always know. I am always right, you know." She snatched a napkin from the table, sending silverware flying.

"Here is your wine, your ladyship." Mrs. Jenkinson offered the glass to Lady Catherine.

"I do not care for wine!" She flung it at Mrs. Jenkinson who shrieked as it hit her face.

"Would you care for something to eat instead?" Mary shooed Mrs. Jenkinson out of the room.

"No food! No wine! I want answers!"

"Pray ask your questions, Lady Catherine." Mary stood in front of her. If she could hold Lady Catherine's focus on herself, there was a chance she might yet regain composure.

"Has Mr. Collins inherited an estate?"

"Yes, he has." Mary dropped her voice to nearly a whisper.

"I want to talk to him. Where is he?"

"He is away on a long journey. You may write to him."

"I do not wish to write. I would see him immediately. Is he visiting that damned estate?"

"No, madam, he is not."

"Good. Good." Lady Catherine relaxed a little and allowed Mary to help her sit. "Then you will write to him. Tell him he is not to do so. I will not have him leaving his post here. I appointed him to the Hunsford Parish, and here he shall stay. He has no business going elsewhere."

"I will write to him as you ask, your ladyship."

"See that it is done today. You are a lazy girl. I do not want you dawdling!"

"As you say, madam." Mary exhaled a long, slow breath.

"And you," Lady Catherine whirled on Charlotte. "You will satisfy me at once. Are you increasing?"

"No, your ladyship." Charlotte shook her head, ghostly pale.

"Good, good. I did not give you leave to do so. Children are inconvenient, bothersome little creatures. Collins has no need for an heir. What has he to pass on? A vicar has nothing of his own. And his income is small. Best not waste it on the raising of children."

Sir William and Lady Lucas turned to one another with wide eyes.

"You look tired, your ladyship. Do you wish to rest before dinner?"

Lady Catherine planted her elbow on the table, hard. "I do not wish to rest, I demand satisfaction! I heard something said about you going somewhere, Miss Bennet? I will not have it, not at all. I have not authorized that, and it will not be. Nor you, Mrs. Collins. Your place is in the parsonage. A house is never well-maintained without a woman present."

"Of course, your ladyship," Charlotte stammered.

"Good ... good." Lady Catherine leaned back in her seat, breathing heavily.

"Perhaps you should rest, madam. You wish to be at your best for your guests, do you not?" Mary reached for her.

"I am very weary."

"Let me help you to your room." Mary tucked her hand under Lady Catherine's arm and helped her up.

Lady Catherine insisted on a tour of the gardens and the stillroom before they finally made it to her chambers. Mary barely got Lady Catherine into her bed before she fell asleep.

Thank heavens for small mercies.

Mary shut Lady Catherine's door behind her and braced hard against it. Someone should sit with Lady Catherine. Where was Mrs. Jenkinson?

"Miss Bennet?" Parkes held out a letter. "The post just came. Since this was addressed to you, I thought you would want it directly."

That was Elizabeth's hand! "Yes, yes, thank you." She took the letter and hurried to her sitting-room-turned-office and shut the door. That was usually enough to ensure a little privacy.

She pulled one of the armchairs a little closer to the window and curled up in its soft blue embrace. A fresh bowl of flowers, roses this time, graced the table nearby. Exactly the right scent to accompany a letter from Elizabeth. Though Elizabeth preferred lavender, it was roses that reminded Mary of her.

How long had it been since Elizabeth's last letter? So much had happened, it seemed a lifetime ago.

My dear sister,

Such news has reached me! I hardly understand it all, much less know what to say. We have heard of the tragedies at Rosings. Is it true—and I fear that it must be—that Mr. Michaels has been lost? And Mr. Collins as well?

Mary pressed the letter to her chest until the burning in her eyes passed.

The unspoken admonition stung, but Elizabeth was correct. She should have written to them of the news much sooner. Had Fitzwilliam sent them word?

Should what I fear be true, then you have my deepest condolences, my dear sister. Mr. Michaels was the best of men, and his loss will be deeply felt. Pray offer our condolences to Mrs.

Collins as well. I am certain she is near her time now, which must surely make this situation worse.

No doubt, Mrs. Collins will be returning to her parents' home soon. I am worried what you will do then. Where will you go?

Mr. Darcy and I have discussed the matter at length, and I want you to know, regardless of everything else, you will always have a home with us. You will be welcome at Pemberley and Darcy House whenever you wish and for however long you desire.

Everything else? What everything else? Discussed it at length? What could require a lengthy discussion?

I must ask you, though. Is it true, what we have heard? If it is, I know Darcy shall be most put out with Fitzwilliam, and I as well. We trusted him with you at Hunsford and it will be hard to forgive him.

Of what? Forgive him for what?

Her heart thundered in her ears, shaking her hands so hard it was difficult to read.

We heard that Fitzwilliam was injured in the fire and that you were part of his rescue. While I can believe in your courage and strength to do so, imagine my wonder when I heard that in the process you were compromised by giving him the kiss of life.

Cold spread from her face and coursed through her body. Compromised? Who would have spread such gossip? But then, this was Rosings—there were any number of persons who had crossed paths with Lady Catherine, or even with her father, who would bear grudge enough to do so.

Compromised!

Darcy and I are convinced that you are innocent of any

wrongdoing. Utterly and completely. I have no doubt that Fitz-william owes his life to your quick intervention and for that we are grateful.

But now, what must be done for you? I have heard some insist that a marriage between you two is the only solution.

That sounded like something Father would say.

I am not blind to Fitzwilliam's nature, as fond as Darcy and I are of him. I would not have you marry to satisfy the machinations of the gossips. You do not deserve to be tied to someone so wholly incompatible…

They were not at all incompatible.

No wonder he stayed away.

A chill snaked down her back, burrowing into her heart. She was compromised, and he knew it. Any further association with her would affect his chances of marrying the heiress he so needed. So, he kept away.

A soft rap at the door make her look up. She dabbed her skirt over her eyes. "Yes, come in."

Charlotte slipped in. "Is Lady Catherine—"

"She sleeps now. I expect her to sleep a good deal of the day." Mary folded Elizabeth's letter and tucked it up her sleeve.

Charlotte nodded and perched on the sofa near Mary, not quite making eye contact. "My parents, they are unsettled by her outburst. They fear it might be dangerous if she hears or sees the babies."

"I understand. It is difficult to know how she will react moment by moment. We can put a footman in the hall—"

Charlotte threw up open hands. "No. I think it is time for us to go. My parents want to leave in the morning, early. That will have us in Meryton by after-noon."

"Of course. I understand."

"Pray, come with us." She touched Mary's arm. "I worry for you when Colonel Fitzwilliam returns. You will be alone in the house with him …"

That was hardly likely now. Mary bit her lip. Just how tightly could her insides knot before they pulled her into a taut little ball?

"You have no obligation here, and really, you must think of yourself for once." Charlotte squeezed her fingers.

Think of herself?

"Perhaps … yes. Yes, I will go with you."

Charlotte threw her arms around Mary's shoulders. "I am so glad to hear it, so very relieved. Hertford-shire will be good for you, I am sure."

Rain, rain, more rain. Flooded roads, mud, and trees down. Had the entire world conspired to keep him from Rosings? Certainly it must have.

Mother would be gratified to know her influence extended so far as to control the weather when she was sufficiently vexed. Lady Catherine would be jealous of her power.

Seven days! A se'nnight complete to travel what should by all rights have taken three days! And as if simply to mock him, the weather cleared on the last day. Kent and its surroundings were a veritable paradise of good weather, as if simply to rub salt in the wounds.

He relaxed into the soft leather of the carriage squabs as it dipped and swayed across the puddled, rutted road. Dirt and drying mud coated the floor-boards and it had picked up a slightly musty odor—it would need a thorough cleaning once at Rosings. The outside was solidly caked in muck, obscuring the family crest—disgraceful really. But bright sunshine filtered through the dirty side glass, the curtains pulled as wide as possible to admit it. He stretched, kicking the seat in front of him. Yes, this would indeed be a good day.

How would Miss Bennet react when he told her the news? No doubt she would be quite put out by the surgeon's untoward actions. She had every right to be so.

She would not carry on when he proposed. It was not her way. That was a little disappointing, but still, perhaps the surprise of it would provoke some small reaction from her. Surely, she would, at the very least, be pleased to receive his offer. It was apparent she liked him, in a subtle, odd, Miss Bennet sort of way.

Why else would she tolerate all the thousand times he had annoyed her, ignored her advice, even teased her on occasion? Why would she hold her ground so vehemently and yet not turn away from him? If those were not signs of her affection, what were? Why bother to argue with him and correct him if she did not intend to stay with him?

Granted, it might not be the most conventional way in which one might be liked, but it somehow suited him very well indeed. As did she.

How soon would they be able to marry? An ordinary license was not strictly necessary, but it would be faster than waiting for banns to be called. She might be willing to take on the expense. It should not take long to obtain her father's approval—or had she not just turned one and twenty? That much he needed to find out. In any case, it should be soon and then …

Then he would truly be able to consider himself Master of Rosings Park. He would be married—fully a man in the eyes of all who saw him. Even Andrew would have to acknowledge him …

That used to be important, but somehow now it felt hollow when compared to having a friend and companion by his side and a family of his own.

No wonder Darcy seemed so bloody content.

Rosings appeared on the horizon, growing larger, silhouetted against the setting sun. It had never been an attractive house, but today it held a fresh appeal. It was about to be his home, not just the place he lived, but his home. His. Free and clear from his father's influence. He would be the making of it—or the cause of its final demise.

A knot rose in his throat. Dear Lord, just how sentimental could he be? Utter pap this was!

But still, it would be home, especially when Miss Bennet welcomed him with one of her all-too-rare smiles.

He bounded up the front steps, giddy as a schoolboy home on holiday. Parkes met him at the door, but he waved her off and headed directly for his study. Miss Bennet spent a great deal of her time in the evenings there.

Not even a fire greeted him. Only stark, ominous neatness and order.

"Begging your pardon, sir, I shall have a fire laid immediately." Parkes bobbed in a curtsey.

"Where is she?"

"Lady Catherine is in her chambers, sleeping, sir."

"Not her! Miss Bennet." He whirled on Parkes.

Her mouth opened but no sound came forth.

"Where is she?"

"I believe she left you a letter, sir, on the desk. She asked that she be allowed to explain herself rather than one of us." Parkes pointed.

Squinting into the dim room, he made out a folded, sealed letter in the center of the desk. He snatched it and tore up the stairs to his room.

Where was she? What disaster had befallen that she should be away?

He flung his door open, startling the young maid laying the fire. He stalked along the perimeter of the room, a caged animal with prey dangling just outside his reach. He must read that letter! At last she scurried through the servants' door and disappeared.

Good riddance!

The heavy wingback squealed along the floor as he shoved it near the fireplace. He fell into it, tearing away the seal.

Colonel Fitzwilliam,

I hope your travels have found you well and you have resolved the pressing matters that drew you away from Rosings.

He grunted under his breath. Without her presence, resolution would have to wait.

Below you will find a list of issues which will require attention immediately upon your return.

… damaged hedgerow … tenant dispute … roof damage to eastern barn … possible sick sheep … selection of a new vicar …

All mundane concerns, which mattered not at all in this moment.

Mrs. Collins' family have assisted her move to Longbourn with the babies. The parsonage is ready for a new occupant at any time. The solicitors have been informed of Mrs. Collins' new situation and are instructed to direct correspondence to her there.

I have reviewed the character letters of several possible companions for Lady Catherine. Below, you have my notes and my recommendations. Mrs. Jenkinson has agreed to stay another month complete. Her son will be arriving from Surrey after that to take her to live with them, so it is imperative that you have arrangements made for another companion by then.

Just how long did she intend to be away? He skipped through several more paragraphs, estate matters, staff issues, suggestions for menus to make the kitchen budget go farther.

Why would she be telling him of that? She handled those things.

His hands trembled, making the words difficult to read. He smoothed the paper over his lap and peered at the final lines.

I thank you for the hospitality you have extended to me during this tumultuous time at Rosings. I fear, though, I have overstayed my welcome, and it is long past time for me to stop imposing upon your generosity.

What imposition? She was never an imposition. What could possibly have given her such an absurd idea?

So, I shall take leave of you now and offer all my best wishes for you and the future of Rosings.

MB

That was all? No word of where she was going? He jumped up and threw the letter on the chair. Why would she have gone and left no way to reach her?

Because it was not proper for him to write to her in the first place. They were not directly related, nor were they betrothed.

But they should be. Damn it all, they should be.

Had she done what she should have and stayed here, waiting for him, they would be betrothed by now.

Bloody hell, why would she have gone? Had Lady Catherine finally driven her away? Had the servants tried her patience too far? None of those things seemed to have been a problem before.

He stopped mid-step and pounded his palm into his fist.

She knew.

Dash it all, she knew.

But what exactly did she know beyond the impertinent accusations of a wretched maid?

He fell into the nearest chair, mostly tucked into the shadows in the far corner, one he usually used to drape shed clothing upon.

Did she know she was considered compromised— or worse? Did she consider herself ruined and beyond the bounds of polite society?

He braced his face in his hands. Did she think he thought that of her? Was that why she left? It made sense. She was made of heartier stuff than to be driven back by the mere hint of rumor. But if his opinion of her mattered ...

By Jove and all his pantheon! His opinion mattered to her! For a woman of her ilk to care for his opinion—who would have thought it possible? And such a woman would not get away from him quickly nor easily.

He bolted into the dark hall, shouting for Parkes.

She trundled down the hall toward him, candle held high, huffing for breath.

"Where is she? Where has she gone?"

"Who sir?"

"Who else? Miss Bennet."

"She does not say in her letter?"

"If she did, why would I be asking? Surely you know where she has gone?" He suppressed the urge—almost overwhelming—to shake the woman.

"I do not know, sir. She did not say."

"She must have said something. Tell me exactly what she told you."

"All I know for certain is that she left in the Lucas' carriage with them, bound for Hertfordshire and the estate the boy inherited."

"So, she is there with them?"

"Perhaps, sir."

"Where else might she be?"

"She spoke of many things. Of visiting relations in Meryton, I think a solicitor there is some connection to her. She has an uncle of some sort in London, I think. She could go to Darcy House in London as well, or Pemberley? Might she not visit her mother near Matlock? I believe she has friends in Surrey and others in Norfolk, and some even in Bath." Parkes wrung her apron.

"Friends?"

"Yes, sir. She is not without friends."

"She never mentioned them to me."

"I do not know where she is, sir. Perhaps, she does not wish you to know."

He grumbled. "I expect to be traveling soon. First thing in the morning, I will need your assistance preparing the estate for my absence."

Parkes' mouth hardened into a narrow little line. "As you wish, sir."

He owed it to Miss Bennet to ensure Rosings would not suffer during his journey, until he could bring her back to her proper place, helping him to run Rosings.

Chapter 13

CHARLOTTE HAD BEEN entirely wrong about one thing. Eight hours confined in a crowded, dank coach with two month-old infants, even with four women to tend them, was neither simple nor easy. To be fair, the babies slept much of the way, but when they did not—which was in the places where the roads were the foulest—they cried. Loudly.

By far, the worst moments were when they had to leave the carriage and walk beside it lest it become bogged down in the mud where the road had nearly washed out in recent rains. They took turns toting the babies, but even a quarter mile carrying an infant—a wailing, soiled one—was a very long way in the mud and mist.

Then it began to rain.

Good sense had warned her it would be this way. She would have listened to it and stayed behind at

Rosings had there been any other alternative.

But there was not. Not now.

Did Charlotte know?

Something about the way she looked at Mary, and the way she avoided eye contact suggested that she did. But no word of it escaped her lips. Was that kindness or self-interest? A widow with infants, moving into the neighborhood would be subject to much speculation, even if she had been raised there as a girl. Bringing along a friend with a tarnished reputation would do her no favors. It was in her favor if the matter were kept as quiet as possible.

How had it come to this? Lydia was always the romping girl. The one expected to ruin her reputation. Not her. Yet, now it was Lydia who was respectably married, and she who was fleeing across the country from scandal.

But what choice had she? Fitzwilliam would be dead now had she not acted as she did. Would his death be worth her respectability?

No.

And not just because a human life was more important than her reputation.

His life in particular was worth a very great deal.

She should not think of that now. And possibly—probably not ever again. Now was the time to sort out what was to become of her and how that was to happen, not pine over what she had lost.

After she got Charlotte sorted out at Longbourn. Perhaps then.

The next two days were spent at Lucas Lodge recovering from their journey. The third day, Mary accompanied Charlotte and Sir William to Meryton proper to meet with Mr. Philips, the solicitor for Longbourn and the current Mrs. Bennet's brother.

Uncle Philips greeted her warmly and promised her an invitation for dinner soon. Aunt Philips would no doubt wish to host a tea to introduce her to the local families of quality. While it might easily be a double-edged sword, still, it was a kind sentiment.

Charlotte seemed surprised, even a mite put out that Mary should have connections here, beyond the Lucases, of course. But it was nice not to be solely dependent on the benevolence of that family. They were kind to be sure, but their first loyalty would always be to their daughter.

The following day, they toured Longbourn with Uncle Philips. Papers were signed, decisions made, and instructions issued. Charlotte and the babies would take possession immediately.

Which was to say, Mary would coordinate the entire affair, setting up the nursery and Charlotte's chambers, hiring a nursery maid, and overseeing all the unpacking. After only two days, Mrs. Hill the housekeeper answered as readily to Mary as she did to Charlotte.

How familiar it all felt—almost as if she had never left Rosings at all.

Longbourn was a modest estate, with a modest house to match. Larger and better appointed than the parsonage, it was no Rosings. Still, it was more than adequate for Charlotte's needs.

The morning room faced east, sunlight pouring in through two large windows onto blue-green walls. Flower vases stood on dark painted half-tables in three corners, filled with sweet-smelling garden flowers. The chairs around the table bore floral embroidered cushions, and a still-life painting of flowers hung over the flower-painted sideboard. At least flowers were not as garish as an overabundance of ormolu.

Mary looked up from her seat near the windows, the letters she had brought with her from Rosings tucked into the ribbon-tied notebook on her lap. Charlotte settled into the seat at the round table nearest the door. Mr. Collins had usually chosen that spot. Mrs. Hill trundled in a few moments later with a pot of chocolate and fresh toast, nearly burnt. Neither the overcooked toast nor the bland chocolate were to Mary's taste, but it seemed the kitchen had no coffee, so she drank the chocolate anyway.

Longbourn had a lovely set of chocolate cups, commissioned lately by the previous owner's wife. The saucers sported little braided rails to support the tall, narrow cups covered in blue and yellow flowers, with gold-overlaid lids. They were a bit fancy to Mary, but pleased Charlotte very much.

Mrs. Hill handed Charlotte a tattered-around-the-edges leather-bound journal to review—the household accounts and menus for the next week.

"Pray come sit with me, Mary, and help me examine these. I do so value your opinions." Charlotte poured a second cup of chocolate and pointed to the chair beside her.

Mary refolded her letter and tucked it and her pencil into her notebook and tied the dainty ivory ribbon around it. Charlotte raised her eyebrow.

Yes, the hint was a bit obvious, but they had been in close quarters recently. Hopefully a few subtle gestures would help change that.

Charlotte pulled the chair beside her out just a bit.

"What do you think of the morning room?"

"Very charming and, if you will forgive me, more agreeable than the one in the parsonage. Perhaps simply because, here you are free to arrange things to your liking." Mary set her notebook on the table and rose.

"It is a pleasing situation, I must agree. Would you believe though, I am reluctant to alter anything, wondering what Lady Catherine would say if I did?"

Mary chuckled as she sat in the chair Charlotte insisted she use. "I can well imagine, but I think it is safe to say, Lady Catherine is unlikely to arrive unexpectedly and offer her opinions on your housekeeping."

Charlotte's face fell. "I feel sorry for her. How difficult it must be to lose a child. I have been a mother only a month, and yet …"

Pray not this maudlin discussion again! "I am sure such thoughts cannot be at all beneficial to you."

"Forgive me. Surely, you have no desire for such mawkish companionship."

She was right.

"Do not be so hard on yourself." Mary forced a smile. Hopefully that would not encourage her to continue.

Charlotte sipped her chocolate and spread jam on her toast. "Tell me, what do you think of what Hill has brought me?" She pushed the book toward Mary.

Did she believe it escaped Mary's notice that she had not even looked at it herself? Mary pressed her eyes with her thumb and forefinger and held her breath, so she would not sigh.

Hill had a neat hand and kept her accounts well. Mary leafed through several pages—each supplier had a set of dedicated section. Six years of butcher's orders took four pages. The prior Longbourn family seemed to have a taste for pork.

And a taste for sweets.

But that was not what Charlotte was asking. No, she wanted to know what style of housekeeping she would be expected to maintain in order to be considered appropriate for a house such as this. Why did she not consult with her mother on the matter?

She flipped to the menus Mrs. Hill suggested, tracing down the page with her fingertip. "For two women unlikely to keep company, they are more extravagant than necessary—not wildly so, but it would not hurt to cut back the number of dishes served."

"I had wondered about that. But perhaps, do you think that being new here, I should entertain?"

"I hardly think it fitting. You are still in deep mourning not to mention you have barely recovered from giving birth!" Mary shut the journal sharply.

"But consider the role Longbourn plays in the community. I am no longer just a vicar's wife. The Mistress of Longbourn is much more than I was before."

And so much less than she thought it meant. "Even among families of this station, mourning is recognized, especially among the leaders of society. I would be surprised if you would be accepted here if you failed to honor Mr. Collins' memory in the way society expects."

Charlotte leaned her head against the chair back and closed her eyes, sighing. "I am so relieved to hear that. Truly relieved. I do not feel up to entertaining, not now. Just trying to manage such a house feels like more than I can accomplish at the moment."

Which was why Mary was doing most of the work. "Of course it does. It is a great deal of change all at once. You did leave Hunsford with little preparation."

"I am so glad you came with me. I do not know what I would do without you." She clasped Mary's hand firmly.

Another forced smile; this one more difficult than the previous.

"You will be a dear and speak to Hill, will you not? I trust you will know just the way to make her understand what must be done."

That wistful look that could not be denied. She had tried just yesterday. Mary took the household book and her own notebook, and left the morning room.

Yes, Charlotte might think her complacent and willing, but how else to escape before she said something utterly untoward?

She slipped out the front door and found a worn dirt path, lined with squat bachelor's buttons and leggy snapdragons, leading back toward the kitchen garden. Fresh morning air, with a hint of dew still lingering, just the thing to clear her mind.

Was this why Charlotte had asked her to come— to run her house as she had run Rosings? It might be construed as a compliment—perhaps she should assume the best of Charlotte. She was a friend, after all.

But to be expected to be something that defied definition—part housekeeper, part companion, and part friend? What kind of life was that? Did Charlotte offer it because she thought Mary could expect nothing better?

Mary stumbled and braced against the side of the house, crushing blue bachelor's buttons underfoot.

No, no! This was not to be. It would be easy, too easy to fall into Charlotte's hospitality, become what Charlotte required, and lose herself in her efforts. But as soon as Charlotte remarried—and that would no doubt happen—Mary would once again be an awkward guest, tolerated because of her prior usefulness, but not really wanted. She would bounce to another connection in need, only to repeat the cycle once again. Welcome when useful, and a burden otherwise.

There had to be another way, some other alternative. She needed time to think.

A lopsided wooden bench, just outside the kitchen garden, with white jasmine twining up a lattice behind it, caught her eye. Behind the scullery, Charlotte would never see her there, but neither would she have the appearance of hiding.

She sat down and closed her eyes. Bees buzzed in the jasmine as the heady perfume settled over her. If it proved as secluded as she hoped, this would quickly become her favorite spot at Longbourn. She slipped the letters out of her notebook.

The first two letters bore condolences from Lydia and Jane. The former was warm and genuine, sounding just like Lydia did in person. The latter had been copied out of a letter writing manual, neatly and beautifully written to be sure, but the sentiment rang hollow for it. At least Jane had written to her—that was worthy of note, was it not?

The third letter was from Michaels' solicitor requesting she visit his London office as soon as possible, some sort of business needed to be conducted, but he declined to explain further.

She could stay at Darcy House whilst there, assured of privacy to consider her future. Perhaps a trip to London, soon, was a very good idea.

How could it all take so bloody, ridiculously long? Fitzwilliam bounced his fist on his desk, nearly over-turning the bottle of ink. It had been so tidy recently, he dared not ruin that. It was a tangible reminder of Miss Bennet, of Mary, one he could not bear to lose.

Darcy never seemed to struggle with so many preparations before he traveled. But Pemberley was not up to its shoulders in debt, and he had a compe-tent steward to whom he could turn things over when he left. Neither advantage Fitzwilliam shared, though he ought to write to Darcy and ask for help finding another steward. Michaels had been well worth his salary.

Fitzwilliam raked his hair. One more letter re-mained to be written. How many had he already penned?

Too damned many. Every time he was certain he had reached the end of the pile, three more turned up. Or someone knocked on his door needing decisions or instructions. Or Aunt Catherine suffered another tantrum. He rubbed his temples. Just what he needed, one more tantrum.

Miss Bennet would probably scold him for using such an infantile description for her fits, but some-how it made them a bit easier to tolerate. She had no more control than a young child. Thinking of her that way gave him some frame of reference for managing her differently than he had.

And it was helping.

Just one more reason he required Miss Bennet here, at his side where she belonged. At least with her here, he could share a bit of a laugh and some sympathy for the situation. An underrated boon, to be sure.

He set his pen aside and sanded the letter he had just finished. The last one. A few brief meetings with the staff and his major tenants—the newly appointed bailiff needed a few more directions yet—and he might be off. Tomorrow morning. Yes, he would leave in the morning.

That night after dinner, he sipped coffee in his favorite armchair in the gold parlor. He had become accustomed to limited candles in the room—it was even a little restful and relaxing, especially as he listened to Aunt Catherine prattle. She was pontificating on the current state of Parliament, the Whigs and the Tories, clearly forgetting who was who. What a laugh it would be to see their faces upon hearing themselves classed with the wrong group of compatriots! He chuckled under his breath.

"What is that, Fitzwilliam?" She gripped the arms of her chair and turned a falcon-like glare on him. "You laughed. I distinctly heard you sniggering."

He sighed and forced his face into what should have been a pleasant mien. "Only because I agree with you, and it is pleasing to be in the company of someone with whom I share so many opinions."

She sat a little straighter, her chest puffing. "Of course you do, of course." She nodded and continued her muddled diatribe.

Miss Bennet had been correct about how to listen to Aunt Catherine without becoming agitated himself. He should tell her that; Miss Bennet would like that. And she would smile at him. Perhaps even tomorrow. It could be that soon.

"Colonel?"

When had Parkes shuffled in?

"Mr. Darcy is here to see you."

"Darcy? I had no letter from him. What in blazes is he doing here?" He jumped up.

"Shall I tell him you are not at home to him?"

"Surely not. He is always welcome here."

"I am glad to hear that." Darcy sauntered in. "I had wondered just a bit after you left Pemberley so suddenly."

"I would not object if you waited until you were properly shown in, though." Fitzwilliam affected his father's frown.

Darcy chuckled.

"Darcy?" Aunt Catherine rose and hurried to him, voice a little choked. "Darcy, you are here! You gave us no word, no warning. I have no quarters prepared for you."

"Do not fret, Aunt." He took her hands and squeezed them. "Parkes already has the staff readying the rooms I always use."

"Good, good. That is good. It is not Easter, is it?" She cocked her head and peered at Fitzwilliam then back to Darcy. "But if it is not Easter, why are you come? You come every year at Easter."

"Might I not visit my family at other times?" He wore a patient mien that Elizabeth must have taught him.

"But it is not Easter. Why are you here if it is not Easter? Has someone died? Are you bearing bad news? You are not wearing a black band … who has died? Why are you keeping it from me?"

"No one, Aunt…"

"Is it your wife? It serves that doctor father of hers

right if it is. Of course that is it. You have lost your wife." She looked oddly pleased with herself, as if she had just puzzled out something very complex.

"No, Elizabeth is quite well indeed."

"You do not have to pretend with me. I understand, Darcy dear, I understand. I lost my husband—or have you forgotten? It will be well." She patted his arm. "You do not have to worry. Just leave everything to me. I will see to the introductions, and you will be married again by Michaelmas. You will see. Anne is quite ready to marry, now. She will be pleased to hear it. She is strong and well now. It has been months since she has had a spell."

Darcy drew a deep breath, but Fitzwilliam cut him off, frantically shaking his head. "Welcome, Darcy. I was expecting you. It is excellent of you to come to us each Easter. You are as predictable and dependable as the sun itself." His eyes narrowed until he could barely see.

Darcy inched back half a step. "Ah, yes, of course. I look forward to our Easter visits. It is such a pleasant time of year."

Aunt Catherine paused and blinked several times. She glanced back and forth between them. "Foolish boys, playing such games with me. First I say it is Easter, then you say it is not. Now you say it is. You will give me a headache with all your impudence! Stop this at once."

"Yes, Aunt Catherine," they chanted together, hanging their heads.

"Such scamps you are! I can hardly countenance allowing you into the parlor. Really, you do not deserve the privilege! Both of you, up to the nursery and reflect on the bad manners you have displayed." She pulled out her fan and whacked each on the shoulder and waved them out.

Fitzwilliam grabbed a candlestick and led the way to his study, ordering a tray of refreshments along the way.

"That was a spot of good luck." Fitzwilliam chuckled and gestured toward the wingchairs near the fireplace as he lit candles around the room.

"Is that what you call it these days?"

"Trust me, Darcy, it was very good luck indeed. Far better to be mistaken for a small boy than to try and calm her more violent spells when she does not recognize you at all." Fitzwilliam placed his candlestick on the mantel and fell into the nearest chair.

"She has become worse then." Darcy lowered himself into the leather wingback.

"The last six months have seen a serious decline." Fitzwilliam dragged the back of his hand along his stubbly chin.

"You seem to be coping with it better than I had expected."

"I take no credit for it. It is all to Miss Bennet's credit."

Darcy's expression shifted into something unreadable, dark and unreadable. "Where is she?"

Fitzwilliam huffed a deep breath and looked away.

"Where is she?" Darcy leaned forward, hands gripped the chair's arms. "I need to speak with her."

"So do I."

"And?"

"I cannot. I do not know where she is." Fitzwilliam covered his eyes.

"What do you mean? You do not know?" Darcy's voice bordered on a growl.

"How much more plainly can I say it? I have no idea where she has gone."

"When?"

"Whilst I was in Derbyshire. Mrs. Collins' family came to gather her and the infants. Miss Bennet, it seems, went with them." Fitzwilliam dragged his hand down his face.

"Then she is in Meryton?"

"Perhaps. Parkes listed no less than eight different possible destinations where she may have gone, including Darcy House in London."

"And you have done nothing to find her? Give me the list. I must recover her." Darcy reached out as though Fitzwilliam might have such a list in his possession.

"Miss Bennet has not been purloined. I doubt she would appreciate your referring to recovering her like a piece of stolen property."

Darcy rolled his eyes. It could have been good fun if this was not all so serious.

"And you are content to leave her on her own then?" Darcy asked.

"Hardly. I have spent the last se'nnight preparing Rosings for an extended absence. That reminds me, I pray I might have your help hiring another steward."

"Another steward? That is what is on your mind right now?" Ah, there was some of that Darcy anger at last.

"Among a great many other things."

"Well, you can take finding Miss Bennet off that list. I will handle the matter myself." Darcy stood and towered over Fitzwilliam.

Not today. He was not going to indulge in that display today. Fitzwilliam rose slowly, deliberately. "I will deal with it myself."

"What do you intend to do when you find her?"

"Bring her back to Rosings."

"That does nothing to restore Miss Bennet's reputation." Darcy's lecture was beginning to chafe. "You cannot bring her here, to live in the house. It will validate exactly what has been rumored."

"Even if she is mistress of Rosings?"

Darcy's eyes bulged. That probably hurt. "That is no thing to joke about."

"I am not joking."

"You are not?" Darcy leaned in close. "Dear God! You are not joking! But she has nothing."

"Apparently, you agree with Mother and Father, that I require an heiress to be the salvation of Rosings Park? You did not marry expediently."

"I hardly think the situations are comparable." Darcy's jaw tightened and his forehead knotted. "Elizabeth is a very rare, very special woman. You saw that yourself. You, if I recall correctly, pushed me to make her an offer sooner rather than later."

"Then you, of all the family, should understand why I wish to make Miss Bennet an offer."

"Elizabeth is certain we can rescue Mary's reputation without resorting to such measures. We wish to bring her to Derbyshire. She and your mother will begin writing letters and exerting their influence on her behalf."

"I intend to make her an offer."

"You do not have to do that."

"I do not have to. I want to. In fact there is nothing more in the world I want than to make her my wife."

Darcy slowly sank into his chair. "She is wholly unsuitable. You do not even think her pleasing to look at."

"I have long thought her one of the handsomest women of my acquaintance."

Darcy snorted. "You must be joking."

Fitzwilliam balanced on the arm of Darcy's chair. "Have you ever looked at her? Really looked at her? I grant you, at first glance she might seem plain, but when she thinks there is no one looking, her countenance changes. It is quite a remarkable thing. Her face, her figure, they are entirely nymph-like, ethereal. It is rare to catch her in those moments, but when one does, she is stunning."

Darcy blinked hard. "How much have you been drinking?"

"Nothing. I have not indulged since I left here for Derbyshire."

"You think her attractive?"

"Absolutely. But more than that, there is a fire in her that I have rarely seen in any woman."

"What would you call your mother's temper?"

"I am not talking about temper. That I have seen in our family in spades. No, this is something far more. She will stand up to me, go toe to toe as it were, and stand her ground as firmly as any man I have known. It is extraordinary."

"And when she does that, you are entertained?" Darcy tossed his head and looked away.

"Hardly. I am usually annoyed, primarily because she is often right. Even when she is not, she gives me something to think about that I had not previously considered." He raked his hair. "She knows what she is about and is entirely capable of managing damn near anything. Michaels may have been a brilliant steward, but she is every bit as brilliant in her own right."

Darcy rubbed his fist across his mouth. "She has just lost her betrothed. Do you not think this is a peculiar time to press a suit?"

"Did you ever watch them closely? She accepted him because it was a practical, appropriate course of action. She did not love him."

"And you think she loves you?"

"I hope so. Very much, I hope so."

"You fancy yourself in love with her." Darcy's skeptical expression was positively offensive.

"Absolutely not!"

"Then why would you pursue her this way? Because you need her assistance?"

"Damn it, Darcy." He smacked the back of the chair with an open hand. "Listen to me. I do not fancy myself in love. I am in love. There is a great difference. Trust me. I know the difference far better than you think. I had not thought myself capable of love and dismissed it as a fanciful notion. But, I wander about Rosings' halls looking for her. I make up conversations in my head with her and long to know how she would respond. I want her opinion in matters well beyond what should be served for dinner and what is to be done for Aunt Catherine. I am lonely without her here, half-mad I think. If that is not a man violently in love, I do not know what is."

"I understand what you are saying, truly I do." Darcy laid a hand on his shoulder. "But do you not fear she might accept you because she lacks another alternative?"

"You think that the only reason she would marry me?"

"No, but it is a strong possibility."

"Would that be so bad?"

"You would be disappointed to think she married for reasons less than your own." Darcy's tone turned somber. "You know I am right."

Damn him! Damn him!

"I must find her."

"Of course, we must. I promised Elizabeth—"

"No, I must find her for my own sake." Fitzwilliam jumped to his feet and paced in front of the fireplace.

"Are you certain you are not simply being contrary, doing the very thing your parents have insisted against?"

"I am not a child. I know my own mind. I know what I want, and it is not an heiress hoping for good connections."

"I think it imprudent on both your parts."

"You would say this to the man who assisted you in securing your own happiness?" Fitzwilliam slammed his fist on the wall as he passed.

"You put me in a difficult position."

"I put you in no position at all. If you cannot support me, then just give me your word that you will not interfere."

"I must discharge my promise to my wife. I will offer Mary a place with us for as long as she desires."

"Do what you must. If she finds your offer more acceptable than mine, then so be it. But I have no intention of losing my Miss Bennet to you. You already have your own."

Chapter 14

TWO DAYS LATER, Mary steeled herself and strode into the morning room wearing a shawl of determination, rather a stark contrast to the blue-green and flowers that surrounded her. She poured herself tea—bitter and over-steeped as usual—from the sideboard and sat across the table from Charlotte, near the windows. A friendly sunbeam wrapped itself around her shoulders, warm and encouraging.

No point in dragging things out. She blurted out her travel plans to Charlotte.

"Mary, pray reconsider this ill-conceived notion." Charlotte set her chocolate cup in its saucer hard. If she were not more careful, she would end up breaking one or the other and would be cross about it. A few drops of chocolate foam splattered on the white tablecloth.

"I am quite convinced that this is the properest

course of action." And even if she were not, the fact that Charlotte opposed her was sufficient to make her contrary enough to do it anyway.

"Proper? There is nothing proper about you going to London by public coach! It is scandalous. You should wait until Papa next goes into London. It will not be so very long, and he will be happy to take you. Think about what people will say!"

Mary leaned back and folded her arms across her chest.

"Do not look at me like that. You know as well as I, your reputation will be jeopardize if you insist …"

She cocked her eyebrow.

"Oh. You know then." Charlotte wilted back into her chair. "I thought there was a chance I might shelter you from what was being said in Kent."

"Instead of talking with me about it. Somehow it was better to keep it all a secret?"

"I did not want to upset you."

Mary turned, locking her gaze with Charlotte's. "You believed it would be better for me to discover accidentally all that has been said against me? Perhaps after finding someone I liked?"

"Do you truly expect that?"

"Apparently you have already put me on the shelf!"

"Do not be that way. You know I think highly of you." Charlotte's lips screwed into something resembling a pout.

"But not highly enough to be truthful with me."

"You will recall, I warned you of what would happen when you went to stay at the manor."

"No, you warned me that—"

"He would compromise your reputation. That he

had intentions that would ruin you." Charlotte's smug look was nigh on intolerable.

"And he has done nothing of the sort."

"Yes, he has! You have been compromised—"

"But it was not his fault."

"Why do you defend him so?"

Mary clenched her fist under the morning table. "He should not be blamed for what he did not do. It was my choice and only mine. I do not regret it. He should not have had to die for the sake of my reputation, and anyone who would suggest so is a vulgar, vengeful—"

"That may be so, but your father was not well-loved in Kent. There are many who are happy to believe any negative thing they hear."

Mary covered her eyes with her hand and squeezed her temples. "I need to go to London, and it cannot wait."

"Just a se'nnight, please. Papa will surely be going there then."

"No. I will go today. A spinster—as you are determined I shall be—must become accustomed to doing things for herself." Mary stood. It took every ounce of control to rise with ease and grace.

"Do not say such things!" Charlotte smacked the table with her palm.

"I may be a few days. Lizzy has offered me the use of Darcy House, so I shall stay there until my business is complete."

"But I need—"

"Longbourn can very well do without me. The nursery maid is fully capable of managing the babies, and your mother and sisters are but a few miles away."

Control, remain in control. This was, for once, not about what Charlotte needed.

"You have never been so stubborn before."

"I have always been this stubborn, and you have complained about it constantly, or have you forgotten about our arguments over the midwife?"

Charlotte tossed her head with a sharp snort.

"I shall pack and be off to catch the morning coach. I will write to you if I will be more than three days there."

"I still do not like it."

Mary strode out without a second glance, despite Charlotte's desperate attempts to make eye contact.

Her bag was already packed, so it was short work retrieving it. Charlotte did not see her to the door when she left. Not entirely unexpected. She was apt to be petulant when she did not get her way. But if they were to live together, for even a little while, Charlotte would have to reconcile herself to being Mistress of Longbourn not the mistress of Mary Bennet.

The morning was agreeable for a walk—especially one as short as the single mile between Longbourn and Meryton. The road between was rutted and a bit muddy, but it had dried out considerably since their initial arrival, making foot travel quite tolerable. Fences and fields and sheep, with all their familiar scents and sounds, surrounded her on either side, not too different to what one might find in Kent. All in all, Hertfordshire proved a comfortable, homey place.

Perhaps Charlotte was right. She should not take such a cavalier attitude toward her reputation amongst the residents of Meryton. Traveling without a chaperone could cast a shadow upon her character, and if she should make her home there ... But to what point? Even if she took care with that, gossip had a way of spreading. Tales from Kent would sully her. There was little to be done for it.

So, she might as well please herself.

What an entirely scandalous—albeit freeing—thought. She may regret it later, but for now, it would suffice, and she would go to London.

The square red wood-frame coaching station, on the corner of the main street roared with ear-numbing noise, packed to capacity with people of every walk. The noise and the jostling she was prepared for, but the smell of so many, so close together was far more overwhelming than she had anticipated. It was enough to make one reconsider, but not enough to make her ready to face Charlotte's self-satisfied gloating that would surely greet her if she returned now.

So, Mary took a final gulp of fresh outside air and wove her way through the throng to find the ticket clerk. Two men in front of her argued over the one seat remaining inside the next coach to London. Tradesmen both by their dress and their speech, the dispute would devolve to fisticuffs soon. A crowd was forming around them to watch.

Mary ducked around them and quietly procured the ticket. The clerk at the window seemed to take great pleasure in calling out that only roof seats remained.

Spiteful man! She darted outside to wait and nearly ran into Miss Claremont just outside the door.

Miss Claremont, dressed in a smart green traveling ensemble clapped and smiled, her cheeks pink with enthusiasm. "Miss Bennet! How lovely it is to see you!

I have told my mother and sisters so much about you and our stay at Rosings Park!" She slipped her arm in Mary's and dragged her to a shaded waiting-porch on the other side of the building. "Pray come and allow me to introduce them to you. They are waiting just there. We are going to London, you see, to go shopping. Mama says we should all have new gowns—we are all out now—though I know Lady Catherine would not approve—and she wants to make the best of it. Oh, Papa complains mightily about it, you can imagine. I suppose that is why he does not come with us."

The crowd thinned just a bit as they made it to the porch, with some seated on wooden benches near the building, others leaning on the street-side railing, watching for the coach's arrival. Mrs. Claremont, a stout woman in a rust and puce striped traveling gown, and two younger Miss Claremonts converged upon them in a flurry of skirts and bonnet ribbons. All three wore a bit too much lavender water, making them reminiscent of the still room. The elder Miss Claremont made introductions.

"You were so good to our dear daughter in Kent. You were a true comfort you know. She was so anxious about meeting a great lady like Lady Catherine and staying in so grand a house. You made her feel quite at ease, you know. We are to London now—I am sure she has told you. The girls must be at their best—I only wish we knew which are the finest warehouses." Mrs. Claremont fanned herself with her handkerchief, face flushed with excitement. The edges of the lace mobcap under her bonnet fluttered in the breeze.

"If I might be so bold, Gardiner's, my uncle's

warehouse in Cheapside, has an excellent reputation. My sisters, Mrs. Bingley and Mrs. Darcy, shop nowhere else."

The Claremonts' faces lit in uniform glee—similar to Kitty and Lydia when promised a rare shopping trip.

"Then we must go there for certain. Pray, tell us all about his goods whilst we travel. I pray whomever is accompanying you will not mind." Mrs. Claremont smiled from one daughter to the next, all echoing her enthusiasm. "Charlotte is not escorting with you, is she?"

"I pray not! She is dreadfully dull, especially since she married," the youngest, Miss Betsy Claremont muttered. Her ensemble was a match to Miss Claremont's except in pink.

"There was some to-do about there being only one ticket inside the coach left." Mary looked over Mrs. Claremont's shoulder. She was not lying, not exactly.

"Well, neither of you should ride on the roof! Are you traveling on her business, or yours?"

"Mine," Mary whispered.

"Then you might go inside and tell Charlotte that she need not burden herself with a trip to London, you are one of our party now. Go on, we will wait for you here." Mrs. Claremont turned her in the direction of the coaching station door.

Mary wandered into the coaching station, as she had been bid, stayed several minutes and returned to the Claremonts. Perhaps this was the time to keep some details to herself.

The coach arrived, one that had seen many miles on the road between London and Meryton. As many passengers as possible were shoved inside, a bit like cauliflower in a pickling jar. How pleasant it was to sit amongst her friends rather than between the two women carrying hissing geese. Perchance there was something to having a proper traveling companion after all.

Friendly chatter, mostly about muslins, lace and ribbons, made four hours in the coach pass quickly. Once in London, she gave them directions to Gardiner's warehouse, and after they invited her to call on them later in the week and see what lovely things they purchased they thought to part ways. But, by happy coincidence, the Claremonts had taken a small townhouse near the solicitor's office, so they walked most of the way together.

All told, walking with them was a great deal like being back at home with her sisters. Something she hardly had time to miss until now. When she left them at their townhouse, emptiness descended, aching and painful.

But she would conquer this. And it would begin with a call upon Mr. Michaels' solicitor.

"Miss Bennet?" The solicitor peered down his sharp nose through smudged glasses. He stood behind his desk with that familiar towering-over-her posture arrogant men were wont to use.

The solicitor's office smelt of ink and paper, which should have made it appealing. But the room was stark and dusty, painted with shadows from other buildings that blocked the sunlight. The solicitor's huge boxy wooden desk sat at the forefront, desktop stained with two large ink splotches, traces of sand, and drips of sealing wax. She clasped her hands behind her to restrain the urge to dust it off. Even at its worst, Fitzwilliam's desk at Rosings was never left sandy.

Two clerks worked at smaller desks near the back of the room, flanked by an imposing, heavily-laden bookcase, not acknowledging her presence with even a glance as their busy pens scratched.

She pulled her shoulders back and lifted her chin. He was taller than she, but she would not cower before him. "You wrote to me, regarding Mr. Michaels."

"Yes, I know we asked for you to come, but we had no idea you would suddenly appear. It is customary to offer some warning, you know. You did not bring your father with you?"

So this was how it was going to be. Lovely, lovely man. "As I am now one-and-twenty, there is no need."

"It is customary that a guardian—"

"Customary, but is it necessary?"

He ran a finger inside his collar. "I would feel far more comfortable—"

"Is there a legal need that a guardian be here with me?"

"I am sorry, but it is just too irregular. I must insist. I simply cannot do business with you otherwise. Good day, Miss." He shooed her along, veritably pushing her out of the front door, and shut it in her face.

She stood staring at the door, trembling as he closed the curtain across the door's window.

How could he? How dare he?

Easily and with great aplomb. Custom dictated, propriety dictated, and the force of her will alone was not sufficient to overcome. Now what?

She turned her back on the solicitor's office, cold

and numb, and stared down the street as a pair of hackney coaches clipped past. It was not too far to walk from here to Darcy House, assuming she could get her feet to cooperate.

"Why, Miss Bennet!"

She jumped. "Mrs. Claremont?"

The matron and her daughters crossed the busy avenue and scurried toward her, still wearing their traveling clothes. "Imagine meeting you here, whilst on our way to Gardiner's! After all you told us, we could not contain our excitement. Oh, I know we said that we would wait until tomorrow, after the weariness of travel had passed, but one thing has led to another and here we are."

"Oh, Mama!" The eldest Miss Claremont clasped her hands under her chin. "I have the most wonderful idea. Perhaps Miss Bennet might accompany us!"

"Oh yes, please do!" Miss Betsy Claremont and Miss Claire Claremont—what an unfortunate name, all told—rushed in close. "You might introduce us to your uncle whilst we are there. Mama says one never sees the best goods unless one knows the proprietor."

"Girls! Really now—to ask Miss Bennet to come so that we may make use of her connection? That is entirely unseemly. Pray do not think us so base—"

"I have younger sisters, so I well understand their enthusiasm. I do not mind introducing you to Mr. Gardiner, should he be at the warehouse when we arrive."

The girls squealed.

"That is most amiable of you, Miss Bennet, but I am sure you have other pressing business to attend."

"Not at all. I should like to call upon my uncle, and to do so while also performing a service for you seems a good idea. I am delighted." Perhaps not delighted, but it would prove a desirable distraction, at least.

"You see, Mama! Let us go!" Miss Betsy and Miss Claire looped their arms in hers and set off down the busy sidewalk toward Cheapside, dodging children and street peddlers as they went.

The Gardiners were not actually her relations, kin to Lizzy and Jane's mother, not to hers. But, they had told her she was as welcome as Lizzy in their home. Still though, her stomach bubbled up in twisted knots as Gardiner's warehouse came into view.

The street in front of the wide shop window swelled with shoppers anxious for their opportunity to ogle the lovelies Aunt Gardiner had arranged for their pleasure: swells of fabric and lace arranged over embroidered pillows and bolsters; ribbons tied up in bouquets like flowers beside framed fashion plates; silk saris draped on lines behind the display beckoning shoppers to come inside to see what lay behind them. She had quite the knack of it, all told. Much of Uncle Gardiner's success was owed to her artistry.

The Claremonts were by no means immune to the spell and at least a quarter of an hour was spent casting oohs and ahhs over the display, until Mary finally urged them inside.

As usual, the shop was full of serious shoppers milling among the goods displayed, debating the merits of one muslin over another, or perhaps silk would be altogether better. Shop assistants ran from one side to the other, darting in and out of the back rooms, bearing merchandise for consideration.

"Mary! I had no idea you were in town."

She jumped and whirled around. Aunt Gardiner stood just behind her, studying her closely.

"Oh! Forgive me, you startled me so. I have brought some friends to see Uncle's warehouse. May I introduce the Claremonts?" She looked over her shoulder and beckoned them close.

The ladies stepped up for their introductions, curtseying daintily in turn.

"Do come in, ladies, and I shall present you to my husband. We are always happy to meet any friend of our nieces'." Aunt Gardiner swept them along, taking charge of the situation in the comforting, motherly way she always had.

Lizzy took after her aunt. They both exuded confidence and calm, and people just naturally followed after them.

In less than a quarter hour, Uncle had identified the Claremonts' preferences and set them up in a small room for tea and biscuits and a private showing of goods which might be to their tastes. Pray that their purses matched their inclinations, or the entire exercise might be a waste for him. Probably would have been wise to find out more about that before inflicting them upon him.

Aunt Gardiner bumped her elbow against Mary's arm, leveling a penetrating stare at her. "Dare I ask?"

The news had spread to London, too? Mary sighed and dropped her gaze, eyes burning.

"It is as I have heard then. I am so sorry, my dear."

"I have come to see Mr. Michaels' solicitor. He said he has business with me. But when I called upon him, he would not see me without a guardian present." Why had the words just tumbled out of their own accord?

"Darcy is not with you?"

"No, I have come alone."

"With whom are you staying? The Claremonts?"

"No, I had thought to stay at Darcy House. Lizzy—"

"Stay there alone? Heavens child, what are you thinking? You are not without friends here. Pray, stay with us. I grant you, Cheapside may not be as grand as the Darcys', but you would be most welcome." Aunt Gardiner pursed her lips just so.

Mary gulped back a lump in her throat and nodded.

Aunt Gardiner slipped her arm around Mary's shoulder. "Come, let me get you some tea. I have a feeling there has been far too much going on and you have had too little opportunity to speak of it."

At length, Mary accepted Aunt Gardiner's hospitality, relishing the novelty of an invitation without a requirement attached. Truly heady stuff.

After an indulgent day spent with Aunt Gardiner, doing only what pleased them—walking in Tower Green, visiting a tea house, playing with the children, and reading a novel—Uncle accompanied her to Mr. Michaels' solicitor the following morning. The entire affair required nary an hour and had them home just after midday.

Aunt Gardiner greeted them in the vestibule as they walked in. "I have a bit of nuncheon set out in the parlor for us. You can tell me how it all went."

Uncle patted Mary's hand. "Perhaps it would be best for me to leave it to you two to talk." He cocked his head and lifted his brow just so.

Aunt answered with raised brows and a twitch of her head.

He tipped his head and touched Aunt's hand as he brushed past on the way toward his office. "I shall be off to the warehouse shortly."

Aunt led the way to the parlor at the back of the house, overlooking the garden. Mary sat near the windows. Though certainly not on the grand scale of a country garden, it was a bastion of flowers and green in a city overrun by brick and stone. A little like the Gardiners' house overall, a refuge of peace and welcome against the vicissitudes assailing her on every side.

The furniture, a pair of sofas and four chairs, upholstered in something comfortable, soft and yellow, were older pieces, homey, not shabby. Iron bric-a-brac cabinets in the corners beside the fireplace contained trinkets and mementos of life—not fine porcelain figurines and souvenirs from the continent, but a favorite tin soldier, one of their daughters' best paintings, a bilboquet Uncle Gardiner had carved for her when they were courting. None of the items were particularly impressive, but together they made a bold statement that the Gardiners' did not find it necessary to impress anyone—a sentiment Mary could respect.

Aunt closed the door behind them. "I gather your errand was more successful this time?"

"Thanks to Uncle's help, it was." Mary ran the edge of the yellow linen curtains through her fingers, the braided trim nubby under her fingertips.

"Do you wish to talk about it?" Aunt poured two glasses of lemonade and gave one to Mary.

"Mr. Michaels left me a small sum in his will, three hundred pounds." She stared into the lemonade glass.

There was a small lemon seed floating and bobbing on the top. "I wonder though, have I done enough to mourn his passing? I wore black for less than a fortnight. It is just less than two months and already I am traveling and engaging in society as though nothing has happened."

"Charlotte held that against you?" Aunt pulled a chair close to Mary's and sat down. "You and Mr. Michaels had little opportunity to more than like each other, I imagine. Most do not truly become close and perchance fall in love until after they marry. Even then, it may take years. In that time, their lives intertwine and they become dependent upon one another, which is a form of closeness all its own. You had none of those opportunities. I think that would make it difficult to mourn for a protracted period. Perhaps that is why we have no prescription for how a betrothed is to be mourned."

"He was a good man."

"He was, and I do believe that you could have been happy together and could have even learned to love one another. But now though, you must decide what you want to do."

"Is it so wrong that I do not want to be the spinster aunt passed from relative to relative, expected to tend the nursery or the old and infirm simply because I do not have a husband?" Mary set her lemonade aside and balanced her forehead on the heel of her hand.

"You do not wish to marry?"

"I do not think it is a matter of what I want. My position is not favorable for it."

"You have many connections who would be pleased to help make introductions for you: Lizzy,

Jane, Lydia, your uncle and I. But I suspect there is something more."

Mary shrugged. There were some things, some feelings that were not to be discussed, even with Aunt Gardiner.

"You do not need to rush into society. You can return to Meryton if you like. I am certain Mrs. Collins will welcome you back."

"It seems I am useful to her."

"I have no doubt of that." Aunt chuckled. "Is that what you want?"

"No, it is not." Mary wrapped her arms around her waist, rocking slightly. "I do not dislike being useful and capable. I just wish that … that perhaps, just once … I might be welcome for some other reason." She squeezed her eyes shut and cringed.

Aunt laid her hand on Mary's knee. "Of course you do, my dear. It is only right and natural that you should. Until you have decided what you do want, I invite to stay with us, but only if you promise not to be useful to me."

Mary giggled.

"No, I am not mocking you. I am set on the ways my household is run. I have no desire to share the responsibility with someone else. You may play with the children, and read to them if you like, teach the girls some fancy stitches, but no more than that. Those are the conditions of my invitation. Can you accept that?"

"It may be difficult to grow accustomed to."

"Well, if you assure me you will try, you may stay as long as you like. But try to plan my menus, and I will toss you into the mews. Understood?"

Mary laughed despite the serious edge to Aunt's

voice. "I ... thank you. I would like that very much. I think I should return to Longbourn first, though. Charlotte has come to depend upon me, and she will need help—"

"Finding someone to take your place?"

Mary nodded.

"Your uncle has business in Meryton, he can take you the day after tomorrow. How long do you need there? A se'nnight?"

"That seems a such short time."

"Any more and I fear you will become convinced you are indispensable."

Mary chuckled, but her cheeks burned. "A week, then."

"I should go and tell your uncle before he leaves. Excuse me, I will be right back." The door shut softly behind her.

What did she want? That was a good question, but probably not the question to ask now. What she wanted was not possible. Not even wise or sensible.

Who would want to return to the chaos that was Rosings Park? To tolerate the tempers and vagaries that were Fitzwilliam? To endure the challenges of restoring Rosings to solvency, with all the privations the estate might require? To suffer the prejudices of the earl's family, judging her forever for not being high enough for their son?

No, that was a ridiculous thought. No one could actually want that.

And even if she did, it was no more possible than it would be for her to turn into the heiress Fitzwilliam truly required.

No point in dwelling on the impossible.

Or on being in love.

She had an opportunity to begin again in London, and only the most ungrateful wretch would ignore such a gift.

It was time for her to be grateful.

.

❧Chapter 15

DARCY'S ARRIVAL SET Fitzwilliam's departure off one more day. But it was for the best. Darcy had made himself useful in resolving a tenant dispute that would probably have escalated to violence in Fitzwilliam's absence. Perhaps more importantly, he offered Fitzwilliam the name of a Scotsman seeking a steward's position. Excellent reputation, but the man who inherited the estate for whom he had worked took issue with Scots.

His loss might well be Fitzwilliam's gain. Scotsmen made excellent stewards. Assuming, of course, that Miss Bennet approved of him.

Assuming, of course, he found her and assuming, of course, she was willing to return.

Too damn many assumptions!

Fitzwilliam and Darcy enjoyed fair weather as they shared a carriage until their paths diverged: Darcy's to

London and Fitzwilliam's to Meryton.

Cleaned from the earlier traveling dirt and muck, Fitzwilliam's coach was actually quite comfortable, roomy and bright with the freshly polished side glass admitting plentiful sunbeams. The tan leather squabs cleaned up buttery soft, traces of leather polish lingering in the air. With the floorboards swept and the entire body washed and paint touched up, it seemed a different vehicle entirely, one befitting a man who would marry soon. It still rocked and swayed a little too much as it hit ruts in the road. The springs needed replacing. Perhaps that might be a fitting wedding gift for Miss Bennet. A new coach might have been more appropriate, but she would be far more pleased with something affordable.

Hopefully he would find her safely at the Collins' estate, but he had extracted a promise from Darcy to send word if he encountered her in London and give Fitzwilliam a fair chance to make her an offer of marriage before Darcy offered other alternatives.

But would she accept?

On the one hand, she would be a fool not to—what chance was there she would receive another proposal from a gentleman with an estate like Rosings? The size, the prestige, the connections—those were more than a girl in her situation could ever hope for. It was, at least on the surface, a very good offer.

On the surface.

But she was aware of the real condition of the estate and how little income there would be to spare for the fineries and fripperies that ladies liked. It would be several years before they could afford to spend even the Little Season in Town, or even much time there at all. Rosings would consume nearly everything, and whatever Rosings did not, Aunt Catherine probably would.

What kind of jointure could he offer her in the marriage articles? Her dowry was a pittance— certainly not enough to live on. There was little he could add to it. But the estate was not strictly settled. Perhaps if he sold off a small portion—definitely something to discuss with Darcy, once Miss Bennet was found.

Father would rail at the thought of losing any part of Rosings Park, but if it secured his future with her, it would be well worth it.

He slid the side glass open and stuck his head out. Meryton rose up on the horizon. Soon he would be able to talk over the possibility with the one whose opinion mattered most to him. Even if she disagreed, that would be satisfying, too. She was most attractive when offering an animated opinion.

A brief stop at the local pub confirmed the direction to the Collins' estate. Longbourn—and hopefully Miss Bennet—were only a mile away. Were it not for the lingering weariness from his injuries, he would leap from the carriage and run the entire way. But arriving there too exhausted and ill to speak was entirely counter to his purposes.

Half an hour later, he left the coach and watched it disappear around Longbourn house, bathed in the afternoon sun. Squat and square, in a buff-colored stone, flanked by gardens on one side and a prettyish sort of wilderness on the other, it was a wholly unremarkable building, unremarkable save for the possibility it housed a particular young woman. That alone made it worth calling on.

Song birds called from the trees in the wilderness,

as if to approve his errand. The breeze, tasting of fresh country air, wafted subtle perfume from the squat blue and pink flowers that grew along the path near the house. Perhaps, it approved too. With such heralds announcing him, how could he possibly fail?

His boots crunched on the walk to the front door. Gravel in Hertfordshire sounded just like it did in Kent. She seemed to like him there, no reason she should not here as well. Yes, it would be well. How ridiculous to be so anxious. It was not as though women routinely scorned him. But he had not really cared for them, not like he did Miss Bennet.

Dusting off his jacket, he drew a deep breath. What would he say to her, exactly? No doubt she would protest initially—it was like her to do such a thing. But the right argument would convince her. How to express it? He knotted his fingers in his hair.

Bother! Enough of that. He always thought better on his feet in any case.

He marched the last few yards and rapped the doorknocker sharply.

The housekeeper took his card and shut the door in his face, clearly expecting him to wait outside as she sorted out things with her mistress. Such behavior was probably to be expected in the countryside where he had no connections. At least it was not raining. The old hag would probably have kept him standing in the rain.

"Mrs. Collins will see you." The housekeeper opened the door just enough that he could sidle through.

So his presence was tolerated, not welcomed. How considerate of her to let him know. But was that the housekeeper's attitude or the ladies'?

The confining dark front hall contained only a hall chair and small table with a squat bowl of flowers. White paper hangings with green vines might have been an attempt to make the space seem larger, but it was a largely failed effort. The housekeeper led him through a pokey hallway, done up with rose-colored floral paper. Light filtered in from open doors on both sides, but the air smelt vaguely damp and musty—a bit like a garden suffering from too much rain.

She opened a door. "Colonel Fitzwilliam, madam."

The parlor was bigger and sunnier than the one at the parsonage had been. The furnishings seemed newer but definitely not to Aunt Catherine's standards—a bit shabby, she would call it. The arranging of it had little art; orienting the sofa directly into the west-facing window was just poor planning on any count. And everything—every surface, every fabric, every painting was covered with flowers.

What was it about Longbourn and flowers?

Mrs. Collins set aside her sewing and curtsied. "Welcome, sir. I confess I am rather surprised to see you."

"Forgive me if I am a bit direct, but I had really hoped to see Miss Bennet." He scanned the room just in case he had missed her on first glance.

"I am afraid that will be impossible." Mrs. Collins clasped her hands before her, a picture of poise and calm—and haughtiness.

"Might I inquire as to why?"

"She is not here. She had business matters that took her elsewhere. I am sorry you have wasted the effort traveling here."

"When will she be back?" He paced along that inconvenient west-facing window. Floorboards squeaked beneath him as though afraid of his wrath. Perhaps they were wiser than their mistress.

"I do not know. I am not her keeper." An edge of irritation sharpened her voice.

"Where did she go?"

"Why should I tell you?"

"There is no need to be impertinent."

"I am not impertinent, sir. I am being prudent and concerned for her welfare." She cocked her head with that sort of all-knowing look his mother wore. The kind of expression that made him scream as a child and in his adulthood demanded the greatest of self-control.

"She is my dear friend. I only want to make sure she is well cared for." How dare she be so damned smug?

"Then you and I have similar aims."

"I hardly think that is the case. If I may be very blunt with you, and even if I may not, your reputation does precede you sir. Your character with women has not been an honorable one."

"What do you know of my character? There is not a single gentlewoman—" He stomped on a particularly squeaky board.

Hands on hips, she leaned in toward him. "Precisely what I am concerned about. I would not have been considered a gentlewoman by your estimations. You would have freely ruined me, then walked away, thinking no harm had been done."

"Hardly, madam." He would never have given Mrs. Collins, a second glance, much less have dallied with her.

That aside, women of her status held little appeal—too likely to want to attach themselves and too much trouble when they did not. No, any woman he lingered with had left his company with no regrets.

"You are well aware of what you have done to my friend." Oh, that maddening, judgmental glare. How dare she!

"I am cognizant of the gossip that has been spread."

"And you blame her for it?"

"I blame that damned surgeon for it. And I blame her father for leaving so much ill-will in his wake that even Miss Bennet's many virtues could not compel Peters to behave like a gentleman."

"But you do not blame her?" Her eyebrows arched.

"I am alive because of her actions. You can hardly think I would fault her for them. I am concerned for her welfare."

"One never knows with those accustomed to rank and privilege." What an insolent little shrug. "What do you intend to do for her?"

He ground his teeth until he mastered the burgeoning epithets. "That is none of your business."

"You plan to set her up somewhere, to bring her under your protection? Just how long would your arrangement last? How long until you tire of her? She is not the kind of woman who would keep your interest. She is plain, and her manners are not polished, knowing nothing of the coquette's art. How long until you decide the expense not worthwhile? Then you would cut her off, and she will be even worse off than before. What sort of friend would I be to subject her to such a fate?" Mrs. Collins all but shrieked the last few words in his face.

"And what are you offering her? The chance to be

your unpaid companion? Or perhaps you would allow her to run the household for you as well, so you can concentrate on getting your figure back and attracting another husband? I saw how you used her at the parsonage. Under the guise of assistance during your increase, she slowly took over your tasks, until you had little to trouble you. That sort of help is as compelling as laudanum. How easy it would be to have her do the same for you here. And what would you offer her? Would you keep her here after you married? Perhaps expect her to entertain your husband as a governess might? Maybe she would serve as governess as well? All with great economy to you!"

"She is my friend! I would never—"

"If she is your friend, truly your friend, then do not stand in my way."

"You mean to offer marriage?" She laughed, bitter, maybe even jealous. "Your family, your connections would never accept her. They barely tolerate Elizabeth whose manner and beauty make her much easier to admit."

"Then it is good that they will not have to live with us."

"You are serious?" Her jaw dropped just a little.

"Tell me where she is."

She looked aside.

"I will find her. Be certain of it. I will." He headed for the doorway.

"You will be the ruination of her. You will make her love you and then break her heart. She does not deserve that."

"Good day, Mrs. Collins." He stormed out.

He met his carriage halfway up the drive and climbed in. "To the inn."

A night spent in that dreadful looking establishment would be proper penance for believing any of this could be so easy.

Should he bother? Was it possible that Mrs. Collins' predictions might be true? That he would only ruin Miss Bennet's hopes for happiness?

No, no! She had agreed to marry Michaels, a practical choice if there ever was one. Surely he could make her at least as happy as Michaels could have—if only by showing her that he had learned to listen to her. And he would. He definitely would.

The next day, near dawn, Fitzwilliam left for London. A few hours later, his carriage pulled up to Darcy House. At the center of the street, the terrace house sat slightly forward of its neighbors, the largest of the street-long group. Fresh white paint on the façade and black on the ironwork railings—fresh enough to still smell it if one paid attention—reminded one of a maiden with a new gown at a ball, standing out in a crowd. It boasted five floors and a generous garden in the mews, as notable here as Pemberley was in Derbyshire.

He bounded up the front steps. It was foolish to place too much hope that Miss Bennet would be here, but a little hope was a good thing. Or at least that was what he had been told.

The housekeeper opened the door and let him into the wide, paneled vestibule.

"Miss Bennet, is she here?" He held his breath. Answer woman, answer!

The housekeeper, a wizened little woman with a craggy face and sharp shoulders, squinted and peered up at him. "Do you mean Mrs. Darcy? No sir, she is not."

"No, I mean her sister—"

"Mrs. Amberson is not here either."

"Damn it, woman, I am not talking about her!"

The housekeeper's brows knit together. "Mrs. Bingley—"

"Not her, either!"

"Fitzwilliam!" Darcy clomped down the main stairs and stalked into the vestibule. "I will not have you barging into my home and abusing my staff."

"Then simply give me an answer. Is Miss Bennet here, Miss Mary Bennet?" He craned his neck to see into the corridor behind Darcy.

"She is not here." Darcy beckoned him to follow.

Fitzwilliam trotted after Darcy down the long hall on the far side of the house. He bit his tongue until the office door shut behind them. No point in providing gossip for the servants. There had already been enough trouble with that.

The room resembled Darcy in every way: neat, traditional, overstuffed with information and instructions—the bookshelves looked nigh on collapse—and private—with neatly curtained windows guarding against intrusion from the street. If there were answers to be found, this would be the place for them.

Darcy leaned against his broad desk and folded his arms over this chest. "Miss Bennet is not here, nor has she been here."

Fitzwilliam raked his hair back from his face. "Have you any sign that she has been in London?"

"Not yet. But I have not called upon the Gardiners." Darcy pointed him towards a substantial leather armchair.

He dragged the chair across the thick carpet to the front of the desk and sat. "I shall call upon them directly."

"I shall go with you."

"I do not need a chaperone—or a keeper."

"Have you forgotten I have business with her as well?" Darcy sat behind his desk, looking very important.

"To offer her an alternative to tying herself to me. Yes, I remember it well." His lip curled back. An expression that resembled Andrew far too much for comfort.

"I am discharging a promise to my wife and offering my sister help that she well deserves."

Something about the way he said it— "Is that to say I have your support?"

"I know you better than Elizabeth does. You have never been like this about a woman." Darcy's lips lifted, just a little, and he nodded just as slightly. But for him that was nearly ecstatic applause.

His face heated, the warmth creeping toward his chest. Damn, sentimentality. He pushed up from his chair. "Shall we to the Gardiners' then?"

Dodging traffic on the busy streets proved a good way to consume anxious energy. With nerves so on edge, he needed every help he could find to help him remain civil.

Mrs. Gardiner welcomed them into her parlor, which thankfully was not the floral horror of Longbourn. Tasteful in a homey sort of way, scented with brewing tea and biscuits, it was the kind of room Miss Bennet would have liked. It was easy to imagine her sitting there by the window overlooking the roses, thoughtful and contemplative.

Mrs. Gardiner poured tea for them, everything gracious and poised. "So you have come seeking my niece Mary?"

Darcy sipped his tea and set the cup aside. "We are on an urgent errand to find her."

"I understand why you, Mr. Darcy might be seeking her, but you, Colonel? I think, perhaps, she left out part of her tale. She made no mention of you." Mrs. Gardiner leveled a stern gaze on Fitzwilliam.

That was probably not a sign in his favor. He ran a finger around the inside of his collar. Darcy's lips pursed into a small frown.

"The situation is complicated." Fitzwilliam balanced his elbows on his knees and recounted the fire, Mary's valiant efforts on his behalf, and Peters' betrayal of them all.

"You do realize, Mary is aware of the gossip."

"Elizabeth wrote to her—"

"She must have received the letter whilst I was gone. That is why she left!" Fitzwilliam slapped his forehead. "I can hardly think what motives she attributes to my departure."

"The poor dear! That explains so much."

"Then you will tell me where she has gone?" Fitzwilliam leaned so far forward he nearly overbalanced his chair.

"Pray do not think me impertinent, either of you. But, she did not give me leave to disclose such information." At least she had the grace to try to look sorry.

"Why would she have? No doubt, she did not expect to be sought." Fitzwilliam flung his hands in the air.

"Even so, she has trusted my husband and me. It seems a violation of her trust—"

"But I wish to make her an offer of marriage."

"I understand. I will write to her and let her know of your call, and if you wish, your intentions. If she has a message she would like me to pass on to you I will most gladly do that as well."

"That is unsatisfying, you know." That sounded bitter, but it was hard to care.

"I understand, but I believe it is all I am authorized to offer."

Darcy cleared his throat and threw a narrow glance toward Fitzwilliam. "We are grateful for the prodigious good care you take of her."

"I will continue to look for her. You may be certain of that."

"I wish you the best in that endeavor. I truly do. I think it would mean a great deal to her if you were to succeed. For my part though, I will write to her immediately. Where might I direct any messages from her?"

"To Darcy House, if you please. You have been very gracious. You will excuse us then." Darcy rose and bowed from his shoulders.

Gracious, and unhelpful, stubborn and willful. So much like Miss Mary Bennet! He grunted something that approached politeness and followed Darcy out.

Outside, sunshine assaulted their eyes and the scents of passing horses, their noses. Heavily laden carts trundled past, slower than the delivery boys rushing by with their goods. Darcy stopped and turned to face him. "Before you say a word against Mrs. Gardiner, think about it for one moment. She is exactly the sort of friend you would wish Mary to have."

"You are siding with—"

"She wishes to protect Mary. Is not that what you are trying to accomplish? She will send her letter today, and with some good fortune, we will have an answer in just a few days."

"And if she does not wish to reveal her location?" Fitzwilliam's innards knotted.

"Perhaps then you should reconsider your pursuit."

"And you would have abandoned Elizabeth so easily?"

"I did not say that was what you should do. Only that it might be a consideration." Another damned approving smile.

But it brought him no closer to Miss Bennet.

After two days of pacing the halls of Darcy House, Darcy pushed him out of the door and insisted he find some occupation elsewhere. His club might have suited, but he had no money for gambling, no thirst for drink, and little tolerance for vapid young dandies who could hardly understand his concerns.

But, he did have business with Michaels' solicitor; the payment of his last quarter's wages must be made to the benefit of Michaels' heirs.

Yes, he could probably forego the expense and ignore the obligation altogether, but the demands of honor required better than that. The errand would take some time and be some trouble. Exactly the sort of thing he needed now.

And would naturally be denied.

Damn solicitors were so efficient, so well organized, so helpful. The matters were concluded in less than an hour.

Darcy would not permit him back in the house for several more hours at least. So now what?

He stalked out of the solicitor's office and picked a direction. Any one was as good as the next when a brisk walk was all he could hope for. He started walking, as fast as he could through the crush, past one store front, then another. Through a group of dandies, ignoring a tinsmith hawking his wares. A curricle headed down the street at a generous clip. It was tempting to try to race across the street to see if he could beat it, just for the thrill of it.

Miss Bennet would certainly shudder and chide him for the thought.

Surely they would hear from the Gardiners soon. But then what? Would she deny him—

"I cannot wait to show Miss Bennet how well Gardiner's trims look on my ball gown!" A young woman jumped out of his way.

"She was right about Gardiner's. We will go directly there from now on—oh! Pray sir, excuse me!" The matron behind her bumped into him and dropped several boxes.

"Oh, Mama!" Another young woman steadied her mother whilst the first picked up the boxes.

"Pray forgive me, madam. The fault was all mine." He bowed deeply, with his most gallant smile. All three ladies tittered, but his heart raced. Had he heard right?

"There is no harm done, sir, none at all."

"Forgive me for being so forward, but I believe I just heard you mention a friend of mine. Perhaps we have a mutual acquaintance—a Miss Bennet?"

The older girl's face lit and she clasped her hands together. "We do! I met her when I accompanied my aunt and uncle to Kent. She traveled to Meryton with us. A delightful, well-mannered girl!"

"And so thoughtful. It was she who told us of her uncle's warehouse where we have made all these lovely purchases." The mother raised her boxes slightly.

"Is she staying here in London?"

"Her uncle has just taken her and my youngest girl back to Meryton. We feared the town air was not agreeing with her, you see."

"Do you know if she means to be there, in Meryton, for some time? I have business that will take me in that direction, soon. She is … my cousin … you see. I should like to call upon her."

The matron glanced at her daughters who shrugged. "She did not say, but I can hardly imagine she would leave before the assembly next week. She promised to attend with us so that she might see the finery we acquired from Gardiner's."

"Indeed, indeed. That is good news. I hope to see you again and properly make your acquaintance." He bowed once more and hurried on his way.

He turned the corner and paused, gulping air into his lungs as though he had run all the way.

Was it possible? Did he really just have that conversation? These unknown women knew Miss Bennet? It was just as likely it was some other Miss Bennet—wait, the one girl had gone to Kent and met her there—how many Miss Bennets were there in Kent, with a connection to Meryton?

Few enough that it was worth the risk.

❧ Chapter 16

"YOU ACTUALLY MEAN to do this?" Charlotte paced across the parlor's doorway, as though she meant to block Mary's escape.

The curtains were drawn against the afternoon light that streamed through the west-facing windows, adding a stuffy, claustrophobic sense to the room. That alone was enough to make one long for release, that and the unnatural amount of flowers—on every surface—in the room.

At the very least, Charlotte could have opened the windows. What was she thinking?

"You make it sound as though I am taking a situation as an opera dancer or an actress! The local assembly is a perfectly proper event—your own father is the master of ceremonies! How can you object?" Mary marched to the window, past the floral upholstered sofa, three vases of flowers, each on a floral painted table, surrounded by matching floral candlesticks, pushed the curtain with embroidered floral trim aside, and forced up the sash.

It squealed and protested against her efforts, finally giving way. No wonder Charlotte had not opened it.

"Quite easily and on many counts! It is obvious to anyone who looks!" Charlotte threw up her arms, much like Lady Catherine did.

"Well, it is not to me. Perhaps you should make it so." Mary flipped the curtain back into place.

"You have no chaperone." Charlotte ticked the point off on her finger.

"Your aunt, Mrs. Claremont has invited me. She is sufficient chaperone for her daughters. How is she not sufficient for me?"

"You hardly know her."

"I know her well enough to be invited to join her daughters. Since when is the degree of intimacy a requisite for being a chaperone? I thought being a respectable matron was sufficient."

"You are being stubborn." Charlotte glowered at her, but it was nothing to the glares Papa could muster. If she thought herself intimidating, she was sorely mistaken.

"And you are irrational."

"You should be in mourning," Charlotte plucked at her black bombazine, "not attending a ball!"

"You think I am unfeeling?" Mary perched on the arm of the couch and folded her arms.

Why did everyone seem to believe that the possession of good sense quenched one's sensibility?

"It does make one wonder. He has been dead, what, a month? And you are off to a ball? And a public one no less."

"It has been two months and a day. Have you forgotten there is no prescribed mourning for one's betrothed?"

"Two months seems hardly sufficient. What are you trying to accomplish? With your reputation—"

"So that is what this is really about? You are convinced that I am ruined and I should be hidden away from good society."

"The gossip is cruel. I do not want you to be subjected to cuts here."

More likely she feared for her own reputation and what would be said about the new mistress of Longbourn and the company she kept.

It was not unreasonable, if one thought about Charlotte's situation: a widow, bringing back the infant heir to an estate. When neither she nor her husband had been in residence there for some time, of course she would be scrutinized.

Charlotte stepped closer. "I know balls were never easy for you back in Hunsford. You refused to attend at all the last two years to avoid the ignominy of young men snubbing you. After that, I cannot fathom why you would want to go now to a place where you have few acquaintances. Are you trying to secure yourself a husband before the gossip circulates farther? That borders on deception that I thought would be beneath you."

"I am not in search of a husband, only an evening spent in pleasing company." Mary lifted her head and squared her shoulders.

"Is there something you are hiding from me? Are you in need of a husband to provide covering for more than yourself?"

Mary gasped and clutched the back of the couch

for support. "Charlotte! I cannot believe you would ask me such a thing!"

"You would not be the first woman to arrive at the altar increasing. It is a commonly done thing." She looked so knowing, so superior.

"It may be so, but I am not."

Charlotte snorted and tossed her head. "Are you certain?"

"Without a doubt."

"How do you know?"

"Because I did not behave as you did to secure my betrothed's affections."

Charlotte gasped.

It had only been a guess—but obviously an accurate one.

Perhaps that was cruel. Perhaps she should not have spoken so. But neither should have Charlotte.

"I just do not want you to be subjected to malicious talk tonight." She pouted a great deal like Lydia. Why had she never seen the resemblance before?

"The Claremonts will not start any kind of talk. They are far too fond of the Gardiner's warehouse to risk their relationship on idle talk about me." Mary forced a chuckle, a thin hollow one. "They and your family are the only ones who know me or of me. Do you suggest your parents will carry rumors about me?"

"You are cruel to leave me alone like this."

"If you think me cruel, then you know nothing of cruelty. I am going to dress." Clenched teeth and fists helped contain a hundred other ungracious words that threatened to spew forth.

"I am not going to help you."

Hardly an alarming threat. Mary bit her tongue and

strode slowly and purposefully out.

Just few days back at Longbourn and Charlotte's appreciation for her company had devolved to petty jealousy and frivolous demands on her time. It was like being at home with Kitty and Lydia.

Far too familiar.

Tonight, she would burn the letter she had penned to the Gardiners the first night she spent at Longbourn, the one insisting that Longbourn was a most agreeable situation and she would stay there with Charlotte.

Mary closed her room's door behind her, softly, carefully, so as not to arouse further notice. As she had often done at home.

Perhaps Charlotte did have a point in all her ravings. Perhaps it was insensitive for her not to mourn for Michaels longer—if only in gratitude for the inheritance he had left her.

She sat on the edge of the bed and wrapped her arms around her waist, rocking. How often had she been called cold and unfeeling?

Was it true?

Through all the chaos and demands after the fire, her feelings had been so tightly locked away, so controlled. Had she ever really felt anything? Grief, sadness longing?

Somewhere, deep in the midst of those trials, surely she had. Had she not?

Maybe not. She had never cried for him—no, she had, she had. That night, after the funeral.

In Fitzwilliam's arms.

Whilst he criticized Michaels and told her she deserved more.

Hot tears trickled down her cheeks.

Fitzwilliam. He esteemed her as no one ever had. And she him.

She would never see him again. Must never see him again.

Not that she could blame him for it. Despite all of Michaels' careful plans, the surest hope for Rosings was for him to marry an heiress. And he could not do that with her—and her ruined reputation—nearby.

For both their sakes, this was the best way.

The ball tonight was the first step in a new life, beyond the shadow of the Queen of Rosings Park. Even if she were snubbed for a partner the whole night, she was not hiding anymore. There would be plenty of other young ladies to talk to, friends to make. If they were not so friendly, she would be off to London with this first step taken—and survived.

She removed her newly-trimmed white muslin gown from the closet and held it up against her before the looking glass. It had once been Lizzy's—handed down to her three years ago now—but new trims and Aunt Gardiner's particular way with styling them made it look entirely new. Something the old Mary Bennet would have never worn—never dreamt of wearing.

It would do very well, indeed.

The Claremonts' driver handed Mary up into their carriage.

"Miss Bennet!" Miss Claremont took her hands and pulled her into the seat beside her. "I am so happy you could come with us!"

Bright silvery light from the full moon streamed in through the side glass. The coach was well-worn, but clean and comfortable with a welcoming feel about it, just large enough to hold them all easily without crushing their finery. All the Claremont girls were shined and polished for the evening, in similar pale muslin gowns bearing trims she recognized from Gardiner's, pretty pin curls, and cheeks that glowed with anticipation of the delights to come.

"It is a shame that Mrs. Collins cannot come." Mrs. Claremont clucked her tongue under her breath, every inch a doting matron over her charges. Her staid navy blue open robe boasted a sprigged ivory muslin skirt beneath, trimmed with ribbon twists Uncle Gardiner had specifically recommended for this purpose. "I hope she did not sulk about it too much. Even as a child, she always had a petulant streak about her."

Mary glanced away.

"Well, then, let me apologize for her. I imagine she went so far as to refuse to help you with your hair. Selfish little thing! You made quite a good showing of it on your own, I dare say. How you managed those curls and braids by yourself! You are quite clever."

"You must teach me how!" Miss Betsy gushed, perhaps a little too excitedly, but there was a genuine enthusiasm in her eyes. She patted the pale green ribbon, matching the shade of her gown, woven through her pinned up braids.

"Absolutely! We do each other's hair, you see, and are always wild for new ideas!" Miss Claire tucked one of Miss Betsy's curls back into place. Instead of ribbon, she wore short feathers in her hair.

Mrs. Claremont smiled fondly at her younger daughters. "I do not know what your assemblies are like in Kent, but I think you will find ours decidedly pleasant. I shall make as many introductions for you as I can, and Sir William will no doubt succeed where I cannot."

"He is all that is friendly and gregarious, is he not?" Miss Claremont leaned into Mary's shoulder.

"It is a wonder Charlotte could be his daughter, she bears so little resemblance to his temperament. Favors her mother, clearly." Mrs. Claremont flashed an apologetic smile. "Sir William is my twin and quite my favorite brother. You must forgive me if I dote a bit upon him."

They did bear a strong family resemblance.

"You have so many sisters. Have you a favorite among them?" Miss Betsy needed to have her share in the conversation.

Mary gulped and looked away.

"Betsy! That is not the kind of question one asks—entirely too personal! Pray forgive her. Let me tell you about who we expect to see tonight."

In the span of half an hour, she heard the recent histories and family trees of no less than four and twenty families, including her own mother's brother, Mr. Philips—of whom, fortunately, Mrs. Claremont had a favorable opinion.

"There are the assembly rooms!" Miss Claire pointed out the side glass. "And it looks like there will be a good attendance this evening!"

Carriages and finely dressed locals milled around an otherwise nondescript building. A sign, illuminated by the moon, hung above the door declaring in fine white script: Meryton Assembly Rooms. Warm candle light poured through the windows and the open door onto the streets, inviting the gathering crowd to come inside.

"I just hope there are enough gentlemen attending." Miss Betsy folded her arms over her chest and slouched slightly. The resemblance to Lydia was a little uncanny. "It is entirely vexing when there are not enough partners to go around."

"Well, perhaps if families did not allow so many daughters to be out at the same time." Miss Claremont narrowed her eyes at her mother.

Mary pressed her lips to stifle a chuckle. "I think Napoleon has much more to do with the lack of partners than too many sisters out at once."

"Still, it would not hurt."

"You are just jealous because Mr. Winston danced with me twice at the last assembly and you only once." Miss Claire shook her shoulders triumphantly.

"Girls, that is sufficient. What will Miss Bennet think of such behavior?"

"I will think that it is very familiar." Mary forced a smile and cocked her head.

That was not to say the behavior was agreeable. Only familiar. Still, one could hardly expect much different when multiple sisters were vying for attention from the same pool of young men. Kitty and Lydia had become more agreeable when she had stopped going to balls. Perhaps …

No, she would not retreat now, nor ever again.

The coach took its place in line, and after a tolerable few minutes, the ladies debarked at the assembly room door, joining the throng waiting their turn to be admitted.

It should not have been surprising that people stared at her even before she entered. The same thing happened back in Hunsford whenever a new face attended an assembly. In a moment—yes, there it was, the whispers began. One matron to another to start.

More would follow. By the end of the night, everyone would have discussed her. That was simply the way things were. Nothing could protect her from it. But she could conduct herself in such a way to influence the talk to be favorable to herself. And the less she danced the easier that should be. That would be simple enough to achieve.

"Miss Bennet!" Sir William pushed through the crowd, his bright master-of-ceremony sash bouncing on his belly, and his cravat tied as tightly as it had been in Kent. "How lovely that you are to grace our humble festivities with your presence!"

At least his eyes agreed with his words. That was some blessing.

He ushered the Claremont party inside with a deep bow and a flourish.

"You must begin introductions for Miss Bennet immediately so she may have a partner for the first dance." Mrs. Claremont flounced up beside Sir William.

Side-by-side, their resemblance was remarkable. If Sir William wore her hat and gown, brother and sister might be nearly identical. The garments would probably even look good on him. Mary smiled in spite of herself.

"I am glad you find the process so agreeable. Most pleased, I must say." Sir William pulled his shoulders back. "Some young ladies, ones that I have regularly encountered here, not the present company of course, pretend such a degree of shyness that effecting introductions is nearly impossible."

Best not correct his assumption.

He trundled off. They pressed deeper into the mauve painted room of swirling skirts and well-brushed jackets. Opposite them, on a small platform at the head of the hall, the musicians tuned their instruments, waiting for the signal to begin. An open doorway on the right revealed a room for refreshments. In all likelihood a card room would be tucked in beyond that. If the walls were green instead of mauve, it might be well be a Hunsford assembly.

A few in the crowd distinguished themselves by the quality of their dress. Those would likely be the leading citizens of the town, among them, the Misses Claremonts. Three or four young gentlemen with particularly smart tailors likely also belonged to that group.

A few stood out in garments of older design, a bit shabby around the hems. They probably did not have a subscription to the balls, but bought individual tickets as they could afford them. All in all though, the majority were indistinguishable from one another. Shopkeepers' daughters might look like lesser gentlemen's daughters, confusing a young man as to whom a suitable partner might be. Lady Catherine detested such events for just that reason.

"Miss Bennet!" Sir William pushed through the multitudes, several gentlemen in tow. "Might I perform my happy service?"

"Certainly, brother! Girls, come closer." Mrs. Claremont waved for her daughters to attend them.

Of course, it would be to their advantage to be with the newcomer, to share in the attention she received. Had that been the motivation for the invitation in the first place?

Oh, that was an unworthy thought. She had been listening to Lady Catherine—and Papa—a little too much.

"I would like to present a new arrival to our humble assembly. Colonel Fitzwilliam of Kent, may I present Miss Bennet and my nieces …"

"Sir!" Mrs. Claremont exclaimed.

"I am delighted to properly make the acquaintance of you and your fine daughters at last." He bowed with a flourish.

Mary's eyes bulged and her heart raced, roaring so loud she could not hear.

It was him. His valet had had his way with him. Every inch was polished, brushed and starched to perfection. How had he ever considered himself plain?

She swallowed hard.

Fitzwilliam fixed his eyes on her. "I must confess, Miss Bennet and I are acquainted from her recent time in Kent."

Acquainted was one way to put it.

"Her family once lived in Hunsford near my estate, but has since moved to Derbyshire."

"Has it been some time since you have been in company?" Mrs. Claremont asked.

"I perceive it as a long time. Perhaps, in honor of that, you might grant me the first set, Miss Bennet?"

The Claremont sisters giggled and blushed. Thankfully they looked more happy for her than jealous for themselves.

"Thank you, sir. I would be pleased to dance with you." What else did one say at such a moment?

He met her gaze and the world stopped. All the noise around them ceased, nothing but his eyes remained. They probed, they sought, they asked, holding her with a strength she could not free herself from—had she wanted to. She should want to. Did he not realize she would ruin him—and if the gossip spread, he her.

But still, he would not release her.

Sir William coughed. "If you will, and pray, I do not wish to disturb you, but there are several other introductions it would be appropriate to make before the musicians begin."

Were there other young men with him? Gracious, yes, two, no three. And they had partnered with the Claremonts—no wonder the girls did not exude jealousy. How thoughtful of Sir William to identify enough partners for them all.

Sir William trundled away, the gentlemen in his wake. They disappeared in the crowd.

"You must tell us more about him." Miss Claremont's gaze followed him into the throng.

"Do give her a chance to catch her breath. You can see she is surprised to see him here. I am sure you or your sisters will have an opportunity to dance with him later tonight. You can learn of him then." Mrs. Claremont laughed.

Why was he here? What brought him to Meryton? The only tie he had to this county was Mr. Collins. Perhaps he wished to provide Charlotte with the final quarter payment of Mr. Collins' living. That would make sense. It was the sort of thing he was likely to do in person—and it would satisfy his curiosity about the estate Collins had inherited.

But on the heels of his journey to Matlock? It made precious little sense.

Sir William opened the assembly and called the dancers to the floor. Mary faded back toward the wall, more out of habit than anything else, but Fitzwilliam, elegant in his skin-tight breeches and impeccably tailored coat, intercepted her halfway there. What a sight he was!

"You have not changed your mind, have you?" He offered his elbow.

"Ah, no, I have not." She slipped her hand in the crook of his arm.

It was the arm he had injured in the fire. He winced, just barely, but it was there if one knew what she was looking for. His steps, though strong and confident, had just a hint of hesitation—no, weariness—in them.

His travels had taken quite a bit from him. Why then would he be dancing? Did he suffer so for lack of company?

Possibly. Elizabeth had said he was a sociable man. Perhaps this was all the society he could afford now.

"You seem distracted, Miss Bennet." They took their place in the line of dancers.

"You cannot be surprised that I might find your presence here a bit distracting."

His eyebrow cocked just so, his teasing little smile playing at the corners of his lips. "I confess, Meryton has not been on my social circuit. But perchance I have missed a hidden gem of the English countryside."

She snickered, probably as he intended. "You should tell Sir William that. I think he would enjoy the compliment to his community."

"He is an excellent ambassador for Meryton is he not? I believe he served as its mayor at one time."

"Mrs. Collins once mentioned that." Actually it was more than once. Much more.

The music began.

He reached for her hand and caught her gaze.

She should never have allowed him that … intimacy. The grey-blue gun metal which could be cold as deep winter when he was angry, tonight, was warm and inviting, like hearthstones around a cozy fire. Intense and sparkling, they held her through each repetition of the steps.

Step together, turn, cast down and away—

Their eyes broke contact, and she gasped for breath—or was it the pain of separation? An upswing in the music and they met again, their palms pressed together—just a moment, not long enough, before the melody made its next demand.

He was a clever partner who took great pleasure in the precision and unity of the dance floor—the best she had ever danced with. But there was more, something more in his eyes. He took no pains to hide it, but never offered it a name.

They parted, turned, once, twice, came back together, and the music faded away.

Applause echoed, very far away. Was there anyone else in the room?

He tucked her hand in the crook of his arm, without asking, as though it naturally belonged there, and escorted her to the side of the room, between an unoccupied cluster of hall chairs, one of the few open spaces.

A bow and polite exit were in order next—had he forgotten? Perhaps he had, given the way he stood and gazed into her eyes, silent, smiling.

"You did not tell us you had the most accomplished partner in the room!" Miss Claremont declared as she bounced up to them, skin flushed prettily with the exercise of the dancefloor.

Mary stared at her dumbly. It would be right and proper to respond, but what did one say?

"You flatter me, Miss Claremont, to be sure. One cannot dance truly well without the right partner, though. Would you not agree Miss Bennet?"

She stared at him, her cheeks coloring. "One's partner does profoundly influence the experience."

Was that a stupid thing to say?

"I am sure you have danced with many proficient young ladies. My uncle, Sir William, has mentioned that you have danced at St. James?"

"I consider it highly overrated."

"You do?"

What game was he about?

His eye twitched in something that might have been a wink at her. "It sounds like it would be a fine affair, and to be sure, it is full of well-dressed, well-mannered people, all on their best behavior. To a man, the dancers are generally excellent, making it quite the sight to behold."

"I would dearly love to behold it someday." Miss Claremont fluttered her eyelashes at Fitzwilliam. She was not a gifted coquette.

His smile widened just a bit and he pressed Mary's hand to his arm.

Gracious! He had not released her. Was that why she felt so oddly comfortable and secure despite the intrusion?

"It is a lovely sight, I am told, if one likes that sort of thing." He shrugged briefly.

"Who would not?"

"It is possible to become bored with such shallow finery, I think. It is hardly a place where real enjoyment might be had, you see. It is a place to impress and to be impressed, not for merrymaking and companionship. One is like a learned pig on display, and it can be entirely tiresome. Granted, at one time I found it rather stimulating, but my tastes have changed, and I much prefer such a gathering as this, full of good company and good cheer."

"Do you profess your own opinions, or the ones you believe we would wish to hear?" Mary leaned back a little and gazed narrowly at him.

Miss Claremont gasped softly.

"What do you think, Miss Bennet?"

"I am not certain. That is why I ask."

"I am astonished you would doubt the word of one who would offer an opinion so freely." Miss Claremont pursed her lips in a dainty, feminine frown. She might be a more accomplished coquette than Mary had given her credit for, after all.

"Perhaps it is only because Miss Bennet has known me that she understands it is proper to question me so."

"You think I have known you so well?"

"What do you think?"

"I believe I asked you first."

He laughed heartily, the way he did when he was truly pleased about something. He did not do it often, but when he did, the way his eyes lit and crinkled at the sides rendered him truly handsome.

"The next dance is about to start." Miss Claremont edged a little closer to Fitzwilliam, wearing a hint of expectancy like perfume—not an entirely pleasing one.

"So it is. Miss Bennet?" He gestured toward the dancefloor, eyebrow raised.

He had not asked her for this dance, at least not

until this moment. But he was asking her now—the first time she had ever been asked for two sets by the same partner.

She smiled—no words were available, and they returned to the dance under a wide-eyed stare from Miss Claremont.

This time the musicians played a maggot—a saucy, flirtatious tune that would never have been performed at a proper society event. He performed his role to perfection, grinning and winking and drawing her out to play along.

It was fun to play and tease. No wonder Kitty and Lydia had enjoyed it so much. But there was a sad hollowness to it. When the music ended, so would this, and they would part—

"People are staring at us? Have you noticed?" Fitzwilliam whispered, glancing back over his shoulder.

Heavens! He was right! Her face flushed so hot it stung.

"Do you know why?"

She had made a spectacle of herself—exactly as she knew she would if she ever tried such a dance. How could he have—

"It is because I have the most agreeable partner in the room."

She must have glowered very sternly. More so than she realized given the way he started.

"You think I am mocking you?" Alarm filled his eyes.

"What else am I to think?"

"Why would you think that at all?"

She stared again, one eyebrow slightly raised.

"How long has it been since you have danced at a ball?"

Did he really believe she would own that?

"I see."

The next repetition of the tune drew them into the flirtatious acts once again. An intensity built in his gaze.

He should be spurning her now, not … this … whatever this was. Hunger, tempered with longing and … what was that?

The music stopped, a sudden, wrenching end, cold and hollow.

He placed her hand in his arm before she could move away, and ushered her toward the refreshments.

"I think we could both do with a glass of punch."

"And I think you should stop playing games with me."

He stopped mid-step and turned to her, eyes dark and serious. "I may have led a gentleman's life, Miss Bennet and enjoyed the company of a number—smaller than you might imagine, by the way—of women, but I have never been a cad. I have never 'played games' as you have put it. You might not approve of my dalliances, but you will not hear me called a bounder either."

"I am sorry. I should not have spoken so." How fast could she get away from him?

"Yes, you should speak out, if that is your concern. Tell me, Miss Bennet, what are you thinking? In particular, what are you thinking about me?"

"I caution you, do not ask a question that you do not wish to have answered."

"Oh, but I do wish an answer. Very much."

"An honest one?"

"That is the only kind you offer, is it not?"

"I cannot make you out. Why you are here?"

He leaned closer, his voice dropping to a whisper. "I think there is a more important question you have not asked."

"You presume to know my mind?"

"No, only to judge you too polite to speak everything you might think. You have not asked me about my trip to Matlock."

"Perhaps, I do not really care."

"Perhaps, you do not care how it was, so much as why it was."

She gasped and stepped back. No, that she did not need to hear, not in this place and certainly not now. She turned in a swirl of skirts and rushed headlong into the crowd.

He might think himself no cad, but neither was he a gentleman to threaten her so.

Why had she thought an assembly a good idea? Charlotte was right—completely and entirely. She was not fit for company, not now, and probably not ever.

She bolted for the rear door.

The chill night air embraced her like a cloak, the moonlight a soothing balm. A few drivers gathered around a small fire near a herd of parked coaches. Several turned to look at her, but on realizing she was not their mistress, returned their attention to the fire and their compatriots.

Yes, this was just what her shattered equanimity needed. A few minutes of anonymity in the shadows to gather her public mask, and she would be able to face—

"Miss Bennet!"

Not him, silhouetted in the candlelight from the doorway. Anyone but him.

But there was nowhere to go except into the dark streets—an only slightly worse alternative than standing her ground.

"Why have you followed me? Can you not see I am not seeking company?"

"Why am I here? To ask you for the next dance." He approached, extending his hand.

She blinked and shook her head to clear it. "But we have already …"

"I am able to count. I know precisely what I have asked."

"You cannot—"

"I can and I have. Little else has been in my thoughts since I left Matlock." He took another step closer, close enough to touch her.

"That cannot possibly be what your family advised."

"Quite the opposite, truth be told."

She turned her shoulder to him. "Then why vex me so?"

"Because I have found doing the opposite of their wishes usually brings me the greatest happiness." He dodged around to face her again. "You do not trust me."

"I do not understand why you left Rosings or why you would ask me such a thing now."

"Asking you to dance is not so difficult a thing to understand."

She stomped, nearly on his toes. "You willfully misunderstand me—or would you see my reputation tarnished in two counties?"

"Finally, now you have come to the crux of the matter."

"If that is what you intended to speak of, then why have you forced me—"

"You are right, that was ignoble of me. Forgive me. I should not have treated you so. I suppose, in that sense, you have also been correct, I have been playing a game."

She bit her lip and nodded.

"But not the one you might think." He raked his hair, something he only did when he was uncomfortable and frustrated—but he deserved to be for treating her so, and if he expected any relief from her, then he needed to revise his behavior.

"When I learned of Peters' letters, I was horrified—I know of no other words for it. I have always been careful never to tarnish a lady's reputation. To have it happen in such a manner—I owe you my life, and this is how you are repaid?"

"There is no guilt on your part. It was my choice entirely, a risk I knew I was taking at the time. Thus, there is nothing to trouble your conscience. I gladly bear the consequences of my actions."

"Gladly?" He tipped her chin up with two fingers.

Why did his touch send a shiver down her spine? "You owe me nothing."

"I owe you everything."

"Do not torture yourself with that. I am not without means. I have some small independence now. Elizabeth wrote to me to say—"

"My parents suggested that I provide you with an independent life—as far away as possible from me— and be about my way. But a better man than I has already promised you nearly as much. So it seems I may ignore their advice with alacrity. Or perhaps you think I should take their advice and provide for you in addition to Darcy?"

"That is nothing but an over active sense of duty."

"I am well aware of what that feels like." He pulled her close until he pressed hard against her. "And I assure you this is nothing like that."

She lifted her chin, her nose nearly bumping his. "And what is this like?"

"Like standing too close to the woman I want to dance every dance with—every dance—and not knowing if she will accept me." He pulled back just enough and only enough to plead with his gaze. "You are the only partner with whom I have never wanted the dance to end. Pray, Miss Bennet, dance with me."

"Are you certain?"

"That is not the answer I had envisioned, but I will accept it, and show you how certain I am." He leaned in and kissed her, warm, hard, and passionate. Quickly enough to be hidden by the shadows, but long enough to leave her aching for more.

She gasped and clutched his forearms to steady herself.

"Now that is precisely the sort of response I had hoped for." He clasped her hand against his arm and began a slow amble into the assembly rooms.

Light and crowd noises assaulted her senses, blurring everything into a surreal scene, whirling and swirling about her. The musicians signaled another set and gentlemen sought their partners along the edges of the hot, stuffy room.

Mrs. Claremont was the first to notice her on Fitzwilliam's elbow, pressing her fist to her mouth to cover her expression. Was it a smile? Astonishment?

Judgment, perhaps? Maybe all of them. But it did not matter. The self-satisfied smirk—yes, it was a smirk—he wore was the only expression that mattered.

Heads turned and tongues wagged as they took to the dance floor a third time—a slow, graceful affair with a fairytale quality about it. They floated around one another in three-quarter time, twirling like peony petals spinning on the breeze. So fitting when all of this felt like a dream.

But still, was this nothing but his contrary streak—the need to be stubborn against his family?

He took her hand and leaned very close. "You are thinking too much, Mary. Far too much."

Was that what her name sounded like, spoken by one who—

"That is much better, Mary. I do so like to say that, now that I may. Mary, Mary, Mary."

It was a caress as much as a name, tenderly stroking her ear, her cheek, the line of her jaw. Heat rose along her neck.

She looked over her shoulder.

He chuckled. "Yes, they have noticed, and yes, they are all looking. By the end of the night the whole of Meryton, possibly the whole of Hertfordshire, will know that we are … betrothed."

Her knees wobbled, and she missed a step, but he caught her elbow and swung her through the turn.

"Fear not, my dear, I have you, and I always will."

Chapter 17

THE NEXT MORNING, before they even had the opportunity to break their fast, Charlotte followed her
upstairs from the morning room, like a hound on a
fox. Mary tried to shut the chamber door ahead of
her, but Charlotte scooted in too quickly.

The modest quarters, another floral masterpiece,
cried out in disarray. Clothes hung from the flower
carved bedposts, the flower sprigged coverlet over the
bed hosted piles of folded garments. A still life painting—a vase with jonquils—hung askance where Mary
had brushed up against it, carrying an armload from
the press in the corner. Three vases of garden flowers
crowded one small table to clear space on the dressing table to fold body linen for the trunk.

"Mary, do be serious." Charlotte closed the door,
as if she thought a closed door would change the
course of events.

"You think I am not?" Mary dragged her trunk from the closet and peered at her over the open lid.

"I cannot permit this. I absolutely cannot."

"What makes you believe you have any say in the matter at all?" She forced her voice into something very soft, but much more of this attitude and she would surely lose her temper.

"I did not deliver you out of Rosings Park for you to go rushing back into the arms of a man who has no honorable intentions." Charlotte folded her arms and tossed her head—something Mama did when she was adamant. It was not pleasing in either incarnation.

"You delivered me from Rosings?" Mary pushed off the trunk and rose, slowly, deliberately.

"Of course, why do you think I invited you—"

"Because you wanted a companion and manager for your home, and quite possibly a governess for your children when the time comes." She probably should not have said that, but even her control had limits.

"How can you say such a thing? I am your friend." What audacity Charlotte had to look so wounded.

"One who does not hesitate to put me to work like a servant."

"You prefer to be usefully engaged. You grow restless when you are not."

"How would you know? You have never asked me my preferences. Never." Mary stomped to the closet and removed the remaining garments.

"You are simply being stubborn now. This will end in disaster." Charlotte stalked her to the trunk. "I have always known you to be so practical. I do not see how you are so utterly unaware of what kind of man he is."

"What kind of a man do you think him to be?"

Charlotte gripped the bedpost. "You have heard his conversations and seen how much he drinks. He loves to gamble as much as the next rich man, and has been far from chaste."

"So you judge him for being one of his class?"

"I judge him against you! I know no one less suited for such a man. Is that not why you accepted Michaels—one of the few men as stiff and starched as you?"

"Starched and stiff? That is how everyone wants to be described. Thank you for the compliment."

"I have never seen you this way! You look to take offense because you do not like what I am saying."

"There is a great deal more to him than you give him credit for."

"And how would you know this—unless you have allowed him liberties that I warned you to guard against." Charlotte slithered between Mary and her trunk, fighting to make eye contact.

"The only liberty he has ever taken was to dance with me more than twice last night—and that was preceded by an offer of marriage!"

"He does not mean it. Surely you must see that. He is toying with you and will repent of it all this morning. Then he will be away and leave you here with your reputation in tatters. You are a fool to expect anything else."

"Perhaps. But he was the one who noticed the … injury … Mr. Collins inflicted upon me, and he was the one who stepped in to try to protect me."

"Protect you? What Mr. Collins did was not wrong in the first place. Did you not expect him to maintain order in his own household?"

"Of course. He was all that was right and proper in a man." Mary ground her teeth.

"He was a far better husband than you give him credit for being."

Mary shut the trunk's lid, more forcefully than necessary. "Shall I take this down myself, or will you call the maid?"

"I am not going to let you do this." Charlotte stood in the doorway, arms crossed. She nearly fell as the door swung open behind her.

"Then I suppose I must insist." Fitzwilliam appeared just behind her, the housekeeper fluttering impotently behind him.

Mary snickered under her breath. He certainly had a flair for the dramatic.

"He just barged in, madam. I could not keep him out." The housekeeper peeked over his shoulder, bobbing like an old hen.

"Indeed I did. The old woman is not to blame. Do not take it out on her. You may scold me all you want." He planted his hands on his hips and stared down at Charlotte.

"You have no shame, sir, barging into my house like this!" Charlotte rose on tip toes.

"And you have no manners, trying to turn me away from seeing my betrothed."

"How dare you play such games with my friend?"

"Who are you to judge such a thing?" Mary sidled around Charlotte to stand with Fitzwilliam.

"I take that accusation personally, and I would thank you not to suggest it again. I am not in the habit of offering marriage to random young ladies only to change my mind in the morning."

"Mary is hardly an heiress. She has nothing to offer you—why would you make her an offer?"

"That you would ask such a question means you are a fool, and I do not answer fools." He shouldered his way past her and grabbed Mary's trunk.

They marched downstairs past a sputtering Charlotte and her housekeeper.

He threw open the front door and led her outside, crushing some of the pink snapdragon border underfoot. She blinked in the bright sun, stumbling a moment as her eyes adjusted. His carriage—had it been freshly cleaned and painted?—waited just in front of the house. He waved the driver over to take the luggage. "Have you anything else in the house?"

"A smaller trunk and a bag."

"I will retrieve them after this is loaded. Pray await me in the coach." His tone carried the force of an order.

So this was how it would be? She matched his posture and stared at him.

His eyes softened just a bit. "I heard much of what she said to you, and I would shield you from more of it."

She squeezed her eyes shut. He wanted to shield her …

"Mary?" He touched her arm.

She opened her eyes. Her vision filled with his face, so close, so concerned. All she could do was nod.

He handed her into the carriage and stalked back into the house, the driver trailing behind him.

In a quarter of an hour, Fitzwilliam climbed inside and shut the door firmly behind him. He grinned, a lopsided boyish grin, and slid into the seat beside her. A moment later, he tucked his arm over her shoulder and pulled her close.

The carriage lurched a little, and she fell into his side.

"Excellent," he whispered.

"So you ordered your driver to do that?"

"I think it best if you believe that." He pressed his cheek to the top of her head.

How comfortable and safe the weight, the warmth, against her.

"I am sorry you had to endure Mrs. Collins. I had no idea she was worse than her husband."

"It was not unexpected. She thinks she is being a good friend. I am certain, in some way, she cares for me and wants good for me."

"She is selfish and judgmental. And not above trying to extend her budget by finding free service from her friends."

"I would not have stayed with her in any case. I saw what was happening and had other plans in place."

He affected a boyish pout. "I would have liked to believe that I rescued you."

"I am sure that would be more appealing for an officer such as yourself. A knight in shining armor, as it were. But you know what I am and could not expect me to indulge you in a false belief. There may be little I can offer you, but I can always give you the truth." She bit her bottom lip. It did not seem like so very much to offer him.

"That is more than anyone else has ever given me. And yes, I know that it is a double-edged sword in some ways. But I shall be grateful for the gift that it is."

"It is a gift few have ever wanted."

"Fools abound in this world."

She chuckled.

"I do so love that sound." He turned slightly, caught her gaze, and kissed her soundly.

Warm and hard against hers, his lips sought, explored, caressed. What was one to do at such a moment? Could he tell she did not know?

"Do not worry. I think you delightful," he whispered, tickling her ear with his breath. "I shall enjoy the journey with you." He pressed his prickly cheek to hers. "I ask only one thing of you for now, my dearest Mary." He took both her hands in his. "And I insist, you must answer me with the full bore of your honestly. I want nothing else."

Her shoulders tensed. "Pray do not ask such a question as needs that sort of preface."

"Do you love me, Mary?" All bravado faded from his countenance, leaving a vulnerable, a very vulnerable, young man staring into her eyes, steeled for a response he dreaded but would accept with the courage of an officer.

She stroked the lines on his forehead with her fingertips and cupped his stubbled cheek with her palm. "Sometimes one needs to hear the words to be sure."

"Yes, one does."

"Yes, Fitzwilliam, I love you. I have loved you far longer than I should have."

His eyes brightened, and the tension in his jaw eased. "How long?"

"Why do you think your life was so important to me that I would risk my future to save it?"

He cuddled her to him, her ear against his chest. How fast his heart beat! Did he really fear a different reply?

"You will not ask me the same, will you?" He tucked his chin over the top of her head.

She pressed against him hard. But he was right. No matter what she might expect, those words, that question was too much.

He held her in warm silence for a quarter of an hour, then rapped on the ceiling of the coach, calling for the driver to stop. The carriage pulled off the road onto a patch of grass.

"What—"

He held a gentle finger to her lips and handed her out onto the soft green carpet.

Just a few steps away stood an ancient tree, with wide spreading shade beneath. He took her hand and tugged her toward it. A soft breeze at her back that smelled of fresh clover encouraged her to go with him. He guided her hand to the gnarled grey-brown tree trunk—did he think she would need such support for what he was about to say?

Her face flushed cold, and her hands trembled. She bit her lip hard. No matter what he said, she could bear it. She would bear it, with poise and grace, whatever it was.

He dropped to one knee before her and took her hands in his, kissing each one tenderly. "I am not a romantical man—you know I never have been nor will I ever be—so what I tell you may not please you, but you can be certain it is true."

Exactly as she would want. Yes, this was the way it should be.

But why did she want to run instead of hear him out?

"That day I came across you at the wellspring, I watched you far longer than you know. I saw far more than I am sure you would have wanted me to. I had never really seen you until that moment, and I was stunned. I could not tear my eyes away for wanting you—a nymph princess in my woods, distressed. You made me think things a gentleman should not think of a lady. I could not rip my thoughts from you since that day. I cannot say it was love at that instant. No, it was something far more base. But when you came to Rosings, allowing me to see more and more of you, love followed so quickly I do not know when it began. I thought Darcy a bit daft when he pronounced his love for your sister. But now, I understand it was the sanest thing he ever did."

She fell back against the tree trunk and slid down to sit beside him.

"I love you, Mary."

How could one answer such a declaration but with a kiss? Awkward and unpracticed, to be sure, but his grin suggested he hardly noticed.

"Now that we have that established, I must discharge a promise. Darcy and I have both been looking for you. But I had to make sure you heard my offer first."

"Offer? From Darcy? You mean the one Elizabeth mentioned in her letter?"

"Yes, but he insists on presenting it to you himself." He laced his fingers in hers and helped her to her feet. "But I trust that you will not find it as compelling as mine."

They arrived in London too late to do anything but announce their betrothal to the Darcys and be trundled off to guest chambers—wonderful, luxurious guest rooms not adorned with wall to wall floral motifs.

Late the next morning, Elizabeth—she was no longer Lizzy, not in this fine place—tapped at her door and invited Mary to take breakfast with her in the parlor. Her eyes accused Mary of avoiding her. She was not wrong.

Mary trailed after her, purposefully keeping her steps soft on the polished hardwood floors. Somehow, such noise would be offensive here, even though Elizabeth took no such precautions. How long had it taken her to become so at ease in this elegant house? Tasteful landscapes and a few portraits graced the fresh white walls—the faint smell of new paint still lingered in the air—above elegant, expensive hall chairs and console tables. The Darcy family must have been wealthy for generations in order to amass such holdings. Unlike the garish absurdity Rosings espoused. Darcy House did not shout affluence; it quietly wore it at every turn. The effect was quite intimidating.

The sunny second-floor parlor greeted them with a picturesque view of the garden behind the house. A dainty white-lattice gazebo sat nestled among the tall bushes—what were those? They were not flowering, at least not yet. Within the parlor, there could be no doubt Elizabeth had arranged the furniture: comfortable conversational groupings of armchairs and sofas—one near the fireplace, one close to an old pianoforte in the corner opposite the windows, and a final grouping of dainty chairs in a corner nestled between window and bookcase. A smattering of pretty pillows made from fabric Gardiner's sold, and the subtle fragrance of dried lavender completed Elizabeth's signature. Those familiar things should put her at ease here.

But they did not. An interrogation was still an interrogation even if it took place in a pleasant room.

A tea service along with a tempting selection of delicate baked goods—their scent masked by the lavender—awaited them on a low table near the window. Elizabeth took her seat and busied herself preparing tea.

Mary perched on the stiff embroidered cushion of the wood frame chair nearest the window and farthest from Elizabeth. Elizabeth handed her a cup of tea.

"I am not entirely surprised that Charlotte proved less than an ideal friend. But I am disappointed." Elizabeth stared pensively into her teacup. "I suppose I should have warned you of my concerns."

"I confess, it was rather a shocking transformation." Mary sipped her tea, a light blend, somewhat floral. Elizabeth must have created it herself.

"All of this has been so startling."

Mary placed the yellow-flowered teacup bearing the Darcy crest on its saucer and pulled her shoulders back, sitting very erect. "You mean I am startling."

"You must admit, from the outside, all of this," Elizabeth glanced over her shoulder in the direction of Darcy's study where Fitzwilliam likely faced a similar inquiry, "is quite unexpected."

"From the inside as well."

Elizabeth chuckled and met her eyes briefly. "You have moved from Mr. Michaels to Fitzwilliam rather … ah … quickly."

"I expect it does appear that way. I would think you would understand, though. You love Darcy very dearly."

Elizabeth nearly dropped her teacup. It would be a

shame to break family heirloom china. Mary took it from her and set it near the center of the table, a reasonably safe distance from further outbursts of Elizabeth's nerves.

"You love Fitzwilliam? Forgive me, if I find that confusing. You must agree, that, at least from all appearances, you are very dissimilar."

"From outward appearances, I am sure it is so." Mary laced her fingers tightly in her lap. Better to keep them occupied that way than to clench her fists.

"Pray tell me what have you in common."

"You have no right to demand such of me. We do not need your approval."

"I know that. Darcy knows that. But Fitzwilliam is dear to us and you—"

Mary bolted to her feet so quickly she nearly upset the table. "Pray do not mock me by pretending that I am dear to you."

Elizabeth scooted her chair back several inches. That should not be a surprise. She had hardly ever seen Mary's temper. "I deserve that. I was not a good sister to you. I ignored you as much as everyone else. I know it means little, but I was wrong. I am deeply sorry for it. If you give me the opportunity, I do want to make it right with you."

Mary turned her back and took refuge near the corner bookcase, out of the sun's brightness. It was a soothing place for a respite. The smell of old books always calmed her. She ran her fingers along several cracked leather spines. "That is one of the things Fitzwilliam and I share in common. As middle children, we were never of much account to anyone in the family. No one noticed or cared a great deal about us. He was the 'spare,' and I was destined to be a maiden aunt, keeper of someone else's children. Of utterly no worth if or until we were called upon to fill our roles."

"I suppose that does give you quite a bit of common ground. But still, his lifestyle—"

"Has been little different from any other man of his station. I grant you, he is not Darcy—who by that measure—is better suited to me than to you. Stiff and starchy, incredibly dull, I believe we both have been called."

Elizabeth snickered, muffled by something, probably her fist.

Soft steps, muted by the carpet, and the swish of muslin skirts approached.

The back of Mary's neck twitched. She hid it in a shrug. "You can say it. Charlotte already has. I appear prim, rule-bound, and sermonizing."

"She said that to you?"

"And you thought it. Little difference if you really think about it." She turned to face Elizabeth full on. "You wonder how I could tolerate a man who has not been so."

"The thought has crossed my mind."

"Was the person you were in Papa's household a good reflection of who you truly are or a mask worn for the sake of survival?"

"So it has been an affectation all this time?"

Mary stepped back, bracing against one of the shelves, looking for a means of escape. She was not a cornered animal, but the analogy was not wrong, either. "I would not say exactly that. I do prefer things to be in order and according to custom, but not nearly so much as it would appear."

"Fitzwilliam has called you fiery, which I confess,

is not a word I have ever heard to describe you."

Mary pressed her lips, hard. Now was not the time to smile, but still it was pleasing he thought of her so.

Elizabeth had the good graces to widen her eyes and blush. "I suppose then I really have never known you."

"He has, more than anyone ever has. And what is more, he likes what he sees." Her voice broke.

"That is something I can understand. If that is the case, then I must support you, no matter how peculiar it all looks."

Peculiar? That is how it looked to her? The description was far from wholly pleasing. Then again, it was better than many of the alternatives. "I hope Darcy will come to the same conclusion once he is finished interrogating Fitzwilliam."

"Interrogating? That is what he called it?"

"What would you call it? Your husband can be rather high-handed and intimidating."

Elizabeth chuckled heartily. "Point made. Just tell me you have given our offer to you fair consideration." She waved Mary back to their seats.

"It is generous and thoughtful, particularly in light of the historic coolness of our relationship. Truly, I do appreciate it. If I were any less certain of Fitzwilliam, I would accept it without question."

"Even with the specter of Lady Catherine looming over you? That says a great deal of your confidence in him."

"He came after me when I had already given up hope, even as Darcy came for you." Mary held her teacup between her palms. It was still warm; floral notes with a hint of bitterness hung in the air above it.

"Lady Catherine is difficult to be sure, but she does not bear me the animosity she holds toward you. And in that light, she is manageable. Much like a small child, but she is manageable."

"Is that what you want? To manage her? Especially considering the state of Rosings' finances? Are you aware—"

"I have spent many long hours reviewing every aspect of Rosings' holdings. I know what I am walking into. And the plans left for us by Mr. Michaels—"

"Do you believe that Fitzwilliam will adhere to them now?" Elizabeth bit her lip. She was back to treading on dangerous ground, and she knew it.

"He has assured me that he has done exactly that in my absence."

"And you are certain he is telling you the truth?"

Mary gritted her teeth. Better that than let loose with an epithet learned from Fitzwilliam.

The door swung open and Darcy marched in, Fitzwilliam just behind him, not at all unhappy. Considering the lines around his eyes, the examination must have been mild indeed.

Mary rose and turned to Darcy. "Of what did you accuse Fitzwilliam?" She snuck a wink at Fitzwilliam.

Darcy stopped short and stared at her. "Excuse me?"

"You heard me. Of what impropriety did you accuse him?"

"Everyone you can think of, and a few more that I hope are beyond the bounds of your imagination." Fitzwilliam's eyes twinkled as he surged forward and took her hands. "But I will forgive him and insist that you do so as well. His offensive behavior was in defense of you, his sister, something for which I cannot fault him and neither should you."

Darcy snorted and rolled his eyes. Apparently he did have a sense of humor after all.

Mary squeezed his hands. "I shall accept your entreaty this time; however, know this." Her voice lowered to something quite somber. "Going forward, the fact that he has gained my approval shall be enough for you."

"You see, Darcy!" Fitzwilliam wrapped his arms around her and kissed her soundly. "It is exactly as I have told you. I have her approbation."

Cheeky man, he was doing that to taunt Darcy as much as to please himself. Still a kiss from him, for any reason, was very good.

"Just be certain you retain that admiration, and I shall be satisfied." Darcy folded his arms over his chest.

Fitzwilliam laughed heartily, but Mary bristled.

Elizabeth moved to her side and touched her shoulder. "They are like brothers. It is their way. You will have to become accustomed to it. In truth, he has no greater support than Darcy, more so than even his own father or brothers. They are not like … our family. This does not mean what it would among us."

Mary glanced from one man to the other. Both nodded just a fraction. "I suppose it is going to take some getting used to."

Elizabeth gestured for them all to sit.

As many times as they had been up and down already, it hardly seemed to make sense, but they did so anyway.

Fitzwilliam leaned back in his chair next to Mary's and crossed his ankles. "So then, what of the wedding? I am of a mind to acquire a license and get on with it."

"I agree; we should not delay." Mary stared at the table. "The key question, though, is what would be best for Lady Catherine."

Fitzwilliam groaned.

Elizabeth huffed, long and slow. "That is an excellent question."

"Have you given any thought—" Darcy propped forward, elbows on his knees.

"Not a single one. But in my defense, I have been preoccupied with something rather more important." Fitzwilliam caught Mary's eyes.

Oh, that expression! Just bordering on improper for company. Would he always be like this?

She raised an eyebrow, just enough.

He took her hand and kissed it.

"Besotted," Darcy whispered under his breath.

"Enchanted. Utterly and completely." Fitzwilliam murmured back to Mary.

Elizabeth cleared her throat. "Regarding Lady Catherine …"

"Our aunt has never been appreciative of change—"

"Especially change that she did not have a hand in creating." Fitzwilliam muttered.

"Especially that. I am concerned about what will happen when you wed. You will recall her reaction when—" Darcy glanced at Elizabeth, a pained look in his eyes.

"I do not think any of us can forget that." Mary shuddered. "Even so, she is not the woman she once was."

"If the wedding is held at the Hunsford church, I do not know how it could escape Aunt Catherine's notice, not to mention a wedding breakfast at Rosings will be expected." Fitzwilliam drummed his fingers along the worn wooden arm of the chair.

"It would be good for the neighborhood to be able to celebrate with us." Mary chewed the edge of her lip.

Fitzwilliam opened his mouth, but closed it again. After a few seconds, he drew another breath to speak. "It is difficult to imagine my aunt behaving tolerably at such an event. I expect so many people would confuse her, and she would easily become agitated." He suddenly stood. "Forgive me, Elizabeth, but pray, would you allow us a few minutes?" His voice carried the weight of an order.

Darcy hesitated, but Elizabeth took his hand, and they withdrew.

Fitzwilliam sought Mary's eyes, but it was too much intimacy, too much intensity for the moment. She rose and retreated toward the bookshelf. Three heartbeats later, he followed, standing behind her, not touching, but close enough for her to feel him. Pursuing her still.

Long, strong arms wove around her waist and pressed her against him. He smelt of sandalwood and shaving lather. "I lied."

"I know. She is never far from your mind any more than she is from mine."

He kissed the top of her head. She leaned into him.

"I imagine you have a plan that you do not wish to subject to Darcy's scrutiny?"

"Or Elizabeth's." His chest rumbled with a deep chuckle. Hopefully, she would hear that sound often.

"Forgive me, but your sister can be every bit as formidable as he."

"I quite agree. What do you have in mind?"

"Whilst you were gone, I received a letter from a Mrs. Tennington. She is one of the ladies to whom Elizabeth had suggested you write, an old school friend of my aunt's. She seemed interested in both the position as companion and in assisting her old chum."

"I remember writing that letter, thinking a familiar person would be so much easier for Lady Catherine to accept."

"At about the same time Mrs. Tennington's letter arrived, whilst working to resolve a tenant dispute, I rediscovered a cottage at the distant edge of Rosings' boundaries. I had totally forgotten about it—it has been unoccupied for some time. Happily it seems to only require a thorough cleaning and a few minor repairs. I set staff to restoring it for habitation, intending to see it rented. Another idea came to me, though. What do you think about setting up Mrs. Tennington in that property and convincing Aunt Catherine that her friend is in great need of her help in running her household?"

"And since being of assistance—"

"And in charge, do not forget that!" He laughed aloud this time.

"… is of great value to Lady Catherine. Are you suggesting she might be persuaded to take an extended visit to see Mrs. Tennington to aid her in the management of her home?"

"Do you think it ridiculous?"

She turned in his grasp and gazed directly into his worried eyes "Not at all. I think there is great merit it in. I could not conceive how she might be swayed to repair to the dower house. She knows it too well to be led to think it is anything but the dower house. But to give her the opportunity to come to the assistance of a friend and yet remain near to us if she is in need of assistance—I think it quite brilliant."

"I expect we will have to convince her that you can oversee the manor in her absence, but I do not think that will be so difficult to manage. Parkes will be willing to assist in that endeavor. Mrs. Tennington is here in London, staying with her daughter, I believe. You, and Elizabeth if you wish, might discuss the idea with her face to face."

"These are excellent plans. I am proud of you." She stretched on tip-toes to kiss him.

He met her halfway and left her in no question of his ardor. "Tomorrow I will acquire a license, and the day after we wed—pray keep me waiting no longer."

"Not a moment longer." Who knew that his impatience could be so incredibly appealing? Or was it the way he nibbled her neck just below her ear? Either way, he was very convincing.

❧ Chapter 18

As Mary Expected, the wedding was not the day after Fitzwilliam acquired the license. Even a man of his determination would have a difficult time carrying things off so quickly.

Though the delay frustrated him, it gave Mary and Elizabeth the opportunity to call upon Mrs. Tennington. She proved to be about fifteen years younger than Lady Catherine, having married an older man, wealthy but untitled. Small and energetic, she was immediately likeable—a little like a terrier really—warm and compassionate, able to talk and listen in equal measure, not quite the docile admirer Mary had anticipated. Mrs. Tennington's husband had suffered an apoplexy and slid into dotage before he died, so she had a fair understanding what she would be dealing with. The challenge of it all gave her pause, but her desire to leave her daughter's house was such that she readily accepted an invitation to visit Rosings and have a trial period as companion to Lady Catherine.

Her firmness of character would make her a better companion for Lady Catherine than Mrs. Jenkinson, but maintaining them in a semi-independent household would be demanding. No doubt it would require regular intervention, at least at first, to make the situation work, if it would at all. But it was the best alternative they had.

Three days later, Darcy and Fitzwilliam presented her with generous settlement papers. How they had been drawn up so quickly was hard to conceive, but it must have required considerable influence on Darcy's part to make it happen.

All that remained was to marry.

The next day, Elizabeth tapped at her door as the first rays of rosy sunlight peeked through her window. This was the day everything would change, forever. No matter what else happened, today would make her a different person, at least in the eyes of the law.

The housekeeper followed Elizabeth in, bearing a tray of chocolate, coffee and toast. Who knew that the fragrance of chocolate and coffee together could be so warm and appealing?

Elizabeth smoothed the counterpane and sat cross-legged beside Mary. The bed ropes groaned beneath them as she sank into the featherbeds. How many had been piled up on the bedframe to make it so soft and inviting?

The entire room was like that: warm and welcoming, declaring that she was a wanted guest. From the fine bed linens and window dressings to the dainty cut crystal water jug and glass on the bedside table;

the elegant mahogany dressing table with polished silver mirror to the fresh peonies in an antique vase on the chest of drawers . No detail had been over-looked.

They chatted companionably and sipped their favorite beverages for half an hour, then began preparing for the wedding. Though Mary still had her best gown, the one she had intended to wear when she wed Michaels, somehow it just felt wrong to wear it to wed another man. A totally impractical thought. Far too sentimental, really. Had she needed to buy another gown because of it, she would have ignored the feeling and got on with things, but since Elizabeth had come to the same conclusion and offered a ready solution, Mary indulged her sensibilities and borrowed a dress from Elizabeth.

They had added two rows of Vandyke trim—a gift from the Gardiners—to the bottom of Elizabeth's pale blue muslin gown to make it long enough, and gathered the bodice a bit to fit Mary's trimmer frame, but all in all, the dress fit well. The gauzy skirts swished and swirled around her feet, suitable for a woodland nymph. Fitzwilliam would approve. Tiny flowers tucked into her hair reinforced the image.

The reflection that stared back at her in the mirror was actually quite pleasing, though entirely unlike the sort of bride she thought she would be. Probably fitting considering she was marrying a man utterly unlike the one with whom she had expected to connect herself.

Half an hour later, she and Elizabeth, in a lovely, but somewhat plain yellow gown—she had done that intentionally, to allow Mary to stand out; a sweet, if overwhelming sentiment—waited in the vestibule for the carriage to take them to the church.

The housekeeper announced the Gardiners' coach had arrived for them. Why the Gardiners' coach when Darcy and Fitzwilliam had perfectly good vehicles themselves? Elizabeth ignored the irregularity, apparently happy for the excuse to see the Gardiners, so Mary put it out of her mind.

No point in finding things to concern herself with on such a day.

Standing at the back of the church, ready to enter on Darcy's arm, Mary's heart fluttered, not like a butterfly, but more like a frantic falcon, back-winging uncertainly toward and away from its goal. The old stone structure with a high, wooden-raftered ceiling left the air inside cool, even crisp and smelling like damp rock. The delicate muslin gown afforded little protection against the chill. She shivered, just a bit, as much with anticipation as with the cold.

Rows upon rows of empty wooden pews, scarred and stained by decades of use, somehow seemed an ominous audience for such an event. Why were weddings only attended by a few witnesses? It seemed odd that funerals were well-attended, even if attendants had to be paid for, but weddings were held in solemn near-solitude. At least the Gardiners were there, standing near the front in the cheery morning sunlight that streamed through the eastern-side windows.

Mama would regret missing the wedding, but more for the fact that Mary was marrying an earl's son than anything else. Elizabeth was right, even if it made her heart pinch just a bit: it was just as well that neither of her parents were there.

Fitzwilliam and the vicar took their places at the front of the church and turned to face her. Fitzwilliam's jaw dropped and blossomed into a rakish, boyish grin. Pray he never lost that particular expression. It suited him well indeed, leaving her in no doubt that he was well pleased.

It was very good to be looked at that way. Especially today.

"I never thought I would see him so happy—and so at peace," Darcy whispered, straightening his lapels, his eyes fixed on Fitzwilliam. "Thank you for giving that to him."

"He has given the same to me."

"Then you two are much like Elizabeth and me. I have great faith that you will find the same kind of felicity we have. It is all that I have wanted for him, but I had given up on him ever finding it."

For a man of few words, Darcy seemed to choose them well.

He escorted her in the slow solemn march down the church aisle and put her white gloved hands into Fitzwilliam's.

The vicar launched into the enduring words of the ceremony of marriage. The familiar litany and voices behind her assured and comforted her—was that not the purpose behind such rituals? This step into a new life was right. They would not be without support. Their marriage would not be without its trials, but it would be well.

Fitzwilliam locked his gaze with hers as he slid a filigreed gold band around her finger. "With this Ring I thee wed, with my Body I thee worship, and with all my worldly Goods I thee endow: In the Name of the

Father, and of the Son, and of the Holy Ghost. Amen."

The ring felt odd now—cool and heavy—but soon, it too would be comfortable, familiar, and right. Like Fitzwilliam,

They knelt on a plain cushion before the vicar, as he led them all in prayer. Then, joining their right hands together, he said, "Those whom God hath joined together let no man put asunder." Then he continued his blessing.

Fitzwilliam gripped her hand tightly. "We are joined now, and nothing shall come between us. Not Rosings, not Aunt Catherine, not our families."

She squeezed his fingers back.

After the final blessings and prayer, the vicar escorted them and their witnesses back to the vestry to sign the marriage lines, and it was done. She was Mary Fitzwilliam, wife of Colonel Richard Fitzwilliam and mistress of Rosings Park.

That last bit was going to take some getting used to. Quite a bit of it.

The Gardiners' coach waited in front of the church for them. Fitzwilliam himself, grinning like a boy, handed her up and followed her in, claiming the seat beside her before anyone could get in his way. Crisp white curtains over the side glass were pulled aside to allow fresh air and sunshine within, altogether comfortable and friendly.

Darcy and Elizabeth followed, sitting across from them. Aunt Gardiner slipped in beside Elizabeth, whilst Uncle climbed on the box with the driver. That was kind of him, but Fitzwilliam was sitting so close that there was plenty of room for him.

"Forgive me for asking. I do not mean to sound

ungrateful, but I do not understand why we are using the Gardiners' coach. It seems as if there is something I am not being told."

Darcy looked at Elizabeth and nodded.

"I hope you do not mind, but we have arranged a wedding breakfast for you." Elizabeth wore a knowing, almost smirking smile that hinted that she had taken perhaps a little too much upon herself.

Not that it was entirely new, but it could be tiresome.

"By that, I imagine you mean you have invited more than just the Gardiners?" Fitzwilliam asked. But it really was not a question. Everything about him screamed he knew more than he was letting on.

"A few more, yes." Elizabeth could not suppress a wink.

"You know I am all in favor of a good party, at nearly anytime, but no one knows we are here in London. Have you just gathered random people off the street?" Fitzwilliam was enjoying his ruse a little too much.

"Not precisely random people." Darcy lifted his brows in an expression that matched Elizabeth's.

"That is where the carriages have been!" Mary turned to Fitzwilliam. "What have you not told me?"

"Do not blame him. It was our idea," Elizabeth said.

"But I fully agreed. You do not need to protect me from my own decisions." Fitzwilliam glowered at them both. "Yes, they suggested it, but I thought it a capital idea and a suitable surprise for you. Your marriage deserves to be celebrated as much as any of your sisters'."

"As I understand, Mama hosted a memorable

breakfast for Jane." Elizabeth's voice became apologetic.

Yes, she had: a lavish affair which strained the family budget and meant Mary and Kitty had no pocket money in the months following.

"Forgive me, but you are entering a new station in life, and it is important to do so in a fitting way. Admittedly, I do not usually like the fact, but it is imperative," Darcy said softly. "Whilst some sobriety in the affair can be credited to Aunt Catherine's condition, to dispense with some sort of breakfast altogether might cause the kind of notice you would rather avoid."

"I am afraid he is right." Aunt Gardiner smiled apologetically. "But your sister has gone to great lengths to consider your preferences as well."

Fitzwilliam entwined his fingers in hers and whispered in her ear. "She truly has. Pray trust me; it will be well. Your parents will not be there, and it will be nothing like the events you remember."

Her view of the coach blurred. That was the crux of it all. Mama's occasions were an opportunity to be marginalized from her prettier, livelier sisters.

She swallowed hard and forced a smile. "Thank you for doing this for us."

The carriage lurched and stopped in front of Darcy House. Fitzwilliam handed her out, and she steeled herself for whomever awaited inside.

Lydia, bouncy and lively as she ever was, greeted them in the front hall.

"Oh, Mary! How well you look! And how handsome your husband! Oh, I am so happy for you! It is truly a wonderful thing to be married. Come, you must meet my James." She grabbed Mary's hand and dragged her to the drawing room at the back of the house. It seemed the only thing that had changed about her was the matron's mobcap she now wore.

Soothing strains from the grand pianoforte calmed her as she entered the room. The most formal room of the house, elegant furnishings and tasteful art from the continent occupied every corner and shelf. Understated though it was, the demonstration of status and wealth was a little overwhelming.

Would that Elizabeth had chosen to use the parlor instead. But then again, that was the point of this exercise, was it not? To display Mary's new connections and status to their guests.

An awkward, angular man sat at the piano, the music a sharp contrast with his person. His suit was well-tailored, but somehow it looked rumpled, though when she looked closely, it was not. His dark mane of hair was tousled and unruly, not in the stylish sort of way, but in the way Fitzwilliam's was when he raked his hair repeatedly.

Was this Lydia's husband? He looked nothing like any of the men she had been drawn to in the past. But the love-struck glitter in her eye said otherwise. If that was not evidence she had changed, nothing would be.

"James!" Lydia bounded up to him and laid a hand on his shoulder.

He stopped playing and turned to them, the look in his eye that of one who had just woken up. "Yes, my dear."

"This is my sister Mary. She just married Colonel Fitzwilliam."

He rose—just how tall was this man? He would

tower over even Fitzwilliam. "I am pleased to make your acquaintance." He bowed deeply, a bit like a stiff adolescent not quite sure of what he was doing. Nothing like Fitzwilliam's smooth gallantry.

"And I yours," she curtsied as Fitzwilliam appeared at her shoulder. "May I present my husband, Fitzwilliam?"

"A pleasure, sir!" Fitzwilliam bowed from his shoulders. "Always glad to meet another connoisseur of the Bennet sisters!"

"They are a rare and handsome breed, are they not?" James winked and slipped his arm around Lydia's waist.

She giggled and batted her eyes at him. But only at him. She barely seemed to notice Fitzwilliam who was by far the more agreeable looking man.

She was still Lydia, but an improved version of herself, just as her letters had portrayed.

The drawing room slowly filled: Mrs. Tennington, the Claremonts—so that was where Fitzwilliam's carriage had been—Charlotte and her parents, the Philipses. A contingent from Kent also appeared: the Hugheses, the Leightons, as well as the Andersons, the vicar and his wife from the parish neighboring Hunsford—in all, some of the neighborhood's leading citizens. Each one was escorted to Mary and Fitzwilliam and formally presented.

Elizabeth was certainly making sure that all the guests knew this marriage was accepted and respected by them, which implied that the rest of the family felt the same. Whether it was true or not—and it probably was not—the appearance would be what people talked about. It was the right sort of gossip for them to start a life on.

Truly a generous and thoughtful gift.

Still, she did not prefer surprises. Fitzwilliam was right, though. He deserved her trust.

After the breakfast that lasted well into the evening, he proved himself worthy of trust once again when he locked the door behind them in their bridal chamber and showed her the reason Lydia and Elizabeth looked at their husbands the way that they did.

She would probably stare at him in the same calf-eyed way now. He would laugh at her for it, but in a pleased, proud sort of way that would make it all right to laugh with him.

She nestled into his shoulder, under the luxurious soft sheets of the grand four-poster bed with turned oak posts. The low fire in the fireplace lit the room just enough to see his face. He smelt of sandalwood and soap, and a touch of leather polish. That must have been from the Gardiners' carriage.

He had rarely looked so tranquil, so utterly content. No, she had never seen him quite like this before.

"You are staring at me." The corners of his lips turned up, and his eyes opened a sliver.

"I am quite allowed to do that now."

"Not just allowed, but encouraged." He snatched her up and rolled her over on top of him in a tangle of limbs and sheets.

She shrieked and giggled. "What am I going to do with you?"

"Love me."

"That I can promise you, dearest." It felt strange saying that word—she was not given to such sentimental language. But after the intimacy of what they had just shared, it was entirely fitting. He was, in fact, the dearest person in the world to her.

"I may not be the most agreeable man, but I intend to show you every day that you are my queen."

She covered her face with a bit of sheet and tittered. "You do realize, or perhaps you do not, that we used to call Lady Catherine that—the Queen of Rosings Park."

His eyes widened, and he chuckled so hard he had to hold her close to keep her from sliding off his chest. "That is far more complimentary than the things I have called her over the years. Darcy, too, for that matter, though I hardly think he would admit it."

"You are not offended?"

"Not at all. But I can see why you might not wish to be my queen. No, that will not do at all. Hmmm, this will require some thought." He held her tightly and rolled them over. "If not my queen, then what shall you be? My duchess, my princess—"

His weight on her should have been uncomfortable, even alarming, but somehow it was safe and secure. "Your love?" she whispered.

"My love. Yes, I think that will do very well. As will we." He hovered over her, staring intently into her eyes.

"Yes, we shall do very well, indeed."

✐ Author's Notes

Home Medicine in Jane Austen's Day

During Jane Austen's day, the practice of medicine as we know it today was still in its infancy. Formally trained doctors were unavailable to many either because of cost or distance. Consequently any of the curative arts were practiced at home. William Buchan's book *Domestic medicine or the family physician.*

William Buchan was born in Scotland in 1729. Even before his formal training he served as an amateur doctor to his village. In 1758 he qualified in medicine. The following year he served as the first surgeon and apothecary to a Yorkshire branch of the Foundling Hospital. Experience gained in this post influenced his MD dissertation for Edinburgh University *On the preservation of infant life* (1761).

Domestic Medicine

In 1769 Buchan published his seminal work, *Domestic medicine or the family physician*. It was the first text of its kind. Previous medical texts were theoretical and written for well-educated readers or were brief manuals not descriptive enough to be helpful. Buchan wrote *Domestic Medicine* in lay terms. It described both the diseases and treatments clearly enough that untrained people could fabricate the necessary remedies.

Priced at just 6 shillings, it was an immediate success. 80 000 copies from the 19 (English) editions of the book sold during his lifetime. Beyond Buchan's native English, *Domestic Medicine* was translated into all the major European languages even Russian. The text remained in print until 1846 in Britain, and 1913 in the Americas.

Unfortunately, many of his remedies were no better than was currently in use at the time. Many of the cures were grounded in the theories of bodily humors, making him a proponent of bloodletting and purging as cures. Moreover, he proposed that too much of any one 'non-natural': air, meat and drink, sleeping and watching, exercise and quiet, evacuations and obstructions, and passions could result in an illness inducing imbalance. Thus, he advocated letting nature take its course by helping a patient reset to a natural 'set point'.

Still, though, he was ahead of his time. More than a third of his book related to the prevention of disease by such (in today's eyes) common sense measures as fresh air, exercise, hygiene, cleanliness and inoculations. He also encouraged breast feeding as a means of reducing infant mortality and opposed the use of stupefactives on children.

On 25 February 1805 Buchan died at 76. He was buried in Westminster Abbey, leaving a legacy on medicine that we still feel today.

Reference

Buchan W. (1784) *Domestic medicine or a treatise on the prevention and cure of diseases by regimen and simple medicines.* (H Chamberlain and others, Dublin), 9th ed..

Dunn PM. Dr William Buchan (1729–1805) and his *Domestic medicine*

Archives of Disease in Childhood - Fetal and Neonatal Edition 2000;**83:**F71-F73.

Land Stewards: Professional help in running an estate.

We often hear about gentlemen employing stewards to help manage their estates. Who were these men, though, and what did they do?

Small estates, like Longbourn of *Pride and Prejudice,* could be managed by the master of the estate with the assistance of a non-professional man, called a bailiff. Typically a bailiff would be one of the major tenants on the estate, hired to act as a go-between to collect tenants' rents. In the era, it would have been considered vulgar for a gentleman to collect the rents himself.

Larger estates, like Darcy's Pemberley or Lady Catherine's Rosings Park, were major economic endeavors that necessitated professional help in the form of a steward.

Qualifications

Where the bailiff simply collected rents for the master of the estate, the steward was responsible for actually running the business of the estate and thus was integral to its success. He had to be an educated man, often the son of clergy, a smaller landowner or a professional man. He needed a head for numbers, scrupulous record-keeping skills, an exceptional knowledge of all aspects of agriculture, and excellent people-skills. Typically he would be university trained as a solicitor, necessary because of his dealings with contracts. A steward was not considered a servant, but rather a skilled professional with a higher status than the family lawyer.

For these reasons, a steward was addressed as 'Mister'. Not long after the regency era, the term 'steward', with its servile connotations, was dropped in favor of the more professional term 'land agent.'

Duties

Stewards were tied to the estate and did not travel with the master of the estate. They managed all the activities associated with making the estate profitable, including record and account keeping, managing contracts, and overseeing the agricultural aspects of the home farm.

A good steward kept meticulous accounts and records of everything—seriously everything. In addition to the expected accounting that would go with such an enterprise, he kept logs of work done, including repairs to buildings, fences and roads, as well as records of the parkland, game animals, livestock and crops. He also maintained a rent roll of tenancies and records of the farm boundaries. Further, an estate employed a number of department heads, such as the head gardener, head gamekeeper, and the like. The steward kept records for all these departments and paid the wages of their workmen.

Beyond these duties, stewards also spent a lot of time touring the estate on horseback, dealing with the people of the estate face to face. He collected rents, found new tenants when necessary and leased land, supervised the tenantry, directed any work and improvements done on the land, settled squabbles that arose among the tenants or workers, purchased animals, seed and so on. (Shapard, 2003)

Salaries

A steward's salary related both to the size of the estate and his expertise. Typically, a steward's salary would range from £100-300 annually. In addition he would have use of a private house on the estate. For reference, Austen's Longbourn had an income of about £2000, which probably put hiring a steward out of their range.

Risks

Although not nearly as hazardous as many professions of the era, working as a steward was not without risks. Although employers relied heavily upon their stewards for their efficient management of their estates, that did not prevent employers from doubting their honesty, especially as the large sums that many of them handled offered opportunities for speculation. Accusations of wrongdoing could ruin a man's reputation and (wrongful) conviction for the same could result in prison time or worse, depending on the amount of money involved.

Since the steward was also in charge of collecting the rent from the tenants, he could be an unpopular figure. Historical records show assaults on stewards and in one case, the murder of one. So, in a very literal sense, his people-skills could be a life-saver.

References

Austen, Jane, and David M. Shapard. *The Annotated Pride and Prejudice*. New York: Anchor Books, 2003.

Karsten, Susan. "The Steward: Guardian of the Noble Estate (Farm)." Vanessa Riley's Regency Life. Accessed May 26, 2014.
http://christianregency.com/blog/2013/09/09/the-steward-guardian-of-the-noble-estate-farm-by-susan-karsten/

Laudermilk, Sharon H., and Teresa L. Hamlin. *The Regency Companion*. New York: Garland, 1989.

LeFaye, Deirdre. *Jane Austen: The World of Her Novels*. New York: Abrams, 2002.

Ray, Joan Klingel. *Jane Austen for Dummies*. Chichester: John Wiley, 2006.

Schmidt, Wayne. "Victorian Domestic Servant Hierarchy and Wage Scale." This and That. Accessed May 26, 2014.
http://www.waynesthisandthat.com/servantwages.htm

Sullivan, Margaret C., and Kathryn Rathke. *The Jane Austen Handbook: Proper Life Skills from Regency England*. Philadelphia, PA: Quirk Books, 2007.

Debt in the Regency Era
Living on Credit is not a new thing

It's easy to believe that living on credit is a modern thing. The news abounds with tales of woe regarding consumer debt, mortgages, student loans, and other lines of credit. How would Jane Austen have reacted to such news? Probably with great aplomb and a declaration that the more things change, the more they stay the same.

During the Regency era "almost all members of the middle and upper classes had accounts with different suppliers, who extended credit to their patrons. … Only if the amount was small or they were traveling did they pay cash. In fact, only the poor did not live on credit in one guise or another." (Forsling, 2017) In fact, more people depended on credit than ever before resulting in perpetual overcrowding in the debtor's prisons.

Although debt, both personal and national, were rife in Regency society, attitudes toward debt were largely divided across class lines. "Aristocratic claims for leadership had long been based on lavish displays and consumption while the middle class stressed domestic moderation. In particular, aristocratic disdain for sordid money matters, their casual attitude to debt and addiction to gambling …, were anathema to the middling ranks whose very existence depended on the establishment of creditworthiness and avoidance of financial embarrassment." (Davidoff, 2002)

Many small and otherwise flourishing businesses failed due to bad debts, especially among the upper classes. Some went so far as to begin refusing credit and to only sell for 'ready money'. The notion that debts of honor had to be paid and paid quickly while debts to merchants could be put off indefinitely only exacerbated the situation.

Robbing Peter to pay Paul

Gaming debts were regarded as sacrosanct which might not have been so significant an issue had there not been so many of them. The Regency was a time when Englishmen, especially the wealthy and high-born, were ready to bet on almost anything. Though gaming for high stakes was illegal by Austen's day, authorities mostly seemed to turn a blind eye to it, (Fullerton, 2004) perhaps because it was considered largely an upper class vice.

Different social classes offered different reasons for the immorality of gaming. The upper classes feared losing their money to the lower class, giving them income without having earned it and opposing the work ethic. The rising middle class also saw gaming as opposing the values of stability, property, domesticity, family life and religion. (Rendell, 2002) Regardless of the reason, there was widespread agreement that gaming was a problem, thus legislation was passed against it.

Unfortunately anti-gaming laws, much like prohibition in the US, only forced gambling from public venues into private clubs where individuals bet on any and nearly everything. Organized sports including cricket, horse racing, prize fighting and cock fighting attracted spectators willing to bet on the outcome. Huge fortunes, even family estates could be won and lost at games of chance. Even the outcome of the

Napoleonic Wars were subject to betting.

Moneylenders and bankers made themselves available at private clubs to assist gentlemen in settling their debts of honor which were not otherwise enforceable by law. The cost of this service though (beyond the interest on the debt of course), was creating a legally enforceable debt from which one had not been so previously.

Debtors' Prison

English bankruptcy laws were particularly harsh, demanding personal repayment of all debt, including business debt, and often incarceration. Ironically, there was no disgrace about being sent to gaol during the era, provided it was for an acceptable crime like debt or libel. (Murry, 1999) The Royal Courts administered three prisons primarily for debtors: the Fleet, the King's Bench and the Marshalsea, though debtors might be imprisoned at other facilities as well. (Low, 2005) At any given time during the era, upward of a 10,000 men were imprisoned for debts as small as four pence. (Savage, 2017)

Debtors were probably the largest proportion of the era's prison population and had privileges not granted to ordinary criminals, including the right to have their family stay with them and to have other visitors. They could also often arrange to be supplied with beer or spirits. (Low, 2005) "During the quarterly terms, when the court sits, (Fleet) prisoners on paying five shillings a-day, and on giving security, are allowed to go out when they please, and there is a certain space round the prison, called the rules, in which prisoners may live, on furnishing two good securities to the warden for their debt, and on paying about three per cent on the amount of their debts to the warden." (Feltham, 1803)

The process of obtaining an arrest warrant for debt was expensive. Often several tradesmen would have to band together to see a writ for debt issued. (Kelly, 2006)

Once the writ was obtained, the debtor (once caught, of course, as it was not uncommon for debtors to flee in the face of a writ, even so far as to leave the country) would first be confined to a spunging or lock-up house. A spunging-house was a private house maintained for the local confinement of debtors to give them time to settle their debts before the next step, debtors' prison. "…For twelve or fourteen shillings a-day, a debtor may remain [at the spunging house], either till he has found means of paying his debt, or finds it necessary to go to a public prison, when the writ against him becomes returnable. We have heard that great abuses prevail in these spunging-houses, and that many of the impositions practised in them deserve to be rectified. … It would be wrong to quit the sad subject of prisons, without observing that such is the bad arrangement of the laws between debtor and creditor, that ruin to both is greatly accelerated by the expensiveness of every step in the proceedings, insomuch that not one debtor in ten ever pays his debt after he enters a prison. (Feltham, 1803)

Why Debtor's Prison?

Given that once a debtor was in prison, they lacked the ability to earn money making the payment of his debt even less likely, this approach to debt seems ridiculous. So why was it done?

First, it was assumed that the debtor's family and friends would be available to help pay off their debts. So imprisoning the debtor might help motivate them to action. Second, it was perceived as a deterrent to getting into debt in the first place. (Clearly, given the numbers in debtors' prison it was a total failure on that count.) (Savage, 2017)

The third reason is perhaps the most difficult for the modern reader to understand. To the people of the time, the issue was bigger than simply insuring the debtor paid off their debts. "The 'moral' imperative to make the debtor aware of their responsibility for not living beyond their means was judged more important. … To understand the mind-set of the time, it's important to remember two things: taking on more debt than you could pay was seen as a form of theft; and, … (t)heft broke the Biblical commandment, "Thou shalt not steal". The causes of becoming too indebted to pay also pointed to the presence of other sins: idleness, covetousness, greed, deceitfulness. … Sin demanded punishment and repentance not support," thus jailing the debtor fulfilled the moral imperative. (Savage, 2017)

Myth of the smock wedding

Just because there was a moral imperative to punish debtors didn't mean that those who owed money accepted their fate easily or didn't attempt creative means by which to discharge their debts. Running to avoid one's creditors was common. Beau Brummell fled to France to avoid debtors' prison. In some cases a debtor could be pressed into naval service in exchange for the Navy to cover their debts.

Marriage, particularly for the upper class, was also a handy means of bringing in quick cash to alleviate a family's money woes. The (disastrous) marriage of the Prince of Wales to his cousin, Princess Caroline of Brunswick in 1795 came about so that Parliament would pay off his debts.

Not all men were happy to marry a woman with debts, especially a widow still responsible for her late husband's debts. Consequently, the practice of a 'smock wedding' came into being. At such a wedding, the bride would be married naked, brining nothing into the marriage. In practice, she usually was barefoot and garbed in a chemise or sheet. The salient point was that she was technically bringing nothing into the marriage, thus her husband-to-be was thought not liable for any debts she might have. (Adkins, 2013) It is too bad that snopes.com was not around in the era, because it could have told them that the 'smock wedding' way out of debt was an urban myth and would not stop the new bride's creditors from knocking at their door.

References
Adkins, Roy, and Lesley Adkins. *Jane Austen's England*. Viking, 2013.

Craig, Sheryl. *Jane Austen and the State of the Nation*. New York: Palgrave Macmillan, 2015.

Davidoff, Leonore, and Catherine Hall. *Family Fortunes: Men and Women of the English Middle Class, 1780-1850*. Chicago: University of Chicago Press, 1987.

Feltham, John. *The picture of London, for 1803; being a correct guide to all the curiosities, amusements, exhibitions, public establishments, and remarkable objects in and near London; with a collection of appropriate tables. For the use of strangers, foreigners, and all persons who are intimately acquainted with the British metropolis.* London: R. Phillips, 1803.

Forsling, Yvonne . "Money Makes the World Go Round." Hibiscus-Sinensis. Accessed July 22, 2017. http://hibiscus-sinensis.com/regency/money.htm

Fullerton, Susannah. *Jane Austen and Crime.* Sydney: Jane Austen Society of Australia, 2004.

Kelly, Ian. *Beau Brummell: The Ultimate Man of Style.* New York: Free Press, 2006.

Laudermilk, Sharon H., and Teresa L. Hamlin. *The Regency Companion.* New York: Garland, 1989.

Low, Donald A. *The Regency underworld.* Stroud: Sutton, 2005.

Murray, Venetia. *An Elegant Madness: High Society in Regency England.* New York: Viking, 1999.

Rendell, Jane. *The Pursuit of Pleasure Gender, Space & Architecture in Regency London.* London: Athlone Press, 2002.

Savage, William . "The Georgian Way with Debt." Pen and Pension. July 19, 2017. Accessed July 25, 2017. https://penandpension.com/2017/07/19/the-georgian-way-with-debt/ .

Domestic Violence in Jane Austen's Day

Jane Austen portrays a wonderful vision of heroines like Elizabeth Bennet who are hardly doormats to their men. It is important to realize though, that our modern views of marriage did not apply to Jane Austen's day, and expectations (and realities) of marriage were very different for women then. These differences applied to many areas of life. One of particular notes was the tolerance for domestic violence.

Warm and affectionate marriages were desirable, but practical considerations were probably the backbone of most matches. Loving relationships were more likely to form after marriage than before, if they formed at all. Whatever amiable feelings might develop did so in the context of a clear hierarchy. In regency society, no one doubted that the husband was the head of the relationship, in charge of essentially everything.

There cannot, indeed, be a sight more uncouth, than that of a man and his wife struggling for power: for where it ought to be vested, nature, reason, and Scripture, concur to declare;

… How preposterous is it to hear a woman say, ' It shall be done!' —' I will have it so!' and often extending her authority not only beyond her jurisdiction, but in matters where he alone is competent to act, or even to judge. (Taylor, 1822)

Under legal coverture (a legal concept that determined the legal personhood of married women of the era women had no legal existence. The husband existed for them both in public life. He owned all property, had custody of the children, conducted all business transactions on the family's behalf, even owned the wife's earnings should she have income of her own.

He even had the right to physically chastise his wife, divide her from friends and family and severely curtail her movements, if he so wished. (Jones,2009) Mr. Darcy, could have legally forbidden Elizabeth from associating with her disgraceful relations had he chosen to do so.

According to Blackstone (1765)

The husband also, by the old law, might give his wife mod-

erate correction. For, as he is to answer for her misbehaviour, the law thought it reasonable to intrust him with this power of restraining her, by domestic chastisement, in the same moderation that a man is allowed to correct his apprentices or children; for whom the master or parent is also liable in some cases to answer.

But this power of correction was confined within reasonable bounds, and the husband was prohibited from using any violence to his wife, *aliter quam ad virum, ex causa regiminis et castigationis uxoris suae, licite et rationabiliter pertinet.* [Otherwise than lawfully and reasonably belongs to the husband for the due government and correction of his wife.] The civil law gave the husband the same, or a larger, authority over his wife: allowing him, for some misdemeanors, *flagellis et fustibus acriter verberare uxorem;* [To beat his wife severely with scourges and sticks.] for others, only *modicam castigationem adhibere.* [To use moderate chastisement] (Translations from Latin, Jones, 1905)

In short, a man had the right to severely beat his wife if he deemed it appropriate. This made proving cruelty very difficult.

So much for Blackstone's (1765) assertion: "so great a favourite is the female sex of the laws of England."

It is comforting to remember that Judge Buller amended this understanding somewhat, with his 'rule of thumb': A man could thrash his wife with a stick no thicker than his thumb.

Ironically, instead of improving women's lot, the ideals of companionate marriage may have made domestic violence worse. The incompatible expectations of men raised in a patriarchal tradition, legal coverture, and the social enlightenment were ripe to create tensions that could easily explode into violence.

A woman could petition the court that her husband inflicted cruel and unjust harm upon her. She could charge her husband with assault and battery or could 'swear the peace' by which a court could order her husband to keep the peace if he had inflicted physical injury, imprisonment or some other cruelty on her. (Laudermilk,1989) But to get the sympathy of the court, women had to paint themselves as passive and dutiful victims of truly inhumane treatment. It could be done, but it was difficult at best as evidenced in that of the three hundred twenty four divorces granted between 1670 and 1857, only four were granted to women. (Wright, 2004)

Though these legal rights might sound like a recipe for creating petty tyrants, Rev. Thomas Gisborne (1797), a moralist of the era, argued that true marital harmony came from the husband taking pre-eminence over his wife. She need not fear though, if he were a religious man, he would follow God's will and be a kind protector for whom she would, in gratitude, be endlessly good tempered and pleasing. Sounds exactly like the marriage the Bennets of *Pride and Prejudice* enjoyed, doesn't it?

Yeah, not so much. It certainly does put a different sort of spin on the world of Jane Austen's heroines, doesn't it?

References

Blackstone, William. *Commentaries on the Laws of England.* Vol, 1 (1765), pages 442-445.

Gisborne, Thomas. *An Enquiry into the Duties of the Female Sex.* London: Cadell and Davies, 1797.

Jones, Hazel. *Jane Austen and Marriage.* London: Continuum, 2009.

Jones, J.W. *A Translation of all the Greek, Latin, Italian and French Quotations which occur in Blackstone's Commentaries on the Laws of England.* Philadelphia: T7JW Johnson&Co. 1905. Accessed August 5, 2015.

http://www.mindserpent.com/American_History /books/Blackstone/trans_01.htm.

Laudermilk, Sharon H., and Teresa L. Hamlin. *The Regency Companion.* New York: Garland, 1989.

Taylor, Ann. *Practical Hints to Young Females: On the Duties of a Wife, a Mother, and a Mistress of a Family.* 10th ed. London: Taylor and Hessey, 1822.

Wright, Danaya C. "Well-Behaved Women Don't Make History": *Rethinking English Family, Law, and History*, 19 Wis. Women's L.J. 211 2004), August 17, 2012. Accessed August 1, 2016.

http://scholarship.law.ufl.edu/facultypub/128

Acknowledgments

So many people have helped me along the journey taking this from an idea to a reality.

Abigail thank you so much for cold reading and being honest! Debbie, Anji, Julie, Susanne and Ruth your proofreading is worth your weight in gold!

And my dear friend Cathy, my biggest cheerleader, you have kept me from chickening out more than once!

And my sweet sister Gerri who believed in even those first attempts that now live in the file drawer!

Thank you!

Other Books by Maria Grace

Remember the Past
The Darcy Brothers

Given Good Principles Series:

Darcy's Decision
The Future Mrs. Darcy
All the Appearance of Goodness
Twelfth Night at Longbourn

Jane Austen's Dragons Series:

Pemberley: Mr. Darcy's Dragon
Longbourn: Dragon Entail

The Queen of Rosings Park Series:

Mistaking Her Character
The Trouble to Check Her
A Less Agreeable Man

Sweet Tea Stories:

A Spot of Sweet Tea: Hopes and Beginnings (short
story anthology)
The Darcy's First Christmas
Snowbound at Hartfield

Regency Life (Nonfiction) Series:

A Jane Austen Christmas: Regency Christmas Traditions

Courtship and Marriage in Jane Austen's World

Short Stories:

Four Days in April

Sweet Ginger

Last Dance

Not Romantic

To Forget

Available in paperback, e-book, and audiobook format at all online bookstores.

On Line Exclusives at:

www.http//RandomBitsofFascination.com

Bonus and deleted scenes
Regency Life Series

Free e-books:
Bits of Bobbin Lace
The Scenes Jane Austen Never Wrote: First Anniversaries
Half Agony, Half Hope: New Reflections on Persuasion
Four Days in April
Jane Bennet in January
February Aniversaries

❧About the Author

Though Maria Grace has been writing fiction since she was ten years old, those early efforts happily reside in a file drawer and are unlikely to see the light of day again, for which many are grateful. After penning five file-drawer novels in high school, she took a break from writing to pursue college and earn her doctorate in Educational Psychology. After 16 years of university teaching, she returned to her first love, fiction writing.

She has one husband and one grandson, two graduate degrees and two black belts, three sons, four undergraduate majors, five nieces, is starting her sixth year blogging on Random Bits of Fascination, has built seven websites, attended eight English country dance balls, sewn nine Regency era costumes, and shared her life with ten cats.

She can be contacted at:

author.MariaGrace@gmail.com

Facebook:
http://facebook.com/AuthorMariaGrace

On Amazon.com:
http://amazon.com/author/mariagrace

Random Bits of Fascination
(http://RandomBitsofFascination.com)

Austen Variations (http://AustenVariations.com)

English Historical Fiction Authors
(http://EnglshHistoryAuthors.blogspot.com)

White Soup Press (http://whitesouppress.com/)

On Twitter @WriteMariaGrace

On Pinterest: http://pinterest.com/mariagrace423/

Printed in Great Britain
by Amazon

72165934R00208